✂ *Sins of the Daughter* ✂

<u>Fiction Series</u>
The Alex Evercrest Series
The River Front
The Girl on The Grill
Missing
Maggot
Racist
Votive Candles
Windy City
Country Road
Pool of Blood
Sins of the Daughter
Body Parts
The Skull Collector
The Vanishing
The Shadow Fighter
Moonshine
Grief's Trajectory
The Magic Touch
Northern Lights
Alex Evercrest Heroine
Alex Evercrest Collection Two
New Direction
A Family Affair
Disruption
The St. Lebuinnus Church Murder

A Brian O'Neil Novel
Hawaiian Phoenix
Moon Curser
Death Broker

The Problem Solver Series
Solutions
Drug Lords
Border Crosser
The Problem Solver Collection

<u>The Taelo Series</u>
Taelo: The Early Years
Taelo: The Golden Feather
Taelo: Journey of Discovery
Taelo: Dangerous Passage
Taelo: Condor Clan Slingers
Taelo: Circumvention
Taelo: The Journey of Sages
Taelo: Collection
Taelo: Future Leaders Journey

<u>A Taelo Story:</u>
White Swan and Quiet Pheasant
The Child's Name
Floating Cloud
Quiet Rabbit
Busy Bee
Little Otter & Talking Wren
Broken Spear
Burley Bear & Meadow Flower
Taelo Story Collection

<u>Science Fiction</u>

The Savitar Series:
Journey's End
Savitar
Confluence
Savitar Series Collection

Bram Nielson Series
The Fold
The Message
Fold Wormhole
Negative Fold
Ripples in Time
Bram Nielson Collection

<u>Single Science Fiction Books:</u>
Current Past and Future
The Event
The Door
Viajante 7

ೞ Sins of the Daughter ಜ
By: *Ron Mueller*

Around the World Publishing LLC
Cincinnati, Ohio

This story is a work of fiction. Names, characters, places, and incidents either are products of the author's imagination or are used fictitiously. Any resemblance to actual events or locales or persons, living or dead, is entirely coincidental.

Sins of the Daughter ©

ISBN 13: 978-1-68223-345-0

Distributed by Ingram
Alex Evercrest Model By: Pi03@ShutterStock
Cover Picture by: HaiGala @ShutterStock
Cover Design By: Ron Mueller

Ron Mueller

Dedicated to Mothers who Love their Children

Sins of the Daughter

1 Zelda

There was no moon, the surrounding forest was silent, about a dozen leather covered recliners supported the reposed audience out in the middle of a small clearing in the forest. The black silhouettes of several very tall pines seemed to be poking their tops into the millions of stars overhead. The air was cool, and Zelda's wind break was exactly what she needed to be comfortable. She was impressed by the indigenous young woman, dressed in a traditional tribal outfit standing on the flat bed of the truck that had brought them all out from the hotel to the clearing in the forest.

The young lady introduced herself as Kaseweetin of the Nehiyawak Peoples Nation or also known as the Plains Cree.

She then looked up, raised her arms and in her language seemed to be praying to the stars.

She then introduced her nimosôm or her grandfather that was up on the platform with her.

She said that her, nôhkom, or grandmother had passed away but that her spirit was present.

After a moment of silence, she use her hand to accent her outfit and said she was wearing the outfit that her grandmother had dressed in for special occasions.

She pointed out the wide necklace and the feather in her hair and added that they had been gifts from her grandmother and mother.

She then added that family life and the social fabric were important to the Cree. She pointed out that her people were no different from so many other societies where family and the interaction with other members of the society were the values that held them together.

Then she paused before pointing to a group of stars and described them as the Grand Mother Spider and that just below the grandmother were the seven sisters known as the Pleiades to most civilizations but to her people they are known as Pakone Kisik and surrounded the hole or place where all her people had come from.

She then paused again and then she shared that the stars held bears, thunderbirds, and more. It held all the spirits of past peoples and animals.

She pointed to the Big Dipper and said that it was known to the Cree as Mista Muskwa or the Big Bear.

In the Cree legend, Mista Muskwa was a massive bear that roamed the land doing whatever he wanted. He was a bully who was defeated by the seven brave birds that formed the ring now known as Corona Borealis.

She said that there was also the story of the moose running in circles after being startled. In Cree it is called mooswa acak "moose spirit" because when a moose is startled, it will run in a big, huge circle, and then continue on its way. That is what Mars does periodically in the night sky.

She stopped for a moment and put her hand on her Grandfather's shoulder. She then said that the Cree had The Seven Grandfather Teachings that formed the foundation of the Cree way of life.

The seven teachings were Wisdom, Love, Respect, Bravery, Honesty, Humility, and Truth.

These teachings were fundamental and were still practiced by the Cree.

She said that;

The Beaver carried the wisdom,

The Eagle that soared so high bestowed the gift of love.

The Buffalo not only gave the gift of food and clothing but also the gift of respect.

The Bear with all of it many rascally habits gave the gift of courage and bravery.

The Wolf was both a symbol of bravery and also of humility.

The Turtle with its hard shell and slow, but stead movement carried truth and bestowed it on all. She added that sometimes it gave truth to those needing to finally finish their journey.

She then explained that the Cree were one of the largest native groups in North America and that the name "Cree" came from "Kristineaux," or "Kri" for short, a name bestowed by French fur traders.

She explained that the Cree land stretched all the way across Canada and that the current population of Cree was somewhere around two-hundred thousand and that at one time it had been close to a million but disease, when they first met the white man, had devastated them.

Zelda was startled when a hand lightly shook her shoulders. She realized that she had dozed off. She had yet to check in at her hotel that was in Saskatoon.

The hour ride in the back of the truck back was lost in thought as she once again relived the fight with her sister Aada.

Aada had followed her out to Middle Cove Beach and caught her making out with her boyfriend. The boyfriend had immediately fled, and she ended up physically defending herself as her sister beat her with a tree limb. She rushed her sister and pushed. He sister tripped on a stone and fell backwards.

The loud crack had startled her. She had watched as the blood seemed to flow out and spread like a red velvet blanket as it covered the stones on the beach.

The evening sun's rays seemed to withdraw and let darkness come across the water and envelop them.

She did not know how long she had stood in silence wondering what to do.

It was hard for her to recall exactly how she had pulled her sister up the hillside to a crevasse where she then dropped her into. The crevasse was at least ten feed deep.

Once Aada's body was down at the bottom of the crevasse, she had thrown and pushed rocks down to cover her and had collapsed part of the crevasse so that Aada was covered by at least four feet of rock. She took the tree limp that Aada had beaten her with and was able to break loose a large slab of stone that was about ready to fall on its own. She said a prayer and wished Aada good luck in which ever realm she had gone. She threw the limb down on top of the stone.

She remembered driving back and parking Aada's car in the student parking lot which was its normal location and then she went to her dorm room and fell asleep.

It was several days later before her mother called and asked if she had seen Aada.

She answered that she had not seen her for several days. She smiled at the fact that she had told the truth.

But her mother was not satisfied with not knowing where Aada was and Zelda not knowing either.

Aada's death triggered an urge in her mind that defied her attempts to control it.

Since Aada's death she had repeated the ending scene on the beach multiple times.

In those scenes she surprised her victim with various ending scenarios. The victims were always male. She thought she understood why. Aada's boyfriend had avoided her like she had the plague.

She went out numerous times to the beach as she visualized killing someone with one of the thousands of stones. Just before her graduation she had gone out and was visualizing and acting out how she planned to kill Dillon when her mother asked if this was where she had killed Aada.

She stopped in shock. Her mother was dressed in one of her best dresses, so Zelda knew that she had followed her for a reason.

She smiled and said that yes she had killed her. She asked her mother if she wanted to see where Aada was buried.

He mother just nodded but did not say a word.

Zelda walked slowly up the hill and took her mother up just above where Aada's body was located. She knew that the stones there were all very loose and constantly falling into the ravine. She pointed down into the ravine.

Her mother stepped forward to look.

Zelda gave her mother a slight push and watched as the stones under her feet gave way and she slid down into the ravine with her legs buried in stones up to mid-thigh. She push more stones with her feet and watched the stones get up to her mother's waist.

Her mother cried out and asked if she were crazy.

Zelda nodded and sat down and with the heels of her shoes she pushed with all her might and felt the slab of stone breaking loose and caught a glimpse of her mother raising he arms as if to stop the stone from crushing her.

Zelda remembered laying back and laughing at the stupidity that such an action indicated.

Getting her mother's car and her car back to the City had taken forever.

She would drive one car a few hundred feet and then run back and take that car past the one in front for a few hundred feet. She had done that all night and had finally gotten her car back to the college parking place then had taken her mother's car to the apartment building. A few days later she had packed up all her mother's belongings and put them in her mother's car and had driven the car out and put it to the bottom of a lake.

That day she had been prepared for the hike back to her campus.

She had graduated the following day. She had watched all the kids signal their parents as they walked across the stage. When it was her turn she smiled and waved just like all the rest.

She had chosen her career based on that urge to duplicate the beach scene. She knew she needed a career that provided the opportunity that would allow her to play out her desire but make it almost impossible to have the act of a missing person be easily connect to her.

She had solved the problem of having a mother she despised for repeatedly making the point of letting her know that she had a name at the end of the alphabet and her sister had one starting with the first letter.

After a few months on the job, she had invited Dillon out for a drink. He was now working as a sales rep for a little company selling fire alarms.

She invited him to her room at a motel near where he had settled. He was still mister, "let me get into your pants." And she did let him, but she took the top. She hit him on the side of the head with one of the beach stones. She took him out to her car and put him in the trunk. She checked out of the apartment.

She went to his apartment and found that he had little in the way of possessions. They all fit in his car and then she drove to the same lake where her mother's car was located and pushed it in. She always wondered how close the two cars sat to each other at the bottom of that lake.

She had had decided that she was going to be number one in as many facets of her life as she could figure out. She was sure that she had reached that position when she buried her last border body.

It was body eighty-two by her count. As far as she could determine every additional body was now going to put her that much farther ahead of any other serial killer on record. And she had many more Canada-US crossings to go.

It had taken three years and three assignment changes. Each assignment moved her ever westward along the border.

She was able to maintain a smooth steady planting of bodies at or near each of the border crossings.

She had not been in a hurry. She was steady and smooth. She consistently located her victim from a pool of men similar to Dillon.

After making sure they were estranged from family, she planned the timing, the method, and the date carefully while making sure that everything she did would be seen as "normal."

The move to her third work assignment had taken a little longer than she had wanted but she was in the Great Lakes region and while she waited she decided to take up fishing to kill some time.

It turned out she liked fishing after all!

She was currently working on her move to the next work assignment that would take her all the way to the West Coast.

A few weeks after her return from her last crossing associated with her current assignment, she was eating lunch in the cafeteria by herself when she overheard two of her co-workers discussing the fact that the department was hiring a detective located in Cincinnati, Ohio, that had the reputation of having solved every case that had been assigned to her.

The RCMP was asking this detective to help them solve what they thought might be the work of a serial killer.

Alarm bells went off in Zelda's mind. She asked the coworker at the next table, what had made the department ask for the help.

The person that seemed to be in the know replied that the department had a list of missing women and the two bodies that had recently been dug up turned out to be people on that list. She had heard that there were at least twenty women on the missing person's list and the RCMP and the FBI had made no progress in the past year in finding or resolving any of the cases.

Zelda was somewhat relieved that the focus seemed to be on missing young women. That would put the hunters into another area and away from her list of people. She decided that she should do some research on the person whose name she learned was Alex Evercrest.

She wondered what made him so special.

She was soon surprised to learn that it was not a male but a female detective. She became concerned as she began reviewing the news reports on this person. One of the reports had highlighted her as "Cincinnati's Black Annie Oakley" and that pushed her over the edge.

She decided that she wanted to see this person live.

She was able to use her department's internal computer to get the address where this detective lived.

She researched the Cincinnati area for tourist attractions and learned there was an amusement park, a botanical garden, several museums, an extensive waterfront park, an aquarium, and some great malls for shopping. She decided to take a vacation and check those places out and as a side see this Alex in person.

She had no intension of having any actual contact, but she wanted to observe and get a feel for the person that might be her enemy.

She decided on a bed and breakfast on the Kentucky side of the river that had a view of the Cincinnati skyline. This seemed to be a way to be on location, be comfortable and be outside of the actual city.

Her boss congratulated her on finally taking some time off and using the vacation days she had been accumulating. She urged her to take several weeks and enjoy herself. She asked where Zelda was planning on vacationing.

Zelda had been prepared for the question, and she held up two brochures. One for a two-week ship cruise in the Bahamas and one to a resort in Cancun.

She did not specify either. It was hard for her to lie but easy to misdirect.

Her boss pointed at the resort brochure and suggested she go there, enjoy the beach, the food, the massages, and the men that frequented the bars.

Zelda nodded and thanked her for helping her make up her mind.

She then went home packed and boarded a flight to Detroit and from there drove to Cincinnati. She felt that by doing so she would not be broadcasting where she had actually gone.

It took her a full day to drive, and she arrived at her rental at the Bluffs of Devou Park late at night.

She ordered breakfast in and spent most of the Saturday morning sitting on the deck enjoying the view.

In the afternoon she took a drive into Cincinnati and stopped at the River Front Park and walked along the river.

She saw only a few black individuals, and most were family groups with several people including children. There was one couple walking and holding hands and one sitting in the swinging seats.

None of the women were Alex.

Zelda had two photos of Alex in her possession so she felt that she would recognize her if she happened to accidently run into her.

Two riders went past along the pathway on high end touring bikes. She was sure that one was Alex but there was no way to know for sure.

It, however, made her more eager to see what Alex looked like in person.

She stopped at the point where she felt she was standing on the spot where the body of the victim of Alex's first case had been located.

She decided to drive to the apartment address she had for Alex and then drive from there to the police station that had been featured in one of the articles and where Alex's office was located.

She drove up the street from the park on the street where Alex had been shot by an angry mother and father that blamed her for killing their hoodlum son.

She drove past the apartment building and then went by the public library where Alex had been attacked by a person firing an AK-15 from the back of a pickup. She recalled that Alex had shot and killed the driver of the pickup and the shooter and had fired only two bullets.

She scouted out a place where she could see both the front entrance and the side entrance to the police station. It only had street parking and at least on this Saturday the street parking was open.

She did not want to attract attention and decided that Eden Park was her next destination. She parked and walked around the Mirror Lake and stopped at the location where Alex had found the clue that had solved her first case.

She sat down on the wall of the lake and thought about how dangerous a person like Alex might be. She planned to keep close tabs on how Alex approached her involvement with the RCMP. If necessary she would make sure that Alex never made it through the case.

She figured that she would end her Saturday venture at one of the famous local rib restaurants that had an Ohio Riverside view.

The view and the food were both worth the stop. She thought about the rest of her stay and decided that she would continue to develop her understanding of the person she now knew was a true and deadly hunter, and a potential adversary.

She had no illusions about how dangerous a person like Alex could be.

She had studied Alex's bodily statistics and in bodily terms Alex seemed frail.

In action she must be a cyclone of action and destruction. From everything that she had been able to learn, if Alex were keeping score of bodies, she would probably best her own current body count.

However Alex had faced those that she killed when they had weapons.

In her case Zelda recognized that she drugged or surprised her victims and then killed them when they were helpless.

A shiver went down her back when she realized that she had just thought of Alex as a number one.

She decided to call it a day but on the way back to her B&B she stopped and bought two bottles of her favorite wine. She planned to relax and think deeply about what might be ahead for her and how she should prepare for it.

She decided that her Sunday would be spent at the amusement park and then she was going to drive out to where Alex had killed three thugs with only the handle of a broken chair.

She was really impressed with this person that was referred to as "Cincinnati's Black Annie Oakley." Her initial impression and take was one of admiration.

She thought about it for a moment and thought that she should be honest and add that she also had an initial feeling that she should be very afraid of her.

<u>2 Unnoticed</u>

*T*he weekend had been a pleasant one. She and Matt had one of their more pleasant weekends. Matt's EMT members had joined them for the first time for a ride from the Ohio river front and on to the Loveland trail. They had started the ride at the River Front Park and biked all the way to Loveland where they had stopped. Alex treated them all to coffee and a muffin at her favorite coffee shop.

The sky was clear, the temperature perfect and there was only a light breeze which would be at their back on the way back. She got to know the team much better, and she got to thank them in a more personal way for having them save her when the angry mother and father had shot her.

The bike ride had been great, but she ended up with a nagging feeling that she was being watched. She kept returning to the beginning of the ride.

As they were taking off, they had gone past the point where the body of the person on her very first case had been found.

She was startled to see a woman standing on the edge of the path in the very same spot that she had stood on that early morning, which seemed like only yesterday but had been several years ago.

It sent a shiver up her back, and it reminded her that she had not recently connected with, Samantha, the wife of, Paul Langley, the victim in her first case. She put calling her on her to do list.

What bothered her was that as she approached the woman seemed to stare at her and when she looked into her helmet bike mirror she saw the woman staring after her.

She thought of going back but she was with Matt and his team.

She had returned from the bike ride, and the thought of the woman came to her again.

Sunday she and Matt went to the park for a picnic and a sat through a concert. They then watched a movie at her apartment and later had a Chinese dinner they had ordered in and then they sat together on the couch and spent the evening reading.

On Monday she and Johnnie followed their normal routine and bicycled in together.

Alex knew that the last several cases had weighed heavily on her and on all of the team. She looked around and watched each of the team members and was relieved to see that they seemed to be well into recovery.

Bill had a cup of coffee and was listening to one of Travis's many tales as they both ate their morning donuts.

Johnnie had biked in with her and was probably the most relaxed of the team. He was a Vietnam veteran that seemed to have nerves of steel. His morning talks and ride in with her had helped her immensely.

She was very aware of her own vulnerabilities but getting regular counseling was of great help. Her very personal and close relationship with Matt put her on solid footing.

The fundamental bed rock that kept her sane was what her parents had always taught her; "Stand on the fundamental principles of honesty, integrity, and treating others the way you wish to be treated." That guidance allowed her to tackle the most extreme cases and come through with only what she considered "flesh wounds," which, over time, healed.

The last series of cases had touched her mind, and she had experienced the effects of PTSD and had a new appreciation of what Trey had gone through after his return from Iraq. The counseling and the support they team gave each other made a significant difference.

She was more worried about her partner, Trey, who was war hardened but who carried his heart on his sleeve. The last few cases had been extremely hard on him.

In one case, he had almost been physically beaten to death, then in the next case his heroics had gotten him so bruised by a shower of bullets hitting his protective gear that the doctor was worried about internal organ damage.

He had a tough exterior and as the doctor noted he also had a tough interior. He had also overcome his PTSD and had coached the rest of the team based on his personal experience.

Alex had suggested that he take several weeks off and go on a real vacation. Today was his first day back from three weeks in Cancun where he had taken Lindsay and Nolan.

Trey walked in with a cup of coffee in one hand and a bear claw roll in his other. He was smiling and was sporting an golden tan. He sat down and asked if she wanted half of the bear claw.

Alex had never seen Trey looking so good and so relaxed. She nodded to indicate she was for half of the bear claw and said that she was looking forward to it, but she needed to go and get a second cup of coffee to go with it.

As she walked to the coffee pot, the Chief came to the door to his office and asked her to come to his office after having her coffee and roll.

The look on his face let her know that he was about to assign a case to her and by the looks it was going to be another one of the different cases. She knew that nothing was happening in Cincinnati, so it had to be a request from some other police jurisdiction.

She was aware that each of the recent different cases had given the department a significant boost to the budget and the politics were now positive and supportive of "hiring" out their detectives.

Alex decided to take her time and enjoy the bear claw and cup of coffee and not worry about going to the Chief's office.

Johnnie was the first to ask what she thought she was going to hear from the Chief.

Then Travis threw out one of his wild theories that a body had been found in the Himalayas that verified that Big Foot ate humans, and the Tibetans were asking for Alex to come and capture it.

Bill commented that he thought that counseling had been helping Travis, but it was apparent that he was still as crazy as ever.

Trey shook his head and commented that they should check Travis's desk to see where he kept his bottle.

Alex smiled and said it was good to see that everyone was doing well, and she was going to go in and see just what the Chief had that would give them all some purpose other than to exchange meaningless libretti.

Travis called out after her and said he did not know what libretti meant and he didn't have a dictionary.

Alex put up both hands and hunched her shoulder as she walked into the Chief's office.

She could hear Johnnie explain what the word meant as she closed the door.

The Chief asked if she needed anything to drink.

Alex walked over to his coffee pot and refilled her cup and then sat down.

The Chief held up a file and said that the request for help had come from the Royal Canadian Mountain Police or as they were now called, the RCMP, via the FBI.

He said that he had gotten a call from their friend Harold Zimmerman of the DEA who had connect him with the FBI Canadian's liaison.

He added that Harold had given him warning that the case was unusual in that it seemed to be a case that encompassed most of the Canadian to US border.

The Chief then then described the conversation he had with a Denton Tremaine of the FBI. Denton highlighted that the case had made no progress since the discover of two bodies along the Canadian US border.

Now after close to a year of joint investigation of more than twenty cases of missing women they were reaching out to see if they could find a way to break the case.

The Chief looked at her and said that Denton said that he had followed several of her cases and was wondering what it would take to get her assigned to the case they were calling the Canadian Stalker Case.

I told him that money talked but he did not assign the cases and told him that you made the call. I agreed give you the details and he would have to personally talk with the two of us before a decision would be reached.

Alex reached out for the case file and suggested a meeting in Cincinnati. She and the team would prepare for the meeting, and it would be a team decision about taking the case.

She pointed out that she had taken all of what she considered her team through a series of very trying cases and she wanted them to be part of the decision making.

The Chief nodded and agreed that it would be a good idea. He asked what she thought of how each of the team was doing.

Alex replied that it seemed that things were back to normal. Each of them was attending individual sessions with their analyst and they were all still having a group session once a month.

He asked her how she was doing.

Alex replied that her life had also returned to normal, and she had enjoyed the quiet and boring few weeks since her return from Hawaii but was already thinking about when she would be going back to her new home there.

The Chief replied that he had rented a week at her new home in Hawaii. Rose was very excited to go and had said that he should take it easy on her favorite detective.

Alex smiled and told him to tell her that he always took it easy on Trey.

He shook his head and said that he would do nothing of the kind. His home life was good, and he was going to keep it that way.

He gave the file folder to her.

Alex thanked him and let him know that she was taking the team into a huddle room to go over the material together in preparation for meeting with Denton.

As Alex reached her desk, Travis commented that he knew a few big words as well but he did not want to embarrass her so he would just keep them to himself.

Alex held up the file and commented that she had a humdinger of a case that they could swot. But they would need to be able to grasp the basics of construing.

Johnnie started laughing.

Bill shook his head and commented that Travis was causing them all to listen to spoken English that he could not understand.

Trey was also laughing and said he knew the basics of construing.

Travis shook his head put his hands up and said, "I give."

Alex smiled and suggested they all go to a huddle room and review a case that was coming to them from the RCMP via the FBI.

Travis replied that he understood what she had just said except he wondered who the RCMP were. He added that he was now getting bored and missed the noise of gunfire.

Alex led the way to the huddle room and after everyone was seated she pulled out the contents of the envelope. She suggested that she take a picture of each page, one at a time and send it to Johnnie who could post it on the big screen, and they could study the report together.

Bill commented that it would be great because then his partner would be able to understand what the case was about.

Alex ignored the comment and took a picture of the first page and sent it to Johnnie. Once the document was on the screen, Alex pointed out the title.

Trey read the title, "The Canadian Stalker Case." He asked what was being stalked.

Alex sent the picture of the next page to Johnnie. She then sent pictures of all the pages before sitting down.

Johnnie put up the next page which was a summary of what the case was about. It highlighted the possibility that up to twenty-three women were the victims of a serial killer. Two bodies had been found but they were so deteriorated that they had yet to be identified. It seemed that the bodies had been brutally bludgeoned to death. The bodies had only been found because the perpetrator must have been rushed or interrupted while covering the bodies and that some animal had dug them up. The bodies were in remote locations. The Mounted Police had only found them when two different Mounted Police had investigated the areas because of vultures flying overhead.

Alex let out a groan. She shook her head and said that the case was going to be a heart breaker. To solve the case, they were going to have to find many bodies and figure out the pattern the killer was using to find the victims and how often and how he had kept the disappearance of twenty women unnoticeable for the length of time he had.

Trey added that they would most likely be slogging through countless miles of woods trying to find bodies.

Johnnie commented that they should think about using the latest technology and do most of their searching with drones. He added that they could search more territory, and they would go into the woods only when they found some promising sign that needed closer investigation. If they could find some sort of signature or pattern that they could discern from the air they might be able to speed up the discovery of the bodies.

He suggested that they use the two bodies as their base points and first search the miles of space between them. If they found bodies, the distance between them might give them a pattern.

Alex complimented Johnnie for a great idea.

Trevor joked that somebody had been feeding Johnnie too much brain food or maybe if the team fed him more he might solve the case before they all had to face the Canadian biting flies.

Alex laughed and reminded everyone that the last time they had treated Johnnie to a barbeque rib lunch and let him watch logs floating down the Ohio River, he had pretty much solved the case they had been on. All the team had to do was to go in and face crazy gun men trying to kill them.

She pointed to the clock and commented that it was close to lunch time, and she was ready to take Johnnie to watch logs floating down the river.

Trey commented that he was through with the report and wondered if everyone was on board on taking on the case.

Alex countered that they should hold that decision until they met with Denton their FBI contact and got more details about the case and how they would work with the FBI and the RCMP.

Bill seconded her proposal and said that it was too early to close on doing the case. He figured they would, but he was sure there would be some bargaining that they would end up doing before agreeing.

He reminded everyone how well the weekend family mini vacations had worked to keep the home fires burning. He was sure that would be one feature he would be wanting the team to repeat. He added that he had no clue what would be available as they searched along the Canadian border, but he was sure that fishing would be one feature that would be available.

Alex agreed and said that she was driving one car. She was going to see if the Chief wanted to join them for lunch. She asked Johnnie which restaurant with a river view he wanted to go to and then asked him to call and make a reservation for six.

She wished that Matt could also be there, but she knew he was on duty. She gave him a call and asked if he wanted to have a carry out lunch for he and his team.

Matt said that he was sure his team would love to get some carryout. He asked if she were paying.

Alex replied that she indeed was, and he and the team could come by and pick up their order when it was ready. She would have the restaurant call them when the pickup was ready.

The Chief said that he would join them for lunch, but he needed to be back to take the call from Denton's boss. He said he wanted to make sure that the financial and authority jurisdiction were clearly defined.

He asked if Alex wanted to join him for the call.

Alex shook her head and said she was much more interested in what Johnnie had to say about his take on the case than worry about the money and jurisdiction.

She added that the Chief knew where she stood on jurisdiction and investigative control, and she trusted him to make it clear that she did not take orders from any other person but her Chief.

The Chief smiled and said she had taught him well and he had her back.

Alex then led the way out to the parking lot. She let everyone know that the lunch was on her if Johnnie did a good job of sharing his vision of how high tech could help them solve the case and which end of Canada they should begin their search.

Travis commented that Johnnie better come up with a good story because he wanted to be treated to a juicy steak and listen to a tale that he could put his arms around.

Johnnie smiled and said that everyone should order from the top of the menu because he had a crazy tale to tell and a journey, of five-thousand, five-hundred and twenty-five miles, that the team would have to travel to solve the case of the Canadian Unnoticed Serial Stalker. He said that they all should learn to CUSS and laughed at his own joke.

Alex shook her head and commented that she had made a mistake and should have taken him to a burger place so she could save the money for her wedding dowry.

Travis complimented Johnnie on improving the name of the case and he was right at home cussing up a storm.

Bill shook his head and commented that they had not even agreed to take on the case and they had two people that were making jokes about a very serious and chilling one.

Travis shook his head and said it would only be chilling if they didn't get done before the beginning of winter.

Bill pushed Travis out of the door and said he needed to ride with Alex in her old car.

3 Extensive

*L*unch turned out to be a very quiet affair. It was a little ironic that the restaurant that Johnnie had selected looked out over the River Front Park to the spot of her first case. As she ate, she kept thinking about that case and the twist that it had presented. The perpetrator had not fit the profile of a murderer.

Johnnie seemed to be focused on his steak as he cut small pieces and chewed slowly.

Alex knew that he was really focused on the case and was most likely not really enjoying the Tenderloin that he was slowly eating. This was the most serious that she had seen him. She wondered what about the case that had hooked him.

The Chief excused himself after eating his porter house and said he had to be back at his desk to take the call coming from the FBI Headquarters in DC.

He commented that he was going to see if the case could be handled out of the Cincinnati FBI offices so that they could all be closer to home and a closer coordination could be achieved.

Alex wished him a good call and let him know that she would record whatever Johnnie finally decided to say.

Travis made a remark that he hoped the Johnnie hadn't lost his voice. He went on and said that it would be OK because it gave him more time to think about what he was going to order for dessert.

Alex saw Matt come in to pick up the lunches for the EMT team. She went over and gave him a hug and asked how the day was going.

He replied that it was a usual day. They had just finished their third run to the hospital and were hoping to be able to sit in the park and eat lunch before they got the next call. He asked about what the team had learned from Johnnie so far.

Alex replied that Johnnie had not spoken a word since he ordered his meal.

Matt shook his head and commented that he was now worried about the case and hoped that it was not going to be too overwhelming. He gave her a hug and said that he needed to have a sane person to share his evenings with.

Alex asked if he was coming over to her apartment when he got off.

Matt smiled and said that he would be at her door by eight thirty.

Alex walked back to the table just as Johnnie put down his knife and fork.

He looked at her and said he had been concentrating and envisioning what a very smart deviant hunter-predator would do if he was targeting his victims in a very specific way with a specific purpose.

He said that he had traveled the length of the Canadian border and figured that there would most likely be a body every one-hundred and eighty-five miles.

The bodies would be about six per province.

The predator had two purposes. He was satisfying his personal urge to kill, and he was taunting the RCMP.

He suggested that they ask how far apart the two bodies that were discovered happened to be and the specific location of each body. The team could then see if they could find the bodies in between and verify his thesis. Then they should start at the very Eastern part of the border and work back toward the West.

He added that if he were right and they could establish a timeline they would want to leap back to the last body to the west and see if they could get ahead of the serial killer. He pointed out that they should establish a regional contact at each RCMP provincial headquarters.

Johnnie said that he knew a few cities that were headquarters for the Mounted Police, but the team should pinpoint each.

He said the two headquarters he was aware of was in Montreal and the other in Vancouver. He smiled and commented that those two would be great for weekend vacations.

Trey looked at Alex and asked if she bought into Johnnie's thesis.

Alex nodded and said that it made a weird sort of sense and if they decided to take the case they would need to begin by verifying what Johnnie had described. She pointed out that neither the FBI or the RCMP would be very accepting of what Johnnie had suggested, and it would be up to them to find the first body in the East where Johnnie was suggesting it would be.

Bill said that he and Travis would locate the RCMP headquarters in each province and they would identify what would be available for a weekend vacation. He figured getting back to Cincinnati from some province and back might take longer than a weekend would allow.

Alex thanked him and suggested he wait until they learned more about the case but that when they took the case she wanted to make sure that they would look at how to keep their lives in balance.

She figured Johnnie's take on the case was going to make it a long one.

The Chief was waiting for their return and signaled for them to come to his office. He shared the fact that Denton Tremaine was a friend of Brian Lexter the local FBI bureau Chief. He would be arriving the next day to meet with the team.

Alex asked what the Chief's take was on the case.

He answered that it was going to be up to the team to figure out how to solve the case. He said that the RCMP had spent several months before contacting the FBI. The FBI had spent several months as well, and both organizations had come up dry.

All they had was the location of the two bodies that were about two thousand miles apart and the forensic evidence seemed to be compromised. He pointed out there might be information that had not been in the report that Denton might be able to share with the team.

Alex nodded and said that Johnnie had come up with a theory and pattern for the killings and the distance between the bodies and it would be crucial for the team to verify his theory. She added that if Johnnie was correct and the distance between the bodies that had been found was a thousand miles, there would be another ten to eleven bodies in between the two.

The Chief blurted out a curse and asked how Johnnie could know such a thing.

Johnnie nodded and said that it was crazy, and he hoped his idea about the killer was wrong, but he had put his theory on the table so that the team would have a place to start when they took on what in essence was a cold case.

Alex supported Johnnie by reminding the Chief that Johnnie was their magician, the hacker that got into and controlled satellites and into areas that were in the grey areas.

He had pulled off some amazing things and if the team took on the case it would start by finding the bodies in between the two that had already been found.

"Yea, I haven't forgotten the escapades and successes of our ancient war veteran. I am just shocked at what he is proposing," the Chief responded.

Alex said that she and the rest of the team was shocked but if they took on the case they all agreed they were going to work first on verifying Johnnie's theory because if the model that he had put on the table was true, then the next step was to find the first body and find out how long the killings had been going on and the frequency at which they had been occurring.

The Chief asked how many bodies Johnnie was projecting.

Johnnie shook his head and said that it would be more than thirty.

This time the Chief bowed his head and said that he saw trouble ahead for the team because both the RCMP and that FBI were thinking that the number might be around six to twelve bodies.

Alex said that the team had already surfaced that concern, and it was a determining factor as to whether they would take on the case. They were going to insist that the entire US-Canadian border was in play and that they would determine where they would hunt for bodies, and they would determine how to catch the killer. It was to be the teams case and all they were looking for was support from both organizations.

The RCMP's and FBI's opinions would be listened to, and their information would be considered but the decision of how to run the investigation would be up to the team.

Trevor smiled and commented that it would at least be up to Alex.

Alex shook her head and reminded him how often his input had resulted in a change of direction and besides this time he already had the assignment to make the case family friendly.

Bill nodded and said that he would take Travis aside and give him a good talking to.

The Chief then made the point that the assignment would be good for the department. It would give a good boost to the budget if the team took on the case.

He smiled and said that he had also heard that there was some great fishing that he could enjoy in Canada.

Alex asked if the Chief had the exact distances between the two bodies.

He responded that he could have the exact distances in a few minutes. He would put in a call to get that information.

Alex suggested the team go back to the huddle room and figure out where the RCMP headquarters were for each province and then figure out where the bodies would most likely be.

She added that Johnnie should look for the technology that they would need to be able to sit comfortably in the control van and search for bodies.

Trey spoke up and said that he had an acquaintance that dealt in the drone technology, and he would contact her and ask her to recommend the best technology.

Alex nodded and said she liked that approach because it let Johnnie coach them on how to figure out the location of the first body and then the potential spots as they went west.

The Chief had been online and said the information was on the department computer and the team should get out of his office.

He added that he had to align the local politics and begin the advertising campaign for the case and the team.

Alex smiled and said that she wanted to make sure that he didn't over sell the case.

He responded that the team's reputation sold itself. All he had to do was to make sure he figured out how the politicians could earn recognition from the teams good work.

Alex said that it was up to him. She and the rest of the team would focus on organizing the case and then getting the perpetrator into court and then to jail.

She warned him that the only thing she would later try to extract was extra time off.

When they got to the huddle room, Johnnie put up a map showing the Canadian-US border. He pointed to each of the provinces. He point out that Quebec was the Eastern most province that they would be interested in, and that Montreal was where the main RCMP's headquarters was located.

He then went to Ontario, pointed to London, Ontario, and said that it was located halfway between Detroit and Toronto.

The next RCMP headquarter was located in Winnipeg, but the bodies would now most likely be right on the US-Canada border. Then the next headquarter would be in Regina. The next would be in Edmonton. The final one would be in Surrey, a suburb of Vancouver.

Alex said she had the location of the two bodies. One was located just west of where highway eight three crossed the border into the US. The other was near Wild Horse a short distance off highway forty-one. She commented that following Johnnie's model there should be two or three bodies in between.

Bill asked if they were going to need a RCMP contact in every province.

Alex nodded and said she was going to ask that one senior RCMP person in each province be identified and then brought on board the team's effort. She wanted to make sure that as they moved along the border they would not run into barriers put up be the provincial leaders.

Trey commented that he had sent a message to his friend that represented several companies that made drones, and she had already responded with several that would have flight ranges that extended to ten miles if enough elevation was maintained. She had shared that one of the more expensive models had the ability to use GPS to aid in navigation.

He said that if he gave her the type of use, she would be happy to show him two or three drones and demonstrate their use.

Trey said that he had arranged for a demonstration for the coming week. She would bring the drones to the River Front and demonstrate their use. She said that most of the drones she was going to show would require some training.

Alex looked around and asked for each person to voice their opinion about the case and the pros and cons for taking or not taking it on.

Travis led off with the fact that it seemed like a challenging case. It had stumped two leading police agencies. It seemed like a case where there would be fewer gun battles then a couple of their previous cases.

He smiled and said he was in.

Bill spoke up and agreed he added that it would be a chance for most of them to get an exposure to Canada that most Americans never would.

Johnnie said he was for going after the serial killer and he wondered if they could move fast enough to prevent any additional young women from losing their lives.

Trey nodded and said he agreed with all of the points made. He said that the pivotal point for him was not to allow the team to get mired down in the politics of working between two powerful agencies and two countries.

Alex nodded and said that she thought they would be ready to meet with Denton and who ever came with him and get agreement to how they would all work together.

She reiterated the fact that they had the lead in the investigation approach but if it came down to apprehending and arresting the perpetrator, she would push for either the RCMP or the FBI to take the lead. It would depend on which side of the border they apprehended the individual.

She suggested that Johnnie select the locations that they would survey to look for additional bodies. She asked that he try and get pictures of what an actual grave might look like from the air.

She asked Bill and Travis to figure out what they would do each weekend of the investigation and how family members could be at the selected venue.

She said that she wanted to be involved in setting up the use of the drones.

She added that the teams mode of transportation should be a bus converted into a mobile home that could sleep all of them and that could tow the equipment that they would be using to hunt for the bodies.

Trey wondered whether they might be able to arrange to have a driver so the five of them could focus on finding graves.

Alex said that she liked the idea of a driver, but she thought it should be more than one person and that they should also take on the cooking and be responsible for keeping the bus clean.

She added that they should probably include having several motorcycles to use when they had to go and check out a potential grave site.

Travis commented that if they were going to do the initial digging at a potential grave site they would need to be carrying several shovels and maybe picks.

Alex smiled and said that she was going home to visit her mother and father. They were two people that had made several long trips and who were great organizers.

She added that her father had a friend that was into converting buses and would most likely have the bus the team would love to have. She bet he would have one that had a roof based sitting area that would be a comfortable place to sit, launch their drones, and have their control center.

Travis laughed and said that something like that would cost a million buck.

Alex nodded and said it would be expensive, but they were worth it.

4 Contract

That evening Alex shared the outline of the case with Matt. She said that she was going to spend some of her own money and outfit the team with a comfortable bus converted into a mobile home. She was going to go home over the weekend and work the two items with her father and mother.

Her father had a friend in the business of building mobile homes in regular Greyhound like buses and she was going to see if he would build one to her specifications.

She was looking for one that could comfortably sleep at least six in single beds and also have a master bedroom in back.

She wanted the roof to have a railing around it and be set up to have people sit and fly drones from it.

She was going to have her mother draw up a contract that clearly spelled out how the team would interact with the RCMP and the FBI.

She wanted complete control of the team's activities and movement. She did not want interference from either organization.

She was looking for their assistance, and she wanted them in any action that might transpire when they were about to capture the criminal she was after.

She was also seeking to have a designated RCMP contact in each of the provinces that the team would be traveling through.

She asked if he wanted to go to home to Evanston with her.

Matt grimaced and said that there was no way he was going to be able to take the time off. He explained that two folks were off sick and that they left the unit two EMTs short.

Alex said she was sorry and that she had thought about going out to the apple orchard to see how the apples were growing.

Matt knew that was her way of reminding him that the last time they had gone out to the apple farm they had uncovered an organization, SLATE, which was kidnapping young women and then when done with them, they killed them. It was an organization that then came after her. She had survived the attempts on her life, but she was shot while attempting to capture one of the chief Slate leaders.

He had worried about her for the entire time that she was traveling across the country as she shut down SLATE and brought their leaders to justice. He hoped this new case would be less challenging. This case seemed to be the work of one person versus several organizations with multiple members.

He also knew that she was surrounded by team members that were fearless and had gone into multiple gun battles with her. He knew that because of her planning had come through with only bruises caused by the bullet hits they had experienced.

He knew of no one who had such fierce protectors.

Matt was also reassured by the fact that Trey was fearless and super protective of Alex. Matt himself had earned a medal of honor for his service in Iraq. He knew that Trey had also earned that and a purple heart. He had been a sniper and was a dead shot with any weapon that he held.

It made Matt feel better about Alex's habit of rushing towards trouble even when she was weaponless. Trey was always there to have her back.

Matt was also aware that Alex had Trey's back and had saved his life. She had overpowered four thugs with only a broken chair handle. Three of those thugs lost their lives by underestimating the lithe, slender, athletic, black female that took one thug out by ramming the point of the broken chair handle through his neck and then using his gun to take out the brutal thug that had almost beaten Trey to death. And then did not hesitate to shoot the third thug who tried to shoot it out with her.

The fourth thug was the person taking pictures of Trey's beatings and when he refused to give her his bosses name and location, she shot him in the leg and then put the gun to his head.

Matt knew that Alex at that moment might have pulled that trigger. She had been desperate to get Trey out of the freezing water where she had hidden him while she took on the thugs.

While Trey lay in the hospital, her other fearless friend Johnnie, an old but still very capable Vietnam Marine veteran, had backed her up as she pursued the boss of the thugs.

That boss had made the mistake to think that he could outgun her and ended up with a bullet between his eyes.

He recalled Alex saying that she had thought that she had closed things down but when a helicopter gunship turned her room into nothing but flying splinters she knew that she had triggered the ire of the person at the very top of the drug cartel.

She had two incidents of facing gunships and she had prevailed in both battles.

She then had taken the fight into the lion's den and confronted the leader of that cartel. He too underrated her and when he went shoot her in the back she turned and put three shots into his body: two in the chest and one through the forehead.

Ironically, she became friends with the cartel boss's wife who had prayed for someone to kill her husband. To this day that person, known as "The Angel on the Hill," sent a yearly million dollars to Alex who was referred to as the "Black Angel from the North."

The wife had wanted her husband killed because he had killed her parents. She regarded Alex as having been sent by the all-powerful.

All Matt knew was that he and Alex shared a warm, soft, soul-lifting relationship. He was always amazed about her tenacious, attack mode of operation that left him emotionally breathless when he learned what she was doing.

They had become close to Trey, his wife Lindsey, and his son Nolan.

They were also close to Annie Scotts, a person who had been abducted as a twelve-year-old and held prisoner for more than twelve years and who had two babies by her abductor. After Alex rescued Annie, she had become wealthy from the paintings that she had produced during her years of captivity.

Alex had convinced a friend to exhibit and offer the paintings for sale. That friend had helped Annie gain global recognition and her sales had made her independently wealthy.

The two blue eyed, blond girls, Linda, and Laurie, and Nolen were all close friends and they all called Alex "Aunt Alex," and he had inadvertently gained the title of "Uncle Matt."

Matt knew that Alex had ensured that her boss, the first black Cincinnati Chief of Detectives was in a position to negotiate a significant budget for the detective unit. Her continuing successes had earned the department national and now with the new Canadian connection he added International recognition to that title.

She also had an official standing as an Illinois Special Marshall reporting to the Illinois State Lieutenant Governor that she earned by eliminating the Mafia control of the Chicago police department.

On that case the "Angel on the Hill" had sent in a squad from the drug cartel that took out the Chicago Mafia leader when he ignored the warning not to harm Alex. That Mafia leader had underrated the power of the Mexican drug cartel.

She had a very close relationship with the Head of the Illinois DEA. He had been involved in several of her cases and had even gone out fishing with her.

The Sheriff of Loveland, Ohio sent her a bouquet every Valentine's Day. He had been a young deputy when Annie Scotts had been kidnapped and had been haunted for his entire career by that incident. The sheriff was aware that Alex had been shot as she saved Annie.

He credited her with lifting up his soul.

Matt knew that he was hopelessly in love with her and had left his best friend James Kaizer, sheriff of Wiggins, Mississippi, with whom he had served in Iraq.

He had moved to Cincinnati to pursue Alex.

His heart had stopped several times when it was his unit that arrived at the scene of a shooting where she was the target.

His EMT unit had transported Alex to the hospital where she was treated for two bullet wounds that almost killed her.

Then there was the time when he became an observer as Alex commanded the scene dressed in her bike riding shorts and walking awkwardly on her bicycle shoes.

He thought she looked hot.

She had shot and killed two persons that had tried to kill her. She had faced a modified AR-15 to fire like a machine gun. With her standard police issued pistol she had shot only twice, and she had won.

The driver of the blue pickup and the gunner had each been killed by a single bullet to the head.

He had been surprised when she had purchased the farm where she and Trey had faced the drug thugs and turned it into a rehabilitation center for battered women. The "Angel on the Hill" became her partner, and the farm had a full staff and handled twenty distraught young women at a time.

Alex had not stopped there but had purchased two homes in Cincinnati. One home was near the University of Cincinnati, and the other was near a technical training center. The two homes provided a place for up to ten women to attend the two institutions.

He had no clue how she managed to accomplish so much and still be so relaxed.

Matt had no doubt that she would solve the latest case that her team was getting ready to undertake.

He had no doubt that he would take every opportunity to be with her.

He gave her a kiss as he got out of bed to go to work. She put a hand on his cheek but never opened her eyes.

A few minutes later Alex opened her eyes and knew that the kiss that had slowly pulled her from her deep sleep like taffy being slowly stretched and pulled, had been Matt leaving for work.

She got up and poured herself a cup of coffee. She looked at the time and decided it was safe to call her mother and let her know that she was coming home for the weekend.

Rose-Anne was pleased to hear that Alex was planning to come home for the weekend. She asked if there was any special reason and smiled when Alex said she needed parental guidance.

She had long accepted that her daughter did pretty much what she had decided for herself that she was going to do. She was still amazed that the young woman who had been first in her class at Northwestern had chosen to go into law enforcement as a detective.

She had turned down high salary offers and had taken a low paying deputy position in a small town not far from their home.

Later she had transitioned to her current position in Cincinnati and had become nationally recognized for her ability to solve the toughest cases.

She was proud of how her daughter had risen to the top of her field.

She tried to get Alex to share what she needed parental guidance on, but Alex said that she was going to wait until they had breakfast on Saturday morning.

Rose-Anne commented to Russel, that she thought their daughter was planning to come home and engage the two of them in some scheme of hers.

Russel asked what made her think so, but it didn't make any difference because he liked the idea.

She replied that Alex had not wanted to share the reason that she was coming home until she got home and had simply said that she needed guidance from her parents.

"That would be great, I hope the guidance she is looking for won't be too challenging," he replied. I will get her car ready, and I will arrange for a Sunday morning fishing trip.

I hope she is thinking of doing some fishing.

"Well, I will count on the two of you to bring home at least one large lake trout that we can put on the lunch table.

Back in Cincinnati, Alex finished her coffee and then pushed her bike to the elevator and went down to meet Johnnie. They always rode in together but Johnnie insisted on picking different routes randomly so they could avoid getting shot.

Johnnie credited Alex with changing his life for the better and for giving him a purpose that was keeping him seventy-five years young. Even his time as a Marine in Vietnam did not compare with the action that he had been part of as he supported Alex.

Since the time that she had been attacked as they rode in to work where she had been in the lead, he insisted that he be the lead rider.

He recalled her laugh when he had suggested that arrangement and her snide remark that he was too ugly for anyone to shoot him whether he was in front or in back.

This morning Alex sensed that Johnnie had something on his mind. She asked him what was up.

Johnnie said that he wanted to be part of the field team on this case. He pointed out that this seemed to be a case less likely to experience gun battles but one that would entail solving a very complicated puzzle.

Alex thought for a moment and said that it made sense if they could get their transport linked to the internet via a sky link. She said that she was sure they would be doing a lot of specific location analysis, and she figured that the transport she was about to arrange for would have enough space.

Johnnie thanked her and said that he was looking forward to the weekends and getting to enjoy their neighbor to the North.

After they got to the station, Alex changed out of her riding outfit and stopped to get her morning coffee and then went and sat down at her desk. As always, she and Johnnie were the first ones in. She hoped that Bill and Trevor would bring in their usual morning box of sweet rolls.

She always had a half of a bear claw that she shared with Trey. Johnnie normally ate the second bear claw. Johnnie never gained weight no matter how much he seemed to eat. She on the other hand seemed to look at food and then have to run six miles to keep the pounds is check.

The Chief came in earlier than usual and waved to her to come into his office.

Alex knew that he had something about the case that he was going to ask her about.

The Chief greeted her and said that he had received a call from the FBI. He went on to say that Denton's boss wanted to make sure that Denton got to accompany the team to the field. Denton's role would be to be the FBI representative and liaison with the RCMP.

I let him know that if Denton was in the field with you, he would have to be willing to act in the capacity that you decided.

The Chief finished and asked if Alex was OK with Denton being with her team.

Alex thought for a moment and then replied that she was planning to obtain a large, customized bus for the team to travel in as they went along the border. She was sure it would hold six and she had five folks lined up. He could ride along on the bus and be part of her team. In the field he would need to follow the team rules. If the bus could not hold him then he would have to follow along by car.

She thought for a moment and said that it would be good to have a liaison to deal with the various regional RCMP contacts.

The Chief nodded and asked about her bus idea.

Alex commented that when the team was a significant drive from a good hotel accommodation she wanted them to get a good night's sleep and be able to have good meals and refreshments during the day.

He father was friends with a person who made conversion busses and then sold or leased them. She had been to one of his showings when she had been at the University and had been impressed with his product.

She was going to see if he could put a deck on such a bus that would allow the team to sit on top and fly their camera drones as they searched the forests for additional graves.

The Chief nodded and asked how much that might cost.

Alex smiled and said that unless he was willing to pay for a lease, she was going to front the cost. As the case developed, and he got to know the FBI better she would be quite willing to let them pick up the cost.

She added that she was going to have five or six small motorcycles either mounted on the bus or towed so the team would have flexibility in going through the forest or going on some errand.

The Chief commented he liked the fact that the case seemed to be a high tech one as compared to the last few battlefield intense cases.

He then smiled and asked if he could sleep on the couch if he visited the team when they were in the field. He knew that he was not being asked permission about the bus but being kept in the know.

He smiled and added that he cooked a mean Mexican styled breakfast omelet that he was willing to do for the privilege.

Alex liked the Chief's response and let him know that she was flying home that afternoon.

She would be back on Monday morning and let him know how her bus hunting had gone.

She shared that she was also asking her mother to draw up a legal document that would serve as the basis for a contract between the FBI, the RCMP and the Cincinnati Detective Organization. She figured that he would be the main signature, followed by the appropriate names from the FBI and the RCMP representatives. She would bring it back as a draft that he could finalize.

The Chief thanked her and commented that she was going to save him a lot of time and wanted to make sure that she thanked her mother for him.

He smiled and added that he knew that her father would have her out fishing on one of the weekend mornings and he wished her luck.

Alex said that she was looking forward to the fishing that she hoped would only be highlighted by the size of her catch and not the number of bullet holes in the side of the boat.

<u>5 Noodling</u>

She walked out of the office and asked the Chief's support to get her an afternoon flight to Chicago. Then she got a cup of coffee and went to her desk. She smiled when she saw one half of a bear claw under a napkin. She thanked Trey and asked how his evening had gone.

Trey said that both Lindsey and Nolan had sent their best wishes and that they were looking forward to the weekend vacations that you always planned.

Alex looked over to where Travis and Bill were looking her way. She raised her cup, said good morning, and asked Travis how his weekend family outing event identification was going.

Travis smiled and replied that he was waiting to hear that they had an official contract before spending any time getting all excited with what there was to do in Canada.

Johnnie chuckled and said that he had learned that Alex was getting her mother to draw up the contract with the FBI and the RCMP. His only request was that a clause be put in to give them all a bonus.

Bill nodded and suggested that a clause that said they would only work four days a week would also be attractive.

Travis then added that he was not greedy like the other members on the team, and he would settle for a clause that ensured they got to stay in the top suites at the few hotels where they might be staying.

Alex looked at Trey and asked what his special request might be.

Trey thought for a moment and said that he hoped that the trip would be relaxing, the scenery captivating and that Johnnie's theory would be wrong and there would be no more bodies.

Travis let out a groan and asked if the war hero had gone soft. He was with him about the scenery and about relaxing, but he figured if Johnnie was wrong it would most likely be that the body count would go up and that instead of just one killer they would find several.

Alex then shared her vision of the bus she was going home to order. It would be a bus that would hold at least nine and her bedroom would be in the back. They would all have luxurious bunks that would have a video and sound system and be large enough that they could sit, read, and relax there.

It would have a small kitchen area with a microwave, a small oven, small refrigerator, a sitting table for four and a small sink.

The front area would have individual lounge chairs. This front area would be able to expand out by about four feet and make the room spacious.

The rest room would feature a shower, a separate stool area and a separate sink and mirror nook.

She then went on to describe where the team would sit when looking for the graves. She described sitting on a deck on the top of the bus from which they would launch and control their individual drones. She said the seats would be cushioned and comfortable

She then described each of them having a mini-motor cycle that would be carried in the bus's storage area.

Alex ended by saying that except for the deck on top, the bus would be a standard luxurious touring bus.

Bill asked how the Chief had taken to the bus and motorcycle idea.

Alex smiled and said that once he knew that I was fronting the cost until he could figure out how to get either the FBI or the RCMP to pay for it, all he wanted to know was if there was a bunk for him.

She then added that the FBI wanted Denton to be in the field with them. She asked whether there were any objections.

Trey replied that he hoped that Denton would be easy to get along with.

Travis asked if the team could get pictures of the actual bus once Alex had made the arrangements. He was also curious what type of mini motor bikes they would chose.

Alex replied that the team should spend a couple of hours on deciding on motor bikes, drones, and think about any other items that they should be considering.

Travis piped up and said they needed a mini freezer to keep their steaks and spare ribs in.

Alex smiled and said that seemed like a very good suggestion and she wondered whether that could be kept in the luggage area.

Johnnie asked who would be doing the driving.

Alex said that they should each learn to drive the bus, but she wanted a professional driver to do the highway driving. She said that she would check if that was something that the person that she planned to rent the bus from could provide or arrange.

Travis asked if she was going to go fishing on her weekend at home.

Alex smiled and replied that she wouldn't miss it.

Travis quipped that he really wanted to go fishing too. Then after brief pause he said that what he really wanted was to sit by the pool and have her mother feed him some of her delicious spare ribs and share a cold one with her father.

Alex smiled and said that once the case was over she would see about arranging another team outing where they would all go fishing and then afterwards sit by the pool.

Johnnie pointed at the clock and said they should walk to the square and decide which place they would have lunch.

Alex said that was a good idea, but she was first riding back to the apartment to get ready to catch a flight and would meet them at which ever place they picked.

On the way back to the apartment, she decided to give her Dad a heads-up about the bus.

On the walk to the square, Trey brought up to the team the time that Alex had shot the thug that was coming to shoot Johnnie.

Trevor suggested that they see how the place was doing. He commented that it was long enough ago that it seemed that Johnnie might have forgotten what had happened.

Johnnie laughed and said that it was going to take a long time to get the picture of Alex standing up as this huge hulk of a person, which seemed to tower several feet above her head, lifted his pistol to shoot. He remembered clearly the three shots: one to the heart, one to the left chest, one to the forehead. He then watched as the hulk fell to his knees and seemed to bow to Alex and then collapse flat to the floor.

He gave a small laugh and said that, at the time, all he could think of doing was to take another bite of his dessert. He had taken his seat and focused on eating his dessert.

He added that he thought going there for lunch was a great idea.

The person seating them did not recognize them but not long after the manager came over and asked if Alex was going to join them.

Trey responded that she would be in shortly.

The manager smiled and said he had a special treat for her, and he wanted to chat with her as well.

Alex had not expected the restaurant that was selected and wondered who had done the selecting. She never turned down eating at one of Cincinnati's top restaurants, so she walked the few blocks enthusiastically.

When she walked in she knew who had selected where to sit. Johnnie waved to her from the same seat he had been in when she had taken him to lunch the first time. The chair she had been sitting in at that time was open and Johnnie stood to seat her.

She asked if it was to be a nostalgic luncheon.

Johnnie shook his head and pointed to Travis who had suggested the restaurant to have lunch. He had accused him of having had forgotten about the shooting that had happened here. He had just been correcting Travis's memory of what had actually happened.

Alex asked if the orders had already been placed.

Bill replied that they were still reading it to Travis so he could make a choice.

Travis picked up his menu and in a hurt voice complained about his mean teammates were trying to bully him.

Alex smiled and said that she was going to concentrate on getting her order in.

The manager came over and greeted her and said that he was really glad to see her. He then said that he had a request. He wondered if she would once again do an advertisement for the restaurant.

He let her know that her last advertisement had increased his business by at least three-fold for over three months.

Alex nodded and said that she was fine with doing another advertisement.

He held up his new phone and asked if he could do it at this lunch.

Alex said she had no objections.

He then said that lunch was on him, and they should put in the order and once it was served he would take a series of video photos and then ask her for her opinion of the meal.

Alex looked over at Trevor and asked if this qualified as "there is a free lunch."

Trevor nodded and said that she was like a good luck charm.

Bill that pulled out a shamrock symbol at the end of a gold chain and commented that he had added this to his normal attire after surviving multiple Alex induced gun battles.

Alex laughed and said that she didn't wear anything special, she just surrounded herself with special people that knew how to shoot.

Six servers brough out their orders and set up the table so it looked professionally laid out. The manager then took a series of pictures. He then let them know to enjoy and he would take a series of photos.

Alex relaxed and enjoyed the excellent lunch that the manager had recommended for her. The appetizer was a dish with three oysters in a half shell. This was followed by a serving of a plate that had pink grapefruit, avocado pieces, cooked baby carrots and a dish of ponzu sauce. The next course was a dish with scallops in a butter and garlic sauce. The main dish was halibut surrounded with cauliflower blooms. The desert was a pannacotta of pineapple and mango.

Alex had paid attention to her eating because the manager was at hand for each of the servings and he asked her for her opinion after her first bite of each dish.

He thanked her for her willingness to be filmed and said that he would send her a copy of the add when he had it ready.

Alex complimented him on the excellent choice of food that he had served her.

She then let the team know that she was going back to her apartment and getting her things and heading for the airport for an early flight to Chicago. She figured she would get an early start to finding the right bus and she was looking forward to sitting by the pool and having a cold one with her parents.

She looked at Travis and added but her cold one would be sweetened iced tea.

Less than two hours later she was met by her father and led to her beautiful, sleek, shinny, black Jaguar. She had been longing to feel the vibration of its purring engine when she stepped on the gas. The drive home was just what she needed on an early Friday evening. Then driving slowly down the tree-covered lane with the small chubby leaf buds protracting from the limbs overhead seemed to portent a good time ahead.

After hugs and greetings from her mother and putting her things in her room, she went down the back stairs into the kitchen where her mother was looking through the refrigerator.

Alex let her mother know that she had consumed a huge lunch at one of the top Cincinnati restaurants and that she was looking for something light for dinner.

Her mother nodded and said that it was good because she had not prepared anything and was trying to decide whether she cooked or ordered in.

Alex suggested they order in from their favorite Thai restaurant.

Rose-Anne went online and together they selected an order of edamame, an order of seaweed salad, two orders of sushi appetizers, the Thai sampler plate and for desert the pumpkin custard.

Alex figured that they had enough that the three of them would get just the right amount. She prepared the tea and then set up the table out by the pool.

Rose-Anne came out and said that she was dying to know what had triggered Alex to decide to come for the impromptu visit.

Alex said that once they were comfortably seated and eating she would explain the upcoming case that she would be negotiating in the coming week. She wanted help on setting up a contract and she wanted help in setting up transportation.

Rose-Anne sighed and said that she was already more relaxed and that she was now looking forward to an interesting family dinner by the pool.

Alex walked over to her mother and gave her a hug. She said that she had not meant to cause her any anxiety.

Her mother returned the hug and said that she was always on the lookout for the news from the not so sleepy little town that seemed to feature her daughter on the news too often.

Alex reminded her that her last several cases had not been in her home jurisdiction but across several states and the last case was a vacation albatross surprise.

Her mother countered that the only reason the last case was a surprise was because of the exposure her reputation had given her with the police union.

Alex nodded and agreed that Bruce had boasted too much about his excellent team. She went on and said that she seemed to have inherited Bill and Travis on her team. The Chief had consistently assigned both teams to the cases that came to his desk.

Rose Ann commented that it made her feel better that an excellent, brave, and dedicated team surrounded her.

Alex agreed and she was happy that they all got along so well because the upcoming case was going to have them living with each other for many days.

The doorbell rang and Rose-Anne said that they should all go out to the pool, and she would bring out the food.

Alex took the pitcher of sweetened tea and went out to the pool and sat down next to her father. They all enjoyed their portion of the dinner and for once there were no leftovers.

He father informed her that he had talked to his friend Rupert who was in the RV business and that he was ready to show her several busses that he had ready for the road. Rupert had let him know that he had one that he was very interested to get on the road. It was one of his largest ones and had been around for six months and he felt that it was one of the best conversions he had recently done. He would expect to show the busses to Alex on Saturday morning.

Alex thanked him for setting it up and said that she was eager to look at the buses and to see what kind of deal she could get on one of them.

Rose Ann asked what Alex wanted in the contract that she had mentioned. Alex gave her the details and said that she wanted to give the Chief a draft that was ninety-five percent done but would leave him room to make adjustments if he needed to.

The rest of the evening was spent talking about going fishing and what else they might do for the weekend. Alex commented that just sitting by the pool and relaxing would be great as far as she was concerned.

6 Arrangements

lex woke up feeling refreshed and full of energy. She got up and dressed in a casual blue jean and loose dark blue blouse with sleeves that went to the middle of her forearm.

She looked in the mirror and liked the look and turned to ensure that she was not getting a belly.

She felt glad that she had used her old treadmill on the previous night and put in three miles before going to bed. She wondered if it would be worth getting a new treadmill.

She went downstairs and was not surprised to see her mother and father already at the kitchen table. They were sharing the newspaper and drinking coffee. Alex said good morning and walked over to the coffee pot and poured a cup and sat down at the table.

The familiar pile of toast, a jar of strawberry jam and a jar of marmalade and a plate with a one third stick of butter was at the center of the table.

This was the way the Saturday morning breakfast table had been since she was a kid.

She took a slice of toast, spread the butter on, then put on a teaspoon of marmalade and spread it out.

She asked what time Rupert was expecting them.

Her father replied that around nine was the time that he remembered having been mentioned. He asked if she wanted to drive or if he should plan clean the things out the passenger side of his pickup.

Alex was surprised. She had not paid any attention to the cars in the garage and had missed the pickup. She asked when he had started trying to imitate a working man.

Her father laughed and said that a professor at the University had been unsuccessful at selling it. It was in pristine condition, and he figured he would try it out and see if he felt comfortable driving it. He said that he liked it, and it made a good car to take fishing. He admitted that he had not done much fishing as in the past. He smiled and said he needed to cultivate someone to be his fishing partner since his mate had not changed her mind about not wanting to spend that much time out on the water.

Alex asked about Dexter who must be ready to get out from behind the counter in the bait shop.

Her father shook his head and said that he must be a kindred spirit to her mother because he said that even though he had his own power yacht he had never been attracted to fishing.

He said that he would be glad to go out and they had set a date for tomorrow to go out. When he learned that you were going to be with me he got excited and said that he would make it special occurrence.

Alex smiled and said that she had not gone fishing since the last time when she ended up with a bullet wound and Dexter's boat ended up with several dozen holes in its bow and along the side. She figured it was her fault that his boat had received such a beating.

Her father nodded and said that Dexter had taken it the other way around because he had let his friend go out fishing for free only to learn later that his college friend turned out to be a violent fugitive. He felt like he should have sensed something about the fact that his friend had shown up unexpectedly.

Alex shook her head and said that there was no way for him to know how his college friend had changed.

Her father commented that he drove her Jag in once a week to his office. He laughed and said that it was a student magnet. During the warm weather he got more requests for rides then he had ever expected.

Alex smiled and said that her mother should be worried about all the young ladies flocking to get a ride from a handsome, popular professor.

Rose-Anne looked up from her paper and with a smile said and that she had a great law firm that would make sure she got everything.

Alex smiled and said that was a great way to segway to the contract that she would like crafted. Was there anything more needed on her part?

Rose-Anne listened nodded her head and said that by the time they came home she would have a draft that they could look at and review. She planned to pull up one of the many contract templates that she always started with and then put in the specific details. She asked if Alex wanted to put an expense clause that would cover the very necessary travel coach she was going to be looking at.

Alex was quiet for a few moments. She had not thought about how to position the cost of what she was seeing as the observation platform. She mentioned this and asked if it made sense to think about it as a necessity.

Her mother asked if she would be going to look at the conversion van if she had not taken the case.

Alex answered that no she would just go fishing with her dear dad and be very satisfied.

"So, it's in the contract," was the reply she got.

Alex stood up and said she was ready to enjoy the drive to look at conversion buses.

Her father put the address into his phone and put it into a cup phone holder.

Alex drove slowly out of the lane. She had left the top up because though the sun was shining it was only in the low forties. She commented that it looked like it was going to be an early spring.

He father nodded and said that they had experienced quite a bit of snow, but it had recently all melted off.

Alex saw the converted buses parked in an open parking lot in front of a large building with a large black sign that had a signature Rupert Quinlin, and Luxury Conversions, LLC in Gold permanently mounted above it.

She asked about Rupert's personality.

Her father pointed at the sign and said that it clearly shouted Rupert's personality. He was very proud of the work that he did. He added that he should be proud because he was one of the best converters and had won many competition awards.

Alex said that she would be cautious about the comments she made about the conversions.

Rupert greeted them and then waved his hand from Alex's head to her feet and commented that the last time he had seen her was at an Easter party at her house. He stopped for a moment and then added that it must have been when she was maybe ten.

Alex smiled because until he had waved his hand down as he greeted her she had not remembered his name, but she now recalled that she had thought him to be a little eccentric during that party.

She said that yes she recalled meeting him. She swept her arm around the floor of the interior where three busses were in the works and commented that she had heard about his exemplary work and the luxurious vans that he created.

Rupert said that before showing her any of his creations he would like to hear what she had in mind.

Alex shared the fact that she and at least five other individuals were going to travel the US-Canadian border. The case required them to spend almost a year using surveillance drones as they scanned the woods along the border.

She and that team had discussed what they needed during this time.

The conversion bus had been one of the suggestions.

They then had raised the question about whether a platform where they could all sit could be on the roof of the bus.

Another question was whether six mini motor bikes could be conveniently carried on the bus.

A final desire was to have a small freezer somewhere.

Rupert closed his eyes and waved his hand slowly through the air as if he were conducting an orchestra. He then opened his eyes and asked how big a mini-motor cycle happened to be.

Alex shook her head and said they were not very big she indicated how high and long one would be.

Rupert again closed his eyes.

It was clear to Alex that he envisioned what he was doing with his bus.

Rupert said that except for the deck on top of the bus and maybe the brackets to hold the motorcycles he had a beautiful creation that he thought she would be impressed by. He waved his hand and said that it was his favorite conversion that he had not been able to sell or lease because he had gone overboard on it.

He asked that they follow him.

Alex knew immediately that Rupert loved black and gold when she saw a shiny, black conversion with his signature along the bottom trim. The front two thirds of the bus had dark windows, and the back third was solid. It clearly was longer than the other two buses parked on either side of the black beauty.

Ruppert said he was going to begin with the side compartments where he thought the mini motorcycles would be located. He then said that a small freezer would fit in the compartment that would hold the luggage or other tools they might be using.

Alex commented that six small camera drones and whatever support equipment came with them would probably be what the space would be used for.

Ruppert asked how intense the surveying might be.

Alex replied that the team would most likely spend eight to ten hours a day for much of the coming six to eight months doing the surveying.

Rupert closed his eyes and stood silently for a few moments. Then he smiled and said he had it. He could put a flat platform on the top of the bus. It would have rails that collapsed for travel purposes. He said that he would automate the platform so that raising and collapsing it would be simple.

He added that he would also work on having an automated canopy that would provide shade but would have three open sides and that he would make screens on the open sides that could be closed to keep out insects or rain.

Alex said that what he was suggesting was exactly what was needed except that they would not likely be up their during the rain unless they were sitting out to enjoy it.

Ruppert asked about a table and chair for each person. He could have both items automated as well. He added that seat cushions, arm rests and other comfort items would need to be brought up and taken down manually. He said that he would use one of the small top roof windows to make that process convenient as well.

He smiled and said that all that was left was for him to show Alex the luxurious life she would enjoy for the next year if she were to decide to either buy or lease the bus.

Alex decided that Rupert was justified in making his comment. The interior was the opposite of the exterior. It had a light spacious and luxurious appearance.

Rupert pointed out that he had used only the best materials in doing the conversion and that every square inch either provided an open feel or it provided space to store things in.

He highlighted the ten built bunk beds that featured their own entertainment and work center type functions. The sides were a series of storage units where a laptop and various items could be stored. The bed was automated so that it would form into a sitting position in the bunk.

He sat in one of the bunks and demonstrated the features.

Alex commented that the features made the bunks seem better than her personal bed.

Rupert smiled and led the way to the back bedroom that featured a stretch California queen sized bed. He pointed out that the bed was not only very comfortable but had the same features as the bunk. He asked if it would be her bed.

Alex said that it would.

Rupert asked her to lay down and he would show her where all the controls happened to be.

Alex did as he asked. It was clear to her that the features were built in because nothing indicated the kind of features that she had seen in the bunk beds.

Ruppert took a control panel from the bed side stand and gave it to Alex. He pressed the symbol that looked like a zig zag, and her head was elevated. He demonstrated how the height of the lift under the knees could be adjusted.

He then had a surface that could hold a laptop come out. He smiled and said that in his case he would most likely have a book on the stand versus a computer.

He also had the controls for the environment and for the audio on the same surface.

Alex thanked him for showing a part of heaven that she had not known existed.

She knew she had hit the right tone as she watched Ruppert's face and accepted his hand as she got off of the bed.

Rupert said he had one more surprise about the room. He pressed a button, and the bed folded up. He pressed a button that showed a table, and a table rose from the floor that had seats that swung out.

He commented that the room now could be a work and meeting room for six.

Alex said she didn't think things could get better.

Ruppert waved his hand, indicating that she should follow. He went to the lounging area and sat down.

He asked if she had any questions or other requirements.

Alex replied that what he was showing her was beyond what she had imagined and that she was overwhelmed. She then asked if he knew of someone who would be willing to use one of the bunks and drive the bus.

Ruppert asked if she was serious about the buss. He added that the platform would be a onetime cost that would not be refundable, but the conversion bus could be leased or purchased.

He smiled and said that he had a husband and wife driving team that he could arrange to be the drivers, but they would only do it as a team. He smiled and said that they were both great cooks and could be convinced to do some or most of that as well.

Alex asked if she could get a written quote that she could take to and have put into a contract. She would be able to authorize and order by the middle of the coming week if her clients approved.

Ruppert smiled and thanked her and said he would love to have her enjoy the coming year in one of his best creations.

He asked if he could send the quote out electronically to her e-mail.

Alex nodded and agreed that his creation would make the coming year most enjoyable. She gave him her and her mother's email.

Ruppert looked at the e-mail addresses and smiled. He added that if the most famous lawyer in the Chicago area was writing up the contract, he would begin getting the platform started.

Alex replied that he should wait until the customers got over the shock of the cost for getting her to take on their case and signed the contract that she was sure would be iron clad.

On the drive back her dad asked what she thought the price of the bus was going to be.

Alex said that she was guessing that leasing the bus was going to be around three hundred thousand and that the platform would be around fifty thousand.

The husband-and-wife team doing the driving and some of the work would be another one hundred and fifty thousand.

Her father asked if that was something that would be accepted by the FBI and the RCMP.

Alex said she was not sure. She said that she was willing to front the cost for most of the bus, but they would need to figure out the expenses they would face for hotel rooms, the drivers that were not optional. She said that the platform on the top of the bus would be the one item that might be questionable, but it seemed very efficient and convenient.

Alex did some simple calculations on the way home. She ran the numbers in her head and figured that staying in hotels would cost around two hundred thousand dollars, the meal expense would be around thirteen thousand dollars, and the mini motorcycles would be around three thousand.

She finally stated that she bet that without the bus the team expenses would be around two hundred and twenty-five thousand dollars. Plus, she added, there would be lost time leaving a search site and driving to the hotel.

Her father looked at her and asked if she knew where the house happened to be.

Alex smiled and said that the Jag knew the way home by heart, and she didn't have to do a thing but sit in the driver's seat.

Her mother greeted them and said that she had ordered in a pizza, but she had made some sweet tea. She asked what Alex had done to Ruppert. It seemed that he had been impressed by her and that he had offered what seemed like a great deal.

She said that he had offered two variations for the bus. The two versions had the same physical structure.

The bus, with an automated platform on top, a small freezer, and an automated mini motorcycle rack.

The entire unit could be leased for three hundred thousand up front. Or the entire unit could be leased at thirty thousand a month and could be returned on any month.

In either case the two drivers would be an additional and separate contract with those individuals that would cost thirty dollars an hour for their driving service. Additional cooking and cleaning services would be extra.

Alex said that it seemed to be a very reasonable offer and that it made the decision fairly clear to her that using a bus would make the entire operation more efficient as well more enjoyable.

Her mother smiled and said that she had put the thirty thousand per month in and a stipulation that the contract could be switched to the organization that might need to keep the bus in service the longer so they could complete the search for the graves.

Alex said that she had selected the right option because her team would stop the grave search when they captured the killer.

She was not planning to look for and find all the graves and their current approach would only find about twenty per cent of the bodies.

She planned to leapfrog forward and put the killer in front of a judge and jury as fast as she could and then she would host another department fishing trip.

<u>*7 The Golden Goose*</u>

The pizza delivery happened a few minutes after they had set up the table by the pool. They had their seats arranged in the comfort zone of the pool side radiant heaters. Alex was looking over the two contracts that her mother had given her. She read them knowing that her mother was extremely proficient. It made it easy to get through them quickly. The legalese was at a minimum and it seemed to be very clear that the contract allowed the Cincinnati team to end the engagement with the capture of the perpetrator. The agreement could be transferred to the group that would complete the search for the remaining graves. It also allowed for an increase in the costs if the time went beyond a year. She had included Rupert, LLC into the contract for the bus.

She realized that her mother must have asked for the names of the two people that would drive because she had made a contract for the two of them that they would be paid thirty dollars per hour for driving or for sitting with the driver. That meant that when the bus was moving the cost was sixty dollars per hour.

A separate rate for their cooking and cleaning services was twenty dollars per hour. In both cases a log was to be kept and signed off by the leader of the search team.

She asked her father to invite the two people, who would be doing the driving, to go fishing with them.

He called Rupert and made the invitation. He smiled and said that yes, he, Rupert would also be welcome.

He then called Dexter and cleared having three extra people join them.

Alex thanked him for making the arrangement. She commented that it was great that she could meet them now so that she could get a sense of how they would work together.

Her mother nodded and said that it was always best to know ahead of signing a contract.

She then asked what Alex thought of the Oro Bianco Pizza from the pizzeria that she had just bought.

Alex stopped and asked if she had heard the question right and that her mother now owned a pizzeria.

Her mother nodded and said that she had made friends with the owners who had migrated from Naples, Italy and had started their pizzeria when they arrived and found it hard to get work.

Their original pizza recipe became the basis for the Chicago Style pizza.

They had decided to sell their local shop, and she had decided to buy it.

They were still in the process of retiring and still running the restaurant. Her mother said that she was in the process of finding a person to run the place.

Alex asked if an old sheriff that had once hired her would be able to apply for the position.

Her mother nodded and said she needed someone to manage the store, she had a pizza maker already identified.

Alex said that she would call her first boss and see if he were interested.

Alex made the call and invited Sheriff Will Hopper to go fishing. He accepted and asked what time he had be on the dock and gave a groan when Alex said six the next morning.

She added that breakfast would be served on the way out to the fishing spot.

Alex spent the rest of the afternoon looking at the US Canadian border. She decided that she would make sure that a weekend fishing trip would get planned for when the team was below Lake Winnipeg.

She would make sure her parents got an invite to go fishing on that weekend. She would check out what else was in the area that would be of interest on that weekend.

Early Sunday she got into the passenger seat of the pickup, and her father drove to the marina. They walked up to the bait shop where they met Dexter. He had put out the various bait that he was planning to make available.

He greeted them and said that the food was already on board and once they carried the bait down they would be ready to go out. He said he had all the poles on the boat and that he was ready to get everyone on board.

Alex said that she would get the breakfast fixings ready. She would make sure everyone had a morning coffee when they pulled away from the dock.

As they walked out she saw her old boss coming out of the parking lot. Another car was pulling up and she saw three people getting out. She recognized Rupert as he walked under the light.

Rupert walked up and after a hello he introduced Rebbeca and Evan Grinder, his long-time employees who had informed him that they were looking to go on the road for a while.

Alex finished the invitations and suggested they all go to the boat.

Dexter led the way and made sure everyone got on board. He gave a brief tour of the yacht before suggesting that everyone huddle in the eating area and stay out of the cool morning air. He said they would have about half an hour before they would be putting their poles in the water.

Alex made sure everyone was comfortable and then got each person's breakfast order. She limited the choice to eggs and sausage, pancakes and syrup or any combination of the two. Toast and jam was available as self-serve.

Dexter thanked her for bringing up his pancakes and sausage and a hot coffee. He commented that it should be a crisp clear morning. He hoped fishing would be good.

It was not long before she was sitting down with her pancake, sausage and two eggs over easy on top. She slathered on the butter and drowned the pancake in maple syrup. She knew it was going to cost her at least a three-mile jog.

She was looking forward to fishing and in chatting with the folks that were on board.

Her father had engaged Sheriff Hopper, and it was clear to her that he was finding out about his plans.

She was sitting next to Rebbeca and was listening to her describe how they had been experimenting driving semi-trucks to see if they wanted to try that as a retirement gig. It was clear to Alex that Rebecca was really excited about driving the bus for her team.

Alex asked about her driving experience and learned that she was the one that had the most hours behind the steering wheel of semi-trucks. She had moonlighted for the thirty years that Evan had been working for Ruppert. Their only child had often ridden with her. Her son had enlisted in the Airforce and after getting out he had become a pilot and was now flying a private jet for a large company.

Alex asked about Evan's experience and learned that the two of them often shared the gig for a weekend delivery. When that occurred, Evan would do most of the driving to give her a break. He had several hundred hours of driving in his logbook.

Rebecca commented that the offer to pay for cooking and cleaning was the icing on the cake. She hoped that everything would fall into place.

The conversation ended when the boat slowed and then drifted to a stop.

Dexter came down, declared it was time to fish and began to lay out the poles and do the initial baiting.

Alex went to the rail next to where Evan was standing. After she had her pole in the water and was playing her line, she engaged him and asked how long he had been working with Rupert and the type of work that he did.

She noted that Evan was also a veteran angler because he had no trouble talking and at the same time playing his line.

Evan said that he had worked at every type of work that went on from sweeping the floor, designing some of the conversions, the electrical, plumbing and air conditioning were all part of getting the conversion done as efficiently and cost effectively as possible.

He added that now after thirty years and having raised a great son, he hoped that he and Rebbeca could spend more time together in whatever their next gigs were going to be.

He shared that he and Ruppert were close. Ruppert had asked if more money or some other role in the company would keep him. Evan said that it was not about those kind of things and that it had to do with the heart.

That seemed to register with Ruppert. He was a perfectionist about the work, and he was a romantic at heart. He was a romantic that had lost his soul mate to a skiing accident.

Ruppert had let him know about a perfect transition that had just landed in his lap.

Evan looked at her and said that the proposal that Ruppert had sent to her, and her mother was the best that he had seen him make to anyone. He asked what she had done to touch Ruppert's heart because he kept talking about her.

Alex replied that she had let him know that he had a product that most closely gave the impression of having left Earth and entered heaven. She went on to add that it was not her but he and Rebbeca that had touched Ruppert because he had made his offer contingent on accepting an Evan and Rebbeca as drivers.

The conversation ended as they both got a strike at almost the same time.

Her father approached her after she landed a very nice lake trout.

He congratulated her on a great catch. Then he said he had yet to get his pole in, but he had caught one for her mother. Sheriff Hopper, or as he wished to be called, Will, had accepted an interview with her mother.

He was now invited to lunch so he could get the official interview, but he had already indicated that the opportunity was timely, and it came from the right family.

Alex smiled and suggested that he try for a catch from the lake so they would have enough for lunch because she was planning to invite two more guests to lunch.

Rupert had never been much of a fisher, and he was lounging and just letting his line float on its own. Suddenly his pole was almost pulled from his grip. He began shouting and trying to pull his line in.

Alex walked to where he was struggling. She quietly told him to let some line out and then lift his pole and then reel it in as he let the pole down and that he should keep repeating it until he had his monster next to the boat. She let him know that she was returning with a net and a gaff so they could pull in what she knew was going to be the biggest fish that either of them had ever seen.

Rupert was all smiles, and he kept saying that it was working.

When Alex returned she could see that he had landed a very large lake trout. It was large but not as large as the Chief's or hers had been. She commented that he had caught a trophy lake trout, and that Dexter could arrange to get it mounted.

Rupert said that yes, yes he wanted it mounted.

Alex then invited him to lunch at her place. She added that she was also inviting Evan and Rebbeca.

Rupert smiled and asked whether he would have gotten the invitation if he had failed to bring his trout in.

Alex laughed and said that he had hit the nail on the head but even worse had it been a little fish she would have forgone the invitation. She pointed around the deck and made the point that all of his shouting and groaning had caused everyone to stop to watch what he was doing.

He laughed and waved his arm and shout that they should all focus on catching enough fish for lunch.

Alex walked over to Dexter and asked if he was available for a lunch at her house.

Dexter nodded and said that he would love to sit by the pool for lunch. He commented that the last time he had been there was after the shooting, and he had been worried about her. It would be great to just sit and enjoy lunch.

Alex nodded and said that it seemed that the shooting had been in another lifetime. She added that she and her team had been through at least another half-dozen gun battles where every member of the team had been hit multiple times and each of those events seemed to be separate lifetimes.

Dexter shook his head. He said that he would like to hear about a few of the gunfights if it was not too disturbing to her.

Alex shook her head and said that her analyst suggested that each of the team share their stories freely because it helped to relieve the mental stress that when bottled up tended to make things worse.

Dexter asked why she continued to stay in the field.

Alex smiled and said that was the same question her mother always asked. Her answer was that she had been given the gift to put the bad guy in the position that he or she faced a peer of twelve to decide their fate. She and her team were being asked to test that gift to find a bad guy that most likely had killed as many as thirty victims.

She added that Ruppert and his two companions had been invited to come fishing because she was fishing them and thought she had landed them.

Dexter smiled and commented that the Golden Goose seemed to have laid several eggs.

He pointed to the sun and said that everyone had landed at least one fish and that her father had landed two and it was time to get to the dock, clean fish and haul them to the Evercrest kitchen and get them baked or however they were to be prepared.

He said that he would bring over several cases of beer in a cooler to be enjoyed by the pool.

Alex helped get the poles prepared to be put away and then she sat down at one of the tables and enjoyed listening to the chatter about how good the fishing had been.

Sheriff Hopper sat down at the table and thanked her for suggesting him as the manager for her mother's pizzeria.

Alex asked him whether she had ever thanked him for giving her a great recommendation to her current boss that landed her an offer to be a detective in Cincinnati.

She said that one good turn always deserved to be returned. She was glad that the time had been the right time.

She smiled and added that every time she ran across a great pizza she would be sending him the recipe.

As they approached the harbor, she got up and climbed up to the con. She commented to Felix that this was the first time she had come in since the gun battle that the Golden Goose had experienced. She pointed to the landing ramp where Paul Grundle had run the damaged boat up on and had then pushed a worker into the water.

She asked about that worker and how he was doing.

Felix said that the fall into the water must have affected him because he had become the most dedicated employee that he had. In fact, she should ask him how he was doing since he had been tending the counter in the bait shop while they were out fishing.

Felix said that he was considering putting him in charge of running the harbor. After this trip out he might consider featuring a weekly fishing charter on the Golden Goose that he would captain. Then spend other days repairing the various boats needing upkeep.

Alex smiled and said that it hardly qualified as retirement.

Felix nodded and said that he was not trying to retire, he like everyone needed to find something that added a variety to what he or she did.

He asked if that had crossed Alex's mind.

Alex nodded and then added that in her case she wanted to experience boredom versus the variety because variety of action was something that was ever present in her current role. She added that her variety also carried the threat of getting one of her partners killed or her getting killed.

She said that she would follow her mother's advice, "be careful what you wish for, you may get it."

Felix nodded and said she had a smart mother because they were the same words his mother had always told him.

8 Intuition

Monday morning Alex arrived to find the Chief already in his office. He came out to her desk and let her know that he had agreed to a late morning meeting with Denton, in person, his boss online and the RCMP to FBI liaison and his boss. He wanted to make sure that ten thirty worked for her. He said that he had the three contracts that her mother had prepared completed and ready to be signed. He asked if there was a hidden charge for the contracts.

Alex laughed and said that there was and when the case was over he would be asked for the payment. She then said that she was glad that her mother had made it into three contracts because two of them would most likely be in effect for several years, but she planned to change the one that involved the team in just a few months.

When the rest of the team came in Alex shared copies of the three contracts and let them know that if everything got agreement she wanted to get started in a week.

When Denton came in at ten, Alex greeted him and then led the way into the main meeting room. She waved to the rest of the team who then followed. After a few minutes of introduction, Alex shared the three contracts and asked if Denton had any concerns.

He highlighted that the cost for the bus seemed to be high.

Alex replied that the cost for hotels, food and time lost in the search for bodies would be close to the cost of the bus and the way the contract for the bus was written it made a flexible document that could be cancelled when her team solved the case.

Denton nodded and said that her explanation helped. He asked what made her think she would solve the case quickly.

Alex smiled and pointed at Johnnie and said that she had a magician and three additional warriors that so far had batted a thousand and they were planning to keep that record intact. She asked if he had an alternative.

He smiled and pointed at the clock and commented that he was now prepared for the meeting.

The Chief entered and gave Johnnie the number to dial. A few minutes later Denton's boss came online. Then almost immediately after, the RCMP liaison and her boss joined in.

The Chief introduced everyone on his end and the introductions went around to everyone else.

He said that he would like to have Alex describe how her team planned to solve the case.

Alex complimented the hard work that the RCMP and the FBI had done and said that it allowed her team to take the field with a clear vision of what needed to happen next. There was still hard work ahead, but she was confident that the team would crack the case and deliver the serial killer to the docket in short order.

She added that they had developed an attack plan, had figured out the logistics and were prepared to kick things off in the coming week.

She then made the point that Denton would be the person she would count on to keep both the FBI and the RCMP informed on a timely basis. She and the team would determine the pace and the field decisions that needed to be made.

However, when they were ready to apprehend the perpetrator the FBI and the RCMP were to be in the lead. She and her team would corner him, but they would only arrest and take him in.

She pointed out that the contract was in three parts. Her team was in the first contract. The second contract seemed to be the one that was drawing the most attention because of the cost. She made the point that if a comparison was made with the cost of hotels, food and the time lost in travel to hotels and back to the grave hunting sites was made, to the costs of the bus, they would find that it was an almost equal comparison.

She agreed that it at first had seemed high to her too, so she had made that analysis.

She asked how much time and money the RCMP, and the FBI had spent to date.

She then said she was adding a guarantee if her team failed that she would personally pay for the bus.

She asked if there were any questions.

For a moment there was silence.

The head of the RCMP asked what made her so confident about her team's chances of success.

Alex commented that her team was humble, self-doubting, constantly making plans that they had to change and then pushing each other to do better. In the end they pushed each other successfully over the finish line and together celebrated their hard-earned victory.

They were as proud of their record as the FBI and the RCMP were of theirs.

She then smiled and said that her team had one advantage that neither of the organizations on line had. They were small, agile, able to quickly adapt to new learning and they had a magician that provided the magic dust that always led to a solution.

The RCMP Chief smiled and said he was sorry he had asked. He now understood Denton's warning that her team operated independently and very differently.

He then said that he was ready to give it a whirl.

Alex smiled and said that she too was going to give it whirl and have the team using camera search drones to locate graves and for fun they would ride through the Canadian forests, not on the beautiful mounts that the RCMP were privileged to use but on mini motorcycles.

She would have preferred the horses, but she figured the cost of having them along would have scuttled the deal.

When the RCMP liaison asked if she could get a ride on one of the mini-motorcycles, Alex knew that the deal had been sealed.

She smiled and shared that one of the practices that had become a tradition with the team was to plan what they called weekend mini vacations that featured a highlight at each major nearby city where the team happened to be.

She went on to say that she had asked two of her most highly skilled vacation planners to identify the main attractions that would be featured in what the team was calling, "The Canadian Border Adventures." She said that she would make sure that everyone in the meeting would get an invite to those weekends.

The Chief commented that he would incorporate the appropriate signatures to the contracts and would then send out copies of the official copy.

He smiled and commented that now they all knew who he worked for.

Everyone laughed and said they understood and then signed off.

He looked around the room and asked how everyone felt.

Denton asked if by chance he could get some idea what he could do to contribute more than preparing daily or weekly reports.

The Chief pointed to Alex and the team and said that he was sure they would find something he could do.

Trevor said that he was now going to begin identifying the weekend events and that Denton could be part of that effort.

Alex asked if they would consider having a pizza lunch and sit on at the swings at the River Front Park.

She got an immediate yes from Johnnie. The rest all agreed except Denton who said he was scheduled to debrief on the meeting. He added that the meeting had gone very well so he figured the meeting would be short. He asked when he should plan to return.

Alex suggested he give her a call in the morning and that by then the team would be on a roll on the kickoff preparation.

She suggested they all ride down in her luxury car. They all knew that having two new cars blown up or put on fire, she drove the oldest car on the lot. She had also volunteered to be the car disposer.

She parked in the waterfront parking garage and then they all walked over to the swing area. She was carrying a large blanket that she spread out.

She said that she was going to take a walk. Trey asked if he could join her.

She walked slowly to the spot where she had stood and looked down at the body of the first dead person she had ever encountered.

She had a nagging feeling that she wanted to let her mind play out. It was the fact that on the past weekend, she and Matt's team had bicycled by this spot, and a woman was standing where she was now standing. She looked over at the wall and knew that she was standing in the spot she had stood before during her first case.

As she stood, Trey asked what was going through her mind.

She looked at Trey and asked if he remembered that first case.

He pointed at the spot on the other side of the walk and said that he did. He had stood over on the other side nursing a bad headache from drinking too much the evening before. On that day he had felt lucky to get to the station in time to ride with her.

Alex let him know that on the weekend she and Matt and his team had ridden by, and a woman had been standing where she was now standing. Now that she thought about it she felt that it had not been a coincident because on Monday when she went in to work she was sure someone was parked on the street and had watched her enter the station.

She had put it down to still being in recovery but now she was not so sure.

She asked Trey what he thought about the serial killer being a woman.

Trey shook his head and said that nothing about their cases surprised him anymore. He said that they should throw that question to Johnnie and the rest of the team.

Alex nodded and agreed that she would do that but that she was going to wait a few days until they were ready to start proving his current thesis.

She said that she was going to ask Denton to learn to fly a camera drone. She said that in the afternoon they had the meeting with the drone supplier, and she would order an extra. It could be a spare and she would make sure Denton joined the rest of the team learning to fly it.

Trey said that was a good idea and it would give them a spare drone and a spare drone operator.

Alex turned and walked back toward the rest of the team and saw the pizza being delivered.

She took one of the drinks, a piece of pizza, and walked up to an empty swing.

Johnnie came up and asked if he could join her.

Alex smiled and said that he was always welcome.

After a moment he asked her what was up.

Alex looked at him and said that she was saving that information until they ate dinner at his table. She suggested they order in from one of their favorite restaurants and it would be her treat.

Johnnie smiled and said that he figured they were having a picnic because she was having a feeling about the case, and she had stood at the spot of her first case for some ten minutes just looking, and he smiled, and added or just thinking.

He wanted to speed the afternoon along so he could discover the twist that she was going to throw into the case.

Alex said that he was so right and then stood up and said that she was going get back to the picnic while there was still some pizza left.

Alex was listening to Travis comment that the coordinates for the two bodies put them in the middle of nowhere along the Canadian border and that he was struggling to identify what the team would do there over a weekend when she saw Linda pulling a dolly with a large metal suitcase on it. She was escorting a powerful looking woman who looked like a contestant in a women's bodybuilding contest.

Alex suggested they all go and see the type of camera drones they would end up using.

Linda introduced Moira Winters owner of All Things Drone.

Trey went up to Moira and shook hands, and then introduced the team.

Moira explained that she had brought three different drones, and she had a thumb drive that had her presentation on it. She wondered if she could get her presentation up on a computer screen.

Johnnie took the thumb drive, plugged into his computer, and asked what the file she wanted was called. In a few moments, an All Things Drone screen was up.

Moira explained that she was going to show the camera drone that she had decided best fit what Trey had described to her.

She explained that it was the most expensive of the battery-operated ones. She had two more gas powered ones that had more range, capability, and flying time if the battery-operated one did not meet the need.

She had also brought two additional battery models in case she had misinterpreted the need.

She went through three slides that demonstrated the takeoff, the flight maneuverability, and the landing.

She then opened up the suitcase with a green sticker on it and took out a drone that was a little more than a two-foot cube. She pointed to the camera and commented that any camera that met the need could be used. The drone was a platform for the camera of choice. It had great stability in the air and could withstand breezes up to about twenty miles per hour. It was also very maneuverable and could get down near the ground and be able to maneuver through the forest that Trey had described.

Alex walked up to the drone and picked it up. She was surprised by its light weight. She looked at the ring with the rotors and at the battery locate on the bottom below the camera. She asked to be reminded about the flight time that one battery charge provided.

Moira commented that the time was highly variable but that on a calm day, flying level, it would have about one hour fly time. On a windy day, the flight time was closer to thirty minutes. If the drone was maneuvering through the forest and having to make many swerves the operator should be thinking thirty minutes.

Trey asked which camera was currently on the drone.

Moira smiled and said it was the most expensive one.

She added that she was not trying to put them into the most expensive option, but she had focused on meeting his demand for being an eagle in the sky.

It was a camera that took out the swinging motion that might be encountered when flying. It had the highest pixel count, and it had the ability to transmit its images if there was a good relay station close by and if not it had an extremely large memory to store pictures.

She pointed at the other two cases and said that each of the other two were one and two steps below the one she was demonstrating.

Alex shook her head and asked Trey if what was being demonstrated met his specs.

Trey nodded and said it seemed that it did.

Alex asked if she could order six of them and get them by Monday of the coming week.

Moira asked if they should discuss cost.

Alex smiled and said she would be interested in a fifteen percent discount on the purchase of the seven. She wanted to get the training to operate the drones included in the sales price. And she wanted to be forest capable in the coming two weeks.

Moira was all smiles and commented that she had not expected to walk out with a sale. She thanked Alex and Trey and said that she would demonstrate the capabilities of each.

Alex pointed at the door and said they would all follow.

Moira led the way out of the office but then let Trey lead the way.

She demonstrated the preparation, take off, flying and the landing. She then said she would give each of them a quick lesson and give them their first flight.

Alex waited her turn. She had let the rest of the team go first. Trey and Johnnie were the quickest learners. Both Trevor and Bill were about the same.

She took her turn, and Moira warned her that the battery was running low. She said that the drone had battery low landing feature and suggested that Alex bring the drone down to about twenty feet and hold it there until the battery low feature came into action.

The drone seemed to want to stay in the air but then it made a slow vertical descent and turned itself off.

Trevor gave a cheer and said that it had a feature that would probably get used too often.

Alex thanked Moira for the demonstration and asked if they could start the training immediately using her demo drone. They could each have an hour of individual training and by the weekend they could all be three hours more capable of handling the drones.

Moira said that she had two folks that did the training, and she could double their capability and by the weekend they could each be six hours through the twelve-hour training.

Alex said that she had a deal, and her team would all be at the training ground getting as capable as they could. She added that she was interested in more than twelve hours of training if it made a difference in the team's capability.

9 Obdurate Sinner

Zelda had returned from her vacation and shared photos of the scenery that she had enjoyed. They were all some one's true stories just not hers.

She worked hard at establishing back door access to the RCMP directors email account. She was desperate to keep track as to where the hunt for bodies would go. It took every ounce of her capability to achieve her goal. She successfully obtained a copy that had the arrangements that described the relationship that the RCMP, the FBI and the Cincinnati Detective unit would have with each other.

She was relieved when the supporting document shared that the RCMP and the FBI would have the lead when the perpetrator was to be arrested and that he would be put in front of a jury of his peers. It also mention some ten to twelve women whose bodies needed to be found.

They were off on a goose hunt and not the Moose hunt she was worried about.

She slept well that night.

She continued studying the person she considered the most dangerous and as she learned more about Alex Evercrest she became more and more concerned. She wondered how long the misdirection would work.

She felt certain that it would be impossible for Alex to reach down into the Canadian organization and find her.

None the less, she worried and decided that once this Alex was in the field she would learn how the search was being conducted and if the search seemed to be close to discovering new bodies she might need to take direct action.

She had no qualms about shooting and killing her. She figured once she was out of the way the effort would fall into disarray.

She decided that she would pause her monthly body burying activity and let things cool down until she had a handle on the situation. She smiled as she thought that at least the pause was at a moment that she was with a victim that was good in bed.

She studied the two additional contract documents and was impressed with the fact that Alex had gotten the RCMP and the FBI to pay for what seemed to be an exorbitant expense of renting a converted bus.

She went online and looked at the conversion buses offered by that vendor and was surprised at the elegance of the conversions. She then looked at the contract for two professional drivers and knew she was witness to a woman who had the uncanny ability to name any exorbitant price for her services.

She was not sure whether she was super impressed or super jealous. What crossed her mind made her mad because she had again thought of Alex as a number one.

She immediately made arrangements with a local firing range to get training on a long weapon for hunting. She registered for a license for a 7.62 Winchester elk hunting rifle. She had the rifle delivered to the firing range and then made arrangements to get trained on its use and care.

After the first practice she began to relish the time she spent on the range. It took her several weeks before she could consistently hit the target. It also took that amount of time to toughen her shoulder to take the kickback.

When the range master praised the progress she was making she smiled and said that she loved her new weapon. He asked her if she had ever gone out into the forest and hunted.

She admitted that she had not. He suggested that she join in on the hunts that the firing range sponsored. The folks going out on the sponsored hunts were taken to great spots and they got the best coaching of how to be safe in the woods. He made the point that they only hunted deer but that it still provided the experience she would need to hunt the moose about which she was talking.

He asked her if she had put in her name on the list to get a moose hunting permit. He shook his head when she said no. He let her know that there was a two-year waiting list. He said he would submit her name and get it on the list.

Zelda was not too disappointed. The Moose on her table was only about five foot two and black.

She began to think of herself as a good shot and a good hunter.

She was unaware that she was about to be hunted.

Back in Cincinnati, Johnnie led the way as he and Alex went back to their apartment building. Once there he suggested that they meet in about an hour.

He let her know had he a couple of light bulbs to change and one complaint of a leaky faucet that he had to attend to.

Alex said that an hour would be perfect and that she planned to run and then shower and come back down. She took her bike into the workout center and then got on the treadmill and took her jog up to as high a pace as she could. She was surprised when Johnnie waved his hand in front of her.

He chuckled and said that she had about ten minutes until their order for their shared ten-ounce Wagyu Sirloin steak, roasted root vegetables and a simple salad was delivered.

Alex stopped her jogging and realized that once again she had lost track of time as she thought through the case and visualized each part of the plan.

She took her bike up to her room and took a quick rather cool shower and then rushed downstairs. She relaxed when she saw the delivery person walking out the second set of front doors.

Johnnie opened up the door and waved her in. He commented that he had been able to fix a faucet, sweep the entrance area and elevator and had changed four burnt out light bulbs during her jogging time.

Alex complemented him on his productivity and said that she was ready for her half of the steak. He asked her what she would like to drink. She asked for a sparkling water or an ice tea. She accepted the bottle of sparkling water.

Johnnie enjoyed his steak and said that the side salad had a great dressing.

Alex agreed and said that she was glad they were sharing their steak otherwise she would have wolfed down the entire ten ounces.

Johnnie offered to fill some of the void with a scoop of Neapolitan ice cream.

Alex said that she would take a small scoop but what she would really like was a cup of green tea to go with it.

Johnnie put on the pot of water and got the cups ready. He then asked what she was going to ask him to do that she was keeping so secret.

Alex said that over the weekend she had ridden past a woman standing at the exact spot that she had stood on her first case. Then when they had ridden in on Monday morning she got the feeling they were being watched from a parked car across the street from the station.

She had let it pass but she was sure that the person in the park had been there for a purpose.

She looked at Johnnie and asked him how it would affect his model if the woman was the serial killer.

Johnnie slowly poured the hot water into the two mugs and then brought them to the table. He commented that it would be unusual for woman to be a serial killer and to be killing women.

Alex said that she agreed then she made the point that the forensic report had mentioned the fact that there was some uncertainty to the gender of two of the bodies because their seemed to be some contamination. She suggested that they ask for a sample be sent to their lab and have their ever-faithful forensics guru analyze it.

She then commented that if the sites were along the border as he had speculated they needed to get the first two sites pinpointed and see if that gave them any new insights.

If as she suspected she had been the focus of whomever she had seen standing at River Front Park, then she suspected that that person worked in some capacity in the Canadian service, either in the RCMP or some governmental support group.

Johnnie shook his head and commented that Alex had thrown in a huge wrench into the gears of his model. He would be up all night thinking through what that meant. He pointed out that two key pieces of information would be the forensics analysis results and the exact locations of the two bodies.

Alex reminded him that they had the exact coordinates of the two bodies in their e-mail. They just needed to get them put into a map program and they would have the answer before they went to bed.

She said that while he was getting set up she would sent a message to Denton asking him to get a sample of each victim sent to their lab in Cincinnati on a priority basis. She said she would stress getting the best sample possible and getting three samples from different parts of the remains. She would also stress speed and that no expense should be spared in getting the sample to Cincinnati.

Johnnie put the coordinates in and then after zooming in on each one he commented that there must be some mistake because each of the coordinates put them at a Canadian border crossing post. He called up a different Map program and verified that it went to the exact same spot.

He commented that he was already changing where he wanted to look for the next body and that his model was showing a huge weak spot.

Alex nodded that she was going to have problems sleeping too because she now felt she had an adversary that perhaps had an inside track of what was coming down. That person had stumped two major policing agencies so whoever it was they were clever and somehow in a position that provided natural cover.

She commented that whatever they learned it would remain a team secret, and they would not report it to either the FBI or the RCMP.

She was also going to ask Rupert for some additional items for the deck on the bus. She said that she was not going to make them all sitting ducks in a shooting gallery.

Johnnie said that he was now going to have a hard time waiting for the samples to be sent. He added that he refused to talk about his model anymore until they got the lab report.

Alex commented that the two of them should wait to inform the rest of the team until the lab report came to their desk and he could think through the impact it would have.

Johnnie looked at the wall clock and asked if Matt was coming to her apartment and suggested they call it a day. He asked if she wanted breakfast in the morning.

Alex declined and got up and headed for the door.

She had just pushed the lever on her water pot when the familiar palm knock let her know that Matt had arrived.

She opened the door and knew that she was not going to share the problem when she saw the look on Matt's face. She gave him a hug, gave him a kiss, and pulled him toward the couch. She asked whether he wanted a tea.

Matt said he need a couple of stiff drinks, but he would settle for a tea and a few more hugs from her. He said that it had been a brutal and sorrowful day.

His team had six rapid runs, and it seemed that each run was worse than the previous one and three of them were children who had survived gruesome wrecks where either a father or mother had been killed.

Alex had learned not to say anything but just listen, nod, and give hugs. Matt slowly told her about each situation that was gnawing at him until he stopped talking and asked for a hug.

She always broke out some of her home-made raisin and oatmeal, and peanut butter cookies to go with the tea. She knew that he would eat all the cookies she put on the plate and kept it to three of each.

When they got to bed, Matt thanked her for listening and for being patient with him. He said that she provided the support that he needed to keep his spirit viable.

Alex gave him a kiss and said that they provided support to each other and that being able to be in his arms raised her spirit and let it fly.

The next morning, she was surprised that he had been able to leave without awakening her.

She got up and had her coffee before getting ready for her ride in. She remembered that at nine the team was to meet at Washington Park for their training sessions with the drones.

She met Johnnie and asked him how his night had been.

Johnnie smiled and said that one lesson he had learned while he was in the service was to sleep no matter what. It was a "no matter what kind of night" and he felt great, but it was going to be a tough day, and he hoped not to crash his drone.

Alex said he was going to have to train her on his no matter what sleeping technique.

Johnnie commented that he had seen her sleep multiple times, and she already knew the no matter what technique and didn't need any training.

Alex laughed and said that kind of sleep only came when gunship helicopters tried to kill her, and she won.

Johnnie nodded and said that his sleep catalyst had always been the rattle and the vibration of his fifty.

Alex said a quiet, "Hurrah" and said they needed to petal their way to work.

Johnnie led the way to their desks. He pointed to the box of donuts on Alex's desk and commented that she had been promoted to Boss.

Alex thanked Trevor and Bill and took out a half of a bear claw and offered the other half to Trey then offered the box to Johnnie.

Trevor quietly asked what she was keeping from the team.

Alex smiled and asked why Trevor thought she was holding something back.

He smiled and commented that they had watched her, and Trey walk to the exact spot where her first body had been. He smiled and said that yes he had reviewed and walked that case.

He went on to say that he did not want to make all the mistakes she had made.

Alex didn't take the bait. She told him about the woman that she had seen standing in that spot and had walked down to the spot to make sure it was the spot where she had seen her. She said that then she felt that someone was watching her as she arrived to work on last Monday.

Bill nodded and asked what it all meant to her.

She replied that she had asked Johnnie to think through his theory again. She went on to say that she was waiting for the forensic samples of the two persons that were killed to arrive at their lab for testing. She reminded Trevor that there was some uncertainty about the gender of the deceased.

She wanted the test done by one the most competent coroners, Dr. Rogers. In fact, she said that she needed to prepare the request order and go see him. She said that if everything worked out they would have the answer about the gender of the bodies that afternoon . She said that piece of information would determine what she would ask Johnnie to do.

She reminded everyone that they were going to get their flying lessons at Washington Park. She had been told that for a couple of days they would all practice on a small drone that used the same controls as the drones they were purchasing. Their practice drone cost only a couple of hundred dollars so if they crashed them it would not be a major issue.

She held up the order form for the analysis of the samples being sent in and said she would be back shortly.

10 Offensive Defense

D r. Rogers greeted Alex and asked what had happened and that it had been a few months since he had to process a dead body for her.

Alex smiled and said that she had made sure that other coroners kept their employment. She was making sure that he had enough work so that he would remain employed. She handed him the request to examine the incoming Canadian samples and determine the gender and the time of death.

He looked at the order and said that it seemed clear. He asked when he would get the samples and how fast she needed the information.

Alex said that she hoped the samples would arrive by early afternoon and she could use the information as quickly as he could do the analysis because it pertained to the case she was taking on.

He said that it would most likely take him a full day to turn the analysis around. It would also depend on the condition of the samples.

He asked what kind of samples she had requested.

Alex described asking for three slices from each cadaver. One from the shin bone that included the marrow, the bone and as much flesh that still remained. Another of the thigh bone and a third from the forearm.

Dr. Rogers shook his head and said that what she just described was triple the work he had expected. He would give her the early results and the spend a couple of days verifying his initial information. He said he was surprised that she was able to get the samples by just requesting them. He asked what she had over the organization with which she was working.

Alex said that she was not holding anything over the organizations, but they had failed to solve a very complicated case and had asked her and her team to take a crack at solving the case. She had insisted that she would get all the possible support from them and this she guessed was them providing the support.

Dr. Rogers looked at the request and then looked up. He asked how many more bodies and analysis he might be looking at.

Alex shook her head and said she was not sure but the believed body count was beyond twenty.

Dr. Rogers smiled and asked if she had shot any of them.

Alex looked hurt and asked if he thought she was a gun crazy detective.

He shook his head and said that she was just a very deadly one.

Alex wished him a good day and left the lab.

She got back to the office just as everyone was getting ready to go to the park.

She followed and as she walked to the park she dialed Rupert. After a brief hello, she asked if he could add armor to the sitting area at the top of the bus. She asked that the panel behind the sitting area have a bullet proof armor plate that went up about one foot over their heads when they were sitting.

She also wanted the same armor to come up one foot above the table in front of them and then a bullet-proof glass or plexiglass that would be as high at the armor at their backs.

She listened as Rupert said he would add those features to the roof platform, and it would all be automated. He asked if she were concerned about the cost of her request. Alex replied that she trusted him to make the most cost-efficient choices.

She had followed the team to the round oval at one end of the park where the three trainers were waiting.

She then turned her attention to them.

She smiled at the fact that it seemed that the trainers had been selected based on age and ethnicity. One was a young lady of Asian heritage; another was a young Latin American male and the third was a bearded man that was probably in his late fifties or early sixties.

The person that took the lead and introduced herself and the trainers let the team know that they would be flying the drones with the same controls that would be used with the drones that they had purchased.

She then asked each person to put on the name tags that had been prepared.

Alex picked hers up and smiled when she saw that under her name in calligraphy it had "Cincinnati's Black Annie Oakley." It was a moniker that Matt had accidentally given her and one that she knew would be with her for as long as she was in the department.

She put on her name tag and then put her attention to Nabi, who was standing in front of her and Trey and explaining that the controls were exactly like they would be using with their model of drone. She made the point that the small drones they were using were zippier because they were smaller and lighter.

Nabi then stepped close to Alex and said she was going to launch, hover and then land the drone. She would then have Alex copy what she had done.

The entire team was getting this very personalized training and after an hour all of them were able to take their drone up and at about a ten-foot height go across the oval green and return.

Nabi then suggested that everyone fly one behind the other and go counterclockwise around the oval.

Trevor was in the lead, then Bill, then Johnnie, then Denton, Tray, and her.

When they had made a full circle Nabi said they should do it clockwise.

Nabi took them through a series of games and maneuvers. She commented that they had all done exceedingly well and that in the next couple of days they would all be ready to go and try flying in the forest.

She smiled and said that they would continue to use the small drones until they all passed their maneuverability tests under forest conditions.

She said that if everything went well they would all be flying the bigger drones by the coming Wednesday. She added that the training for the larger drones would begin in the park they were in and then graduate to the forest.

Alex asked whether there were fixtures that would allow a drone to be weaponized.

Nabi said that there was, but she would have to check with her boss to see if they sold that feature.

Alex invited everyone to lunch. She added that she was not letting Johnnie choose because she could not afford his tastes. She invited them to the Thai restaurant that was at the corner of the park.

Nabi looked over to Lucas and asked if they were allowed to join. He shrugged his shoulders and said he wouldn't tell if Luca wouldn't tell.

Alex smiled and said that she wouldn't purchase her drones if there were any repercussions.

Nabi smiled and said that she like the choice. She said that they should take a moment and watch how the drones were put into their carrying case. She said that the carrying cases were exactly the ones that their drones would sleep in.

Alex verified that the cases would be the same outer dimensions. When Nabi verified that they were, Alex asked for the dimensions. She wanted to send them to Rupert to make sure the units would fit in the luggage compartment.

Alex and the team were regular customers to the Thai restaurant, and she knew the menu fairly well. She ordered three orders of spicey calamari, a spring roll for each of them, a bowl of steamed mussels, a platter of fried oysters, and a plate of fried rice for the table. She then suggested that everyone choose what they might want and place their orders

A person wearing a Chef's cap came out and introduced himself as Preed Kraisee owner Chef of the restaurant. He looked at and thanked Alex for having lunch at his place. He asked if he could take a picture that he could put in the window.

Alex nodded and said that she always enjoyed eating at one of his tables because the food was so good, and she was pleased that he wanted to put her picture on the window.

Nabi asked if Alex got greeted like this in many places.

Alex commented that it seemed to go in cycles. If she made the news, more people recognized her. She went on to say that at times it became a little overwhelming.

Nabi said that she had been inspired by her and said that she was in her last year at UC, and she had her application in for the next police training academy.

Alex congratulated her but warned her that a detectives or law enforcement role was not glamorous, and you might get stuck with someone like Travis.

Travis bowed his head and cried out, "cheap shot. I get extra desert."

She looked at Nabi and said, "see what I mean."

After lunch she let Nabi, and the two others know that her team would meet them in the same place tomorrow.

She was extending the lunch invite for the next two days. She had a Mexican restaurant and a Burger place in mind for those two days. She commented that if they all made it through without crashing any of their drones, she would let Johnnie pick the restaurant for lunch on their last training day.

Dr. Rogers was sitting at her desk when the team returned. He asked how drone flying had gone. He held up a paper and said that his preliminary report was done.

The samples were still being processed but he had been able to extract two very good specimens from the bone marrow. He was ninety nine percent sure that both victims were male. One was most likely in his mid-twenties, and the other was probably in his thirties. His lab was in the process of refining the ages and how long the bodies had been in the ground or dead.

He shared that the decomposition was due to the use of lye to decompose the body and some other chemical to hide the odor of the rotting body.

He asked if that would earn him a morning donut.

Alex smiled and said that he had earned more than a donut. He was invited to go to dinner with her and Johnnie at a waterfront restaurant of his choice. She added that there might be more people depending on when the day of the dinner happened to be.

Dr. Rogers said he would like that. He said that he would like to bring his wife.

Alex said that would be fine. She suggested that he also ask his staff. She would check with the Chief to see if this could be turned into a department event.

Dr. Rogers said that was a great idea and it made the invitation more attractive to him since he could also label it an official occasion for his lab.

Alex thanked him for the quick turnaround. She said she was still interested in whatever else he and his lab learned about the two victims.

Denton had been sitting at the desk that he had been assigned and commented that Alex already knew more about the case than the two organizations that had worked on it for almost a year.

Alex commented that she was now asking Johnnie to rethink the bodies and his theory. She was willing to make a tray of cookies for him so that he would have the energy to do so.

Johnnie asked if she were willing to go for a long bike ride with him and then have dinner with him at his place when they returned. He wanted to think through this while his body worked to keep ahead of her.

Alex said that she would work very well with her. She liked the idea because it would let her think through the case as well.

Denton looked over at Trey and asked if what he was experiencing was always what went on with the team.

Trey shook his head and said that he was experiencing the quiet, peaceful moments.

Trevor said that normally they had to wear body armor when they were close to Alex.+

Bill added that they had all fallen in love with body armor.

Denton shook his head and said that he had never worked with a group like them. He said he had already enjoyed his short time with them, and things seemed to move so fast that he was wondering if they would make it to the field before the case was solved.

Alex said that she hoped that the case would unravel quickly but she felt that its final resolution was most likely to be years away. She however wanted to stop the killer in weeks not years.

Denton nodded and said that she was so sure about getting the killer but for almost a year there was no inkling who that might be.

Alex smiled and said that she was now in the camp that said the killer was a woman.

The room was silent.

Denton pointed out that it did not fit the profile of the missing peoples list.

Alex said that she thought it was the wrong list. That was what she and Johnnie were taking their bike ride about, that was what they would discuss after dinner and that is what they would get the team to review after their morning of flying drones.

Trevor looked over to Denton and made the snide remark about being in a dark room with Alex. She would hand one person the tail of an animal and ask what the animal happened to be. She would take the next person's hand and put it on something soft ask the same thing.

Then after she had everyone guessing what the animal was she would turn on the light and what everyone would learn was that there was no animal in the room just a variety objects that made no sense. And then as if by magic she would push things together and there before all of them would be a goat.

So, all Denton needed to know was how a goat's nose felt, and he would know how Alex managed her team.

Denton laughed and shook his head.

Alex commented that Travis needed to spend a few more hours with the analyst because even his stories had devolved into gibberish.

Denton was laughing as he said that he was going back to his office at the FBI building and try to recover from working with all of them.

Alex said that she would see them all in the morning with coffee and that she would then share any adjustments to their plans that she and Johnnie might have come up with.

Johnnie said that he would meet her just outside of the side door.

Alex went into the locker room and put on her riding outfit. She saw the new head set that she had bought so the two of them could talk as they rode in to work. She had forgotten to give them to Johnnie. She took them out of the package and powered them up. She figured this was the perfect time to try them out.

She took her bike out of the back of the locker room and pushed it out to where Johnnie was waiting.

She gave him the head set and said they could try it out on their ride. She joked that if they worked well they would most likely solve the case on their ride.

Johnnie shook his head and said that he thought the case had just taken a turn for the worse. He got on and began the ride down to the River Front Park. He entered at the very beginning of the river front walkway and pedaled at a leisurely pace. He commented that he was not going to go as fast as she normally did but they might go far or until he had figured out what their new learning meant.

Alex replied that she was happy to follow and think through how they would go about proving his thesis.

Johnnie replied that it was going to be an extremely unpopular theory, but they might be able to attack it in parallel.

Alex replied that he should pedal hard and simplify his theory.

Johnnie replied that the theory was terrifying in its simplicity. He went on to explain that the theory was that there was a body at every crossing from Canada into the US. If it began at the very point that the border began in the East, there would be some eighty bodies or more that would be buried on the Canadian side.

Alex was shocked and did not know how to respond. She had to pick up her pace when she realized that Johnnie was pulling away when she had stopped pedaling.

She caught up and asked how he was thinking about proving his theory.

Johnnie replied that she was going to ask every crossing station that had an enclosed area to do a body search of their grounds.

Alex gave a laugh and said that he was putting her on the pyre and tying her to the stake and lighting the gas-soaked pile of wood.

Johnnie laughed and said that was the role she was going to need to play. He suggested they turn around and ride back to his place. He said that he preferred to order in so the two of them could work through how they were going to work on a very different project than the original one they had thought about.

Alex suggested ordering from one of the top steakhouses and said she would treat him to a Prime Filet Mignon, some Focaccia, a house salad, Marsala roasted mushroom, some grilled asparagus. She said that the menu she was looking at did not offer desert so she would order it when they got back and sat down at the table with what she had ordered.

11 The Borderline Case

She and Johnnie were just getting to the front door as Matt emerged from the parking garage. He was carrying a bag from her favorite Chinese restaurant. She gave him a hug. Just then an Uber driver got out and said he was delivering the order from the restaurant for an Alex.

She laughed and said that all the good things were coming together like magic. She said that Matt should take all the food into Johnnie's apartment. He should relax and maybe Johnnie would share one of his real beers with him while he waited for both of them to take a quick shower and get to the dinner table. She said she was bringing a six pack down from the apartment.

Matt chuckled and asked if that would be a six pack of sweetened tea.

Alex pushed the button to get to the sixth floor and then pushed her bike to the very corner apartment at the end.

She remembered having to move out of the fourth-floor unit because it had been rocketed by an angry mother, who later tried to shoot her but instead got shot by her own husband who Alex shot and killed but not before he had hit both his wife and her with a round from his shot gun.

That was the time Matt had been holding her when she came awake in the hospital emergency room. She knew at that moment that he was her second half, her soul mate.

Matt had repeated that story several times and how afraid he had been that he was too late. He said that his team still talked about that trip and how useless he had been for the rest of the shift.

Matt's team had also been the one that had arrived when she had been attacked by gunmen at one of the highway underpasses. There she had been wounded as well.

Matt had admitted that there were days that he found himself worrying about her when he thought about her.

He laughed that even going on a vacation trip to her home had ended up in a situation where she was getting shot.

Alex took a quick shower, grabbed the six pack of sweet tea, and headed down to Johnnies apartment.

She gave a knock on the door and then walked in.

She saw that Johnnie and Matt had put all the food out on the table and there was a tall glass of ice where her seat was located.

Johnnie jokingly apologized for not having much food. He pointed at the steak that he had cut into several smaller pieces and put on a platter. The rest of the food had been put on various plates and had serving forks or spoons on them.

Alex helped herself and then opened a sweet tea and poured it slowly over the ice. She asked Matt if Johnnie had described what was happening to the case that they were on.

Matt said that Johnnie had given him a beer and then had refused to tell him anything. He had insisted that the two of them figure out what to do with all the food and any talk about the case would be up to her.

They had both agreed that the soup should go into the frig. They had also put the noodles away. The stir-fried veggies and the rice were on the table.

Alex complimented them on slimming down the amount of food.

She said that she and Johnnie had gone for a long ride so they could sort out the changes that had happened in the last couple of days.

She smiled and said that she thought Johnnie was trying to make the case large enough so it would be the last one that she would have time to take on in her career.

As long as there are no gun battles, I am all for it Matt replied. I am looking forward to a few weekend vacations in Canada Matt concluded.

Alex then asked Johnnie to share his current thinking about the case.

Johnnie nodded and said that the case had changed dramatically, and the body count would increase astronomically. He said his model was very simple. They would find a body at or near every border crossing from somewhere close to where the two bodies had been found all the way to the first border crossing in the East. He added that no one was going to believe in his model until they found enough bodies.

Alex asked what the first steps were going to be.

Johnnie said that they should get every border crossing to look for bodies on the grounds of the crossing facility. Those crossings with fully fenced in areas should use the latest technology to search for bodies.

Alex asked how that should get done.

Johnnie looked at her and said that she should insist that every crossing do an immediate self-check and report their results by the end of the coming week.

Then he went on and said they would want the forensics done on the body farthest to the East to set the time of when the serial killer had started the killing.

Then they would want the forensics on all bodies found so they could determine how often the killings occurred.

They would then move as far West as the western most body found. Then they would see if they could find bodies beyond that point.

What about the killer Alex asked.

Johnnie commented that several things would help them figure out who she was. The starting date of the killings, the frequency of the killings and the identification of a job that would allow for the killer to do the killing and never be noticed.

Alex was sipping her tea. She took a deep swig and said he was really stressing her and that she really needed a cold one but had to settle for tea.

Johnnie smiled and asked if she had figured it all out before he had explained it.

Alex shook her head and said that his reward lunch was safe. She was just overwhelmed by what she was sure they were going prove. It would be something that neither the FBI nor the Royal Canadian Mounted Police would believe until the bodies were found. Then there would still be resistance based on disbelief that it could be possible.

She said that on the following day she was canceling the drone practice so they could spend the entire day communicating with the FBI and the RCMP and urging them to take immediate action. She would push both organizations to put the body search at the top of all actions.

Matt smiled and said that he would be glad to deliver pizza to the station.

Alex smiled and said that they had a pizza parlor that loved to deliver pizza to her office. She said that he was probably right about the pizza unless hamburgers won out.

Johnnie got up and began clearing the table. He commented that he would have food for the rest of the week. He offered to send whatever Alex wanted up with her.

Alex shook her head and said that she had more food in her frig than she would be able to eat for the rest of the week.

She asked if he still had some of the salty caramel ice cream.

Johnnie brought a variety of pints of ice cream to the table and said that they should help themselves to whatever flavor they wanted.

Alex ate her ice cream slowly and said that she would have Johnnie share the case situation that was changing and make sure that the Chief got put in the front.

She had decided that the Chief should insist on an immediate search of the border crossing grounds. She was certain it would put him into the political position that would allow him to be the lead for all three organizations.

Johnnie asked why she was giving him the torch.

Alex smiled and said that doing so put their whole department on a better foundation. It would also make it easier for the Chief to get promoted and to get someone like Trey to be the next Chief.

Johnnie asked what she saw for herself.

Alex nodded and said that when the time came she was going to get out of law enforcement and move into the work that she had underway focusing on helping women who had suffered in some manner due to how they had been treated by spouses, lovers, or society.

Matt commented that he looked forward to that time. He was for it to happen sooner than later.

Alex said that it was time to call it a day and time to sit with her couch buddy and enjoy the rest of the evening.

Johnnie said he would meet her in the morning for their ride into work.

Alex and Matt took the elevator to the sixth floor. As they walked she filled in the details of the change in the case and the steps she was taking to ensure the safety of the team. She described the changes she had made to make sure the team was not a group of sitting ducks when they flew drones from the top of the bus.

Matt said that the changes to the bus platform made him feel great. He said that too often she had been in someone's sights and that she had been lucky to always get the edge and eliminate her attackers.

Alex agreed and she pointed out that she had gone through a series of cases that had its impact on her and her team. She was now trying to shield them and in the process she would be shielding herself as well.

Matt gave her a hug and kiss and said that he was all for having her shielding herself.

Alex smiled and added that luck was a good thing to have on her side, but she did not rely on it.

The next morning, she was up before Matt and had an egg and ham and cheese breakfast sandwich ready.

Matt thanked her, wolfed down the sandwich, and drank half of his coffee and said that he had to run, or he would be late.

Alex finished her breakfast and put all the dishes into the dishwasher. It was not full, but she turned it on anyway. Her schedule was erratic enough that she chose to always have her dishes washed when she got back to her apartment.

Johnnie met her out on the sidewalk, and they rode into work. Their new headphones made the trip different from previous trips. They chatted about their dinner and about meeting with the team.

Alex asked Johnnie what he thought about their ability to talk to each other as they rode.

Johnnie said that on the longer rides it was great but on the short ride into work he preferred not talking.

Alex thought about his feedback and then said that she agreed with him. She suggested that they carry the headphones but save their use for the longer rides or for foot work where they might want to communicate. She suggested they experiment to see if the team should operate more often with headphones.

She led the way into their office area. She noted that she and Johnnie were the first.

Trey walked in with his coffee and greeted them. He asked what might be keeping his half of a bear claw from arriving.

Alex smiled and replied that the bear claw was probably fighting to get out of the box before it was torn in half.

Trey asked if there was any news about the case from either of them.

Alex nodded said that as soon as everyone got in, they would go to the conference room and Johnnie would update the team. She added that it was significant enough that she was calling off their drone flying training for the day. There would be some major redo for how they would attack the case.

Trey commented that he hoped that Trevor and Bill would bring extra donuts

Alex said that they should request a coffee cart with fruit and rolls for the meeting. She got up and intercepted the Chief as he arrived and headed to his office.

She let him know that a major change was happening with the case, and they needed to convene a work meeting. She figured that it should start at nine. She suggested that coffee and refreshments be provided in the main meeting room and that they decide on the lunch menu and get it ordered at the beginning of the meeting

The Chief said that it sounded serious, and he would have his support set everything up.

Alex came back to the desk as Bill and Travis got to their desk.

They said that they were late because the bakery had oven problems, and their bear claws were still in the oven. He said that they had brought three of them so that Alex could have a whole one. It was still warm. They had also brought a bottle of milk for everyone to drink with their roll.

. Alex thanked them and suggested they all go into the main conference room and get comfortable because they were going to spend the day redoing their case.

Trevor shook his head and asked if Johnnie had messed up and they were going to have to clean the mess up.

Johnnie laughed and said he was glad to have a bottle of milk to settle his stomach because the case was giving him indigestion and Trevor was just making it worse.

Alex said that she had arranged for an all-day session. She was going to call their drone trainers and let them know that training was off for today.

She suggested they talk it over and decide what to order in for lunch. She added that lunch was either on the Chief or on her. She suggested they keep it simple with either ordering a sandwich tray or ordering pizza or both.

Bill suggested one large pizza and the sandwich trey and a variety of drinks. Trevor added that a case of beer would go good with the pizza.

Alex said she agreed, and she would order a case of her favorite nonalcoholic beer and a bottle of wine to accompany it.

Trevor replied that he would stick with a sugar coke.

Linda, the Chief's support, pushed in a cart with a pot of coffee and a variety of teas and hot water. There was also a trey of cookies and cupcakes. She asked if there was anything else she could do.

Alex asked Bill what kind of Pizza he had in mind.

He said that a large sausage and cheese pizza would be great.

Alex asked if they could get the pizza and also a sandwich lunch cart with an assortment of drinks for lunch.

Linda said she would arrange lunch for all of them. She asked how many would be in their meeting.

Alex said that with their new FBI member there would be seven.

She gave Linda the heads up that after lunch the Chief most likely would want to have meetings with Denton's FBI boss and the Head of the RCMP.

Linda thanked her for the heads up. She would reach out to the other supports involved and make sure they selected a time when the three were available.

Denton came into the meeting room and commented that he thought they might have left early for their flying lessons, but the Chief redirected him. He said that the Chief had said he would be in shortly. He was reading some reports that had come in from the lab.

Alex nodded and said the reports had identified the two bodies that had been found as two males. One that was probably in his mid-twenties and one in that was in his early thirties.

This information was the beginning of Johnnie's new theory for the case.

The Chief came in and wished everyone a good morning. He held up papers that looked official and said that he had just read through the lab report that seemed to throw a wrench into the gears of their case. He looked at Alex and Johnnie and said that he was dying to hear the new basis for the case. He now understood Alex's push to spend the day getting reorganized.

He wanted to know one thing before they all got into the meeting. Did this change any of the contracts that he had just pushed through and gotten signed?

Alex said that yes it did. The bus was going to be more expensive because she had ordered shielding to protect the team from being sitting ducks in a shooting gallery. She took a moment and explained the changes.

The Chief nodded and said that he agreed with the changes, and he could get that added. He commented that having the contracts ready for immediate signature had worked wonders in getting the leadership to move on.

They had commented that his organization was moving very rapidly. They had learned about the request for body samples and were surprised at the speed that the Cincinnati team was moving.

Alex smiled and said that the Chief would feel empowered when he shared the dramatic change that was going to take place and that the body count would go from the estimate of the twenty females to four times that many bodies, but they would most likely all be male.

Alex looked over to Johnnie and asked him to explain what the new model for the case was and what action the Chief was going to have to take to verify the new model.

Johnnie put a Map of the US-Canada border up on the big screen. He had two red dots where the two bodies had been found. He zoomed in on the location of the body farthest to the west and asked what they all saw.

There was silence for a few moments.

Then Bill asked if the body was under the trees at the edge of the border station property.

Alex smiled and gave Bill a cookie.

Johnnie then zoomed in on where the next body was found.

Trevor shouted out that it was also on the border station property.

Alex smiled and asked what that told Trevor about the case and if he came up with one aspect of the change she would give him a cookie.

Trevor complained that she was being hard on him. He thought for a minute and said that the perpetrator had to be someone in the RCMP organization.

Alex handed him a cookie. Then she said that he might be right, but she doubted that would be the case. It was going to be someone who fit naturally into the scene when they were at the border station and would attract no attention. The serial killer was doing something that fit the role he or she played in some support organization.

She then asked what gender the serial killer would most likely be.

This time Trey spoke up and said that it would most likely be a woman and it would be a woman that did not get noticed because she was doing a job that was routine and was probably ignored by those on the border station staff.

Alex handed a cookie to Trey.

The Chief chuckled and said he wanted to earn his cookie, and he was guessing that he was being set up to communicate the bad news to the FBI and the RCMP leadership.

Alex handed him three cookies. And asked why she was triple rewarding the Chief.

Denton raised his hand and said because there was a second and more challenging thing the chief needed to get the other organizations to do.

Alex handed him a cookie.

She looked at Johnnie and asked him to update the projected body count and how that was to be verified.

Johnnie again projected the border and this time there were many red dots along the border. He said that each border crossing toward the East was where a body would be found. There would be close to ninety bodies. He said that the proof would be relatively easy if the grounds of every border crossing was searched for a dead body.

Alex pushed the cookie tray and the donut box in front of the Chief and said he would need all of them to convince his two partner organizations.

The Chief shook his head and said that he was having a hard time accepting the new model premise.

Alex agreed that it was really hard to accept but it was easy to prove or disprove.

All the Chief would need to do is insist on every Canadian border crossing property undergo a thorough body search.

Denton volunteered that the FBI had a unit that specialized in such searches, and they had the technology to do it quickly and rather easily.

The Chief looked at Alex and asked what time his meeting with the other two organizations happened to be.

Alex smiled and replied that she was not his support and that he should ask Linda.

He laughed and said that he bet that his meeting would be after lunch and by then he would be thoroughly indoctrinated about what the new plan was and how it would be executed.

Alex handed him a blueberry muffin and said they should all take a break while Johnnie set up the next part of their work and planning session.

12 Sniggling

The team spent the rest of the time before lunch doing a quick run through their original plan. Alex accepted the Chief's praise for the team having such a solid plan and that the only significant change was that they were asking the FBI and RCMP to verify that bodies were present in the eastern crossing points. He added that neither of the organization leaders were going to buy into the number of victims.

He wondered if the RCMP would believe that someone in a position of trust could be the most prolific killer in history.

Denton spoke up and said that he was glad that he had immediately joined the team because he would never have accepted what was happening if he had not been part of the process.

He suggested they pick one or two border crossings on the Maine border and suggest searches there.

He added that after bodies were found there they could hold another meeting and give the FBI and the RCMP the list where the team expected the body to be on the border crossing property and the list of where the body would be nearby in the forest.

Alex thanked him for that suggestion and said that after lunch they should develop the upcoming meeting's agenda and messaging. She looked over at the Chief and asked how that sounded.

The Chief thought for a moment and then said that keeping the message simple and the request focused on just two crossing points would make it a much easier sell.

He looked at Denton and said that he would ask for his opinion about the body search. He needed him to sell his boss.

Denton nodded and said he had their backs.

Johnnie smiled and told him that the statement, "I have your back," was sacred with the team.

Denton smiled and acknowledged he was the new outsider to the team and then repeated the statement.

Linda pushed in the lunch cart and began laying out the food. She opened up the pizza box and asked if she could join them for lunch as she took one piece of pizza from the box and put it on a plate.

Alex said she was going to make herself a sandwich and she would get Johnnie to put up an old meeting agenda that they could modify and that afterwards if there was enough time she was going to walk to the park and imagine flying a drone.

Trey got up and began making himself a sandwich and took a piece of pizza and sat back down. He had settled for a glass of ice water and commented that other than the suspect, and the number of bodies, Johnnie's initial concept had been on the right track.

Trevor shook his head and said that a change from twelve bodies to more than one hundred was really just a minor change.

The change from the victims being women to them being men and the killer being female versus male were all rather insignificant.

He then added that he agreed with Trey but that the team was on a different track and the train they had been on had been a dream train and now they were on the train to hell.

Alex agreed that it was indeed a different train, but it was not headed where Trevor thought it was.

It was going to hug the Canadian border, and the team was going to live in luxury and enjoy the majestic Canadian forests, they would relax at various fishing lakes and catch their share of the Canadian bass and trout and on the side they would solve a horrible case and put an end to a serial killer.

She said that it was more like a breather for the team after the last few cases and they should all be happy to have a wizard that could ferret out the critical elements of a case that had stumped two prestigious organizations.

Bill gave Trevor a nudge and told him that he had just been read the riot act in a very gentle and poetic way.

The Chief laughed and said he would need to take lessons from Alex if his more direct way happened to fail him.

Alex pointed to the Agenda that Johnnie had up on the screen. She made an adjustment on the introduction and then added three points.

1. Request for quick theory verification by doing a search for bodies on two crossing point properties on the following day.
2. Immediate autopsies and sharing of samples of the bodies that were found.
3. The location to send a person to pick up the autopsy samples.

She added that all additional discussions should be done after the three points were carried out.

She looked at the Chief and asked for his input.

The Chief looked at Denton and asked if it was sufficient.

Denton replied that he thought it was the best chance to get immediate action. He suggested that when the first objection was raised the Chief should ask the simple question why his organization had been brought online and ask for the time of the results meeting on the following afternoon.

Linda broke in and excused herself and asked if they were done with lunch and that she would clean up and then refresh the coffee and replenish the drink selection. She asked if they were going to want afternoon snacks.

There was a general groan, and everyone agreed they did not need more to eat.

Alex pointed to the clock and said that there was really only enough time for them to take a break and then come back for the meeting.

Linda worked with Johnnie to make the connections to the RCMP and the FBI. Once that was done, she pointed to the Chief.

He greeted his two counterparts and then did a general introduction of the team around the table. He thanked everyone for taking time to get caught up on what was transpiring on the case. He shared that the team needed some immediate and rapid help from the RCMP and the FBI.

They needed a thorough search for bodies at two Canadian to US border crossing. The search was only on the Canadian property associated with the crossing facility and the request was to do an immediate body search since it would affect the direction the case would take.

He then had Johnnie zoom in on the Highway 1 crossing and had him zoom in on the parking backside where there was a six-car parking area. Johnnie put the arrow on a set of trees at the edge of the parking black top. The Chief suggested they begin the search for the body at that spot.

Johnnie then zoomed in on the Houlton-Woodstock Port of entry on Highway 95 and zoomed in to where a service road went by a set of trees at the end of a spit of land between the highway and on the section that the main building was on. Once again the Chief suggested they start at that spot.

He then said that when the bodies were exhumed he would appreciate immediate autopsies. He also would like bodily samples from each victim sent to the Cincinnati office. He had a person ready to bring the samples home but needed the address of where to send that person.

There was silence on the line.

Denton's boss was the first to speak. He asked Denton for his take on the request.

Denton said that he agreed one hundred per cent with the request. He added that his friends on the body finding unit had been complaining about not having enough work. They could easily do what was being requested. They could deliver the bodies to the RCMP facility and there would be no jurisdiction issues.

The RCMP leader thanked Denton for suggesting the help, but he had the resources to do both searches in parallel. He was dying with questions, but he recognized the approach that Chief Johnson was taking, and he grudgingly agreed to it. He would get the search underway as soon as he got out of the meeting and if bodies were found he would most likely be calling immediately to learn what it all meant.

Alex commented that she and the team appreciated his response. If the worst came about and bodies were discovered she and the Chief would share a detailed plan to discover who the perpetrator most likely happened to be.

She said they would not know that individual specifically, but they would have a detailed analysis of the traits of that individual. She said that his leadership team might be able to identify the most likely people.

The RCMP leader asked if she thought it was one of his people.

Alex replied that it was highly unlikely and that it would most likely be some lower-level government worker.

She smiled and said that first she would like to verify the theory the team was working against. Then she would welcome detailed discussions with everyone involved in the case and was part of their next meeting.

Johnnie had been working away on his computer. He went up to Alex and whispered they had a hacker listening in and he needed some more time to pinpoint where the hacker was located.

Alex nodded and on her phone she sent a text to the RCMP leader and let him know there was a hacker listening in and she needed some more time to track them. Could he invite her to come up personally and have some moose or could he weave any other story to keep them online.

She then asked the leader that she preferred using people names and she had to apologize but she had forgotten his name. She added that it was OK for him to answer the buzzing phone.

It was an awkward moment. She was pleased when he looked at his phone and then replied by giving his name. He added that his friends called him Reg. He said that he had been remiss in not having invited her to one of the Canadian specialties.

He would like her to visit him, and they could go out and try his favorite Québécois pie that was packed with a mix of veal and pork meat and got its unusual and Canadian moniker by the cinnamon and cloves that spiced it. He then added that he always also ordered a side salad and enjoyed some sweet Ice wine. He smiled and said that there were so many deserts that he didn't have a favorite but was always trying a new one.

Johnnie gave Alex a high sign and mouthed the words got it.

Alex thanked him and said that she was looking forward to visiting and going out for some Québécois pie. She looked at the Chief and asked him if there was anything that he wanted to add before he closed the meeting.

The Chief had watched the interchange between Alex and Johnnie and knew that something out of the ordinary had just occurred.

He thanked everyone for their time, and he would wait to hear the results of his request.

The meeting ended.

Alex sent a text to Reg and thanked him for his quick reaction. She and her team would spend the rest of the afternoon tracking the hacker and as soon as they had the location and perhaps the hacker's identity, she would share it.

She suggested that he have his office checked for any bugs. She texted that she doubted it would be bugged but caution was the most appropriate step.

She got a simple thx, and WD back from Reg.

The Chief asked what had just happened.

Alex explained that Johnnie had discovered that the meeting was being listened to by some unknown connection. She asked Johnnie to share what he had.

Johnnie said that he had been sniggling behind the scenes to make sure that the connection was not being hacked and was very surprised that the hack was not happening on their side, which was the weak area, but it was happening on the RCMP side.

Trevor shook his head and said there was no such thing as sniggling, and he didn't even think it was a word.

Johnnie smiled and asked how long Trevor had been working with Alex who was always sniggling.

Alex laughed and said that she indeed did sniggle and so did every member of her team. She thought that Trevor should look up what it meant and give the team some examples of how they had sniggled.

The Chief shook his head and said that he didn't want to reinforce Trevor, but he too had no idea of what sniggling was and he wanted to make sure he could approve of such behavior.

Alex asked Johnnie to put up the definition of sniggling.

Johnnie called it up in one of his online dictionaries that defined it as; to fish for eels by thrusting a baited hook into their hiding places.

He commented that Alex was always baiting a hook, pushing it into the eels hiding places and capturing her prey.

Trevor smiled and agreed that Alex was always sniggling.

The Chief nodded and said that they should all get to work and see if they could sniggle the hacker that had been listening in on their meeting.

Alex agreed but said that this sniggling situation was a one-person job, and they should all call it a day, and she would treat her chief sniggler to dinner and reward him with a plate of cookies.

Johnnie shared that the connection to where the hacker was located was in St. Johns in Newfoundland. He added that St. Johns was on the island of Newfoundland.

Alex said they needed to find the physical connection at St. Johns to determine if the hack began there.

Johnnie agreed that it might be a relay to a different location. He bet on the location being in the same city as where the RCMP regional headquarter was located.

Alex asked how they could zero in more closely.

Johnnie said that they should set up a meeting with Reg using his support secretary and set up a meeting directly by calling him and getting him on a video meeting. If both meetings were hacked he would need to think about how to find the hacker but if only the secretary's link got hacked then he would know where to look for the connection.

Alex said they should try it immediately and see if they could figure it out before they went home.

She gave Reg a text and let him know what she was doing and that he and his support should play along, and Johnnie would be doing the hunting.

Reg said that he and his support would play along.

She made the video connection with Reg first and she chatted about the drone training experience. After a few moments Johnnie gave her a thumbs down. She let Reg know that his line was clear and that the next test was with his support.

She asked if her support had a favorite hobby or was into something special. She found out that his support, Ella was an avid fisher in fact a competitive one.

She asked that Ella connect with her on a video link and have a chat about fishing.

When Ella came on Alex introduced herself and said she was calling in response to getting a text from Reg to plan on going out fishing. She shared that she and her father had been fishing since she had been able to walk.

Ella replied that it was the same for her and that now she was into competitive fishing.

Alex saw Johnnie give a thumbs up and knew he had found the hacker. She smiled and said that there was nothing like hooking a fish and playing the line.

Ella nodded and replied that it was always a surprise to her when she played a fish only to find out that it was one that was different than she had expected.

Alex extended an invitation to Ella to go fishing with her out on Lake Michigan in the near future and that she looked forward to doing some in and around Montreal. She commented that it was time for both of them to call it a day and signed off.

She texted Reg and let him know they had a location in Laval. They would see if they could get an address and let him know as soon as they got that.

They might need to do some additional fake meetings with Ella or with him via a connection made by Ella. She said that she would text him about any requests.

She commented that she figured the perpetrator was the person behind the link and it signaled her that they were dealing with a talented as well as very disturbed person.

<u>*13 Debut*</u>

Johnnie chattered on the headset as they rode to the apartment. He said that most hackers put multiple layers of protection to make finding their actual location difficult. So far he was sure he had at least three locations, but he was not sure where the hacker was located. He said he needed more time to nail the location.

Alex had been surprised that Johnnie had even discovered a hacker. She asked him what made him look. He said that the fact that this person had been at what they were doing for a long time and the fact that the team had been called in after two major policing agencies had spent a fair amount of time on the case and come up empty handed made a difference.

He added that the real catalyst was when she had mentioned that the RCMP leadership team might be able to identify the most likely people that a light went off in his head that someone close to the organization would most likely be able to figure out how to set up a way to keep in the know.

Alex commented that she didn't follow his logic, but it was really not critical for her to do so. She asked what it would take for him locate the hacker.

Johnnie replied that he needed more time with the hacker connected to the meeting.

The next morning, she did not remember much about the evening, other than the fact that Matt had a late shift, and the morning coffee had tasted bitter.

Then in the park she almost crashed her drone. She then put her full attention to it and realized that she did not have to look at the drone if she concentrated on the coordinates of the drone. She kept it simple but flew her drone by using the coordinate read out. She launched, flew it, and landed it without looking at the drone.

Nabi had been watching, and she said that she had never seen anyone fly a drone without looking at it.

Alex repeated what she had just done but this time took the drone high into the air and then flew it in a circle and then brought it down in a slow spiral and brought it to a landing at the point from which it had taken off. She knew that she had gained the skill to maneuver through a forest.

Nabi said that she wanted to learn to do what Alex had just done.

Alex said that all she had to do was to be able to understand the coordinate numbers and it was a piece of cake.

Her phone buzzed in her pocket. There was a text from Reg, she smiled at the fact that he was now Reg, and she smiled when she read the simple message, "bodies found. I am ready for the rest of the story."

She held up her phone and let everyone on the team know that bodies had been found. She said that Johnnie had his choice of where to eat lunch.

She said, "thank you Johnnie" and the entire team repeated the thank you.

Johnnie said that he was for some barbeque ribs and a river front view.

Everyone knew the place Johnnie had in mind.

Alex called ahead and made river view reservations for ten people. She made sure Nabi knew where they were going and said that they would meet there in an hour.

She led the team back to the station. She went into the Chief and let him know that bodies had been found and asked him if he wanted to join Johnnie's victory lunch.

The Chief said that he wouldn't miss it.

Alex was about to walk back to her desk when her phone buzzed. She recognized the call by the fact that she had made the ring be the horn of a greyhound bus. She let the Chief know it was about the conversion bus and put the call on speaker mode.

Rupert announced that the bus was ready for delivery, and he was wondering if he and his team could deliver it. He said it would be a great way to make sure everything was working the way he wished. The freezer had been installed, the mini motorcycles had arrived, and they were a perfect fit, and he had made a custom bike holder that was automated. He asked whether Alex had specified the color of the mini motorcycles.

Alex replied that she had not.

He said they were all beautiful black and he had put the team members names on them in gold lettering. They seemed to be part of the design of the bus. He chuckled and said that he had almost painted the stainless-steel freezer black but had controlled his urge to do so.

Alex said that it would be great if he did deliver the bus. She gave him the address of the police station and asked when Rupert was planning to deliver it.

He suggested they drive it down on Saturday. He asked that he be allowed to take her to a dinner at a restaurant of her choice on Saturday evening. He would plan to return to Chicago by plane on Sunday. He said that Rebbeca and Evan would stay with the bus. He asked about a place where they could park the bus.

Alex said that she would find out a good place for the bus and let him know. She let him know how pleased she was to get the delivery.

Once she hung up she commented that her day was turning out to be a very good one.

She walked out and let the rest of the team know about the bus.

Trey spoke up and said that he had an additional piece of good news that all of their drones had arrived and were getting tested The training would now be with the drones they would use.

Alex asked if any of the team knew where they could park the bus other that the police station parking lot.

Bill suggested a place on the river just below Lunken Field. He looked it up, made a call, and reserved a spot for the weekend.

Alex said that they should all go and celebrate over lunch. She would detail what they were celebrating.

They had a room to the back of the dining area with a great view of Ohio that was all theirs. After the order had been given, Alex said that they were celebrating the fact that their case was moving along very well.

Unfortunately, the body count was now frighteningly high. The two bodies that they had asked to be found had been found at the location that Johnnie had suggested they would be. She smiled and said that her new personal friend, Reg had suggested they meet in person in Canada.

The bus that they had ordered would arrive in time to take them to Montreal. They had an invitation to go fishing there. The mini motorcycles had arrived, and they matched the color of the bus and Rupert had painted their names on them.

Trevor's freezer was also on the bus.

Nabi commented that they should also celebrate graduating from middle school and going on to drone high school. She smiled and hoped that their drone college flying that would be done in the forest would not be too expensive.

Alex added that the Chief was so impressed with their progress that he was treating them to lunch.

The Chief acted like he was offended and said that he had not made such an offer, but it was one that if he refused would make him seem ungrateful.

He then added that he was going to extract his pound by going to Canada on the bus with them and go fishing there as well. He would make it all official by asking for a meeting with Alex's personal friend, Reg.

Trevor stood up and pulled up the legs of his pants and said that it was getting pretty deep, and he wanted to keep his pants out of all the bull that was being dished out.

He got the laugh he was after and sat down.

The ribs were brought to the table, and the room went quiet as everyone dug in.

It would have been a joyous celebration for Alex except for the fact that she now had confirmation that close to one hundred victims might be buried along the border.

One of the tasks she was going to take the team through was to identify the location of all the bodies at each of the crossing points. They would also identify the locations they believed the bodies would be buried somewhere nearby.

She was not planning to be part of that effort but felt that she should lay out the road map for the people that would be doing the groundwork.

She wanted to get the time frame of the crimes determined so they could better understand how long the killer had been doing the killing and perhaps figure out how she had kept it all a secret and unnoticed.

Johnnie said he would give a penny for her thoughts.

She was going to reply when Trevor commented Johnnie was not only a penny pincher, but he was also insulting Alex by offering so little for her precious thoughts.

Alex shook her head and laughed and thanked them both for interrupting her morbid train of thought.

She said that it was hard for her to celebrate when they were working on a case that had more poor souls who perished than she could imagine.

The Chief agreed but said she should concentrate on the fact that she and the team were stopping the killing and saving the lives of those the killer would kill if left on the loose.

She said that was always the way, "no unsolved crime, no need for a detective."

She suggested that after lunch they take a quick cut at locating bodies by having Johnnie take them along the border. The goal would be to suggest the body locations to pass on to the RCMP. When they were done, she would get all the information put into a report to be shared with Reg.

She said that they should end the day early and anyone that they desired could be in the parking lot in the afternoon when their bus was to arrive.

Bill suggested sending the address of the park where he had rented a spot for it.

Alex said that was a great idea. It would simplify the logistics and maybe they could practice riding their mini motorcycles as well.

She called Rupert and suggested that he take the bus straight to a van and bus park by the river that had been rented. She would meet him at the waterfront at the Serpentine Wall and then they could go to dinner at a restaurant of choice.

Rupert said that sounded great and it would provide a more permanent location for the bus until she took it for a trip.

Once back at the station, she and the team went into the large meeting room and began the journey along the Canadian border and identified the locations at each crossing where they thought the bodies would be located.

When they got to where the first body had been found she commented that they would stop there, put up a small monument and if by that time they knew the person's name they would add it. She said that she would do that at each site that they visited.

She said then their job would be to jump to the second body out west and do the same. Their next actions were to determine if there were more bodies.

If they found any they would leapfrog the next crossing until they could not find a body. The goal would be to get ahead of the serial killer and stop her.

Alex reiterated that their job was to bring the serial killer in even though she deserved to be shot when captured.

Johnnie zoomed in on seven crossings beyond where the last body had been found. They decide that they should ask that body searches should be conducted so Johnny got the best view that he could, and they suggest two or three spots at the next seven stations.

Alex agreed to send the request to Reg before she went left work.

Trevor commented that having the bodies found before they went out west was a good idea. He figured that fishing would be one of the few things that the team would be doing for entertainment.

He would need to dig deeper to find something more. The weekend vacations might need to be done on the US side where even in the smaller towns there seemed to be a wider variety of entertainment.

Alex agreed and suggested they plan the coming weekends in Montreal, Ottawa, Quebec while they were working the Eastern part of the case.

Trevor replied that he knew they had one fishing date already set. He would focus on what else there might be of interest.

He chuckled and said that there were plenty of museums, parks, and nature centers.

He then said that he felt better because he had found a variety of fun parks that offered the activities their younger members would like to do.

Alex said that they should create a list of all the activities and have everyone select what would make the weekend fun. She pointed out that the team could select to go together or in any grouping that happened.

The parents of the younger set would need to decide how they would handle their situation. She figured that dinner would be a good time to regroup but even that could be done in smaller sets.

She looked at the time and suggested that they break for the day.

She was planning a ride with Matt and a stop for a sandwich with her favorite sheriff in Loveland. Then she planned to spend a quiet evening of reading.

Trey said he was going home and having a backyard barbeque. He said that Annie was coming over with Linda and Lorie and they would all play some badminton. He was also on notice that he was to make smores for a treat.

Bill looked over at Trevor and asked if he was up to doing eighteen holes or maybe having dinner at the driving range.

Trevor said that he could easily do the driving range with the missus, so he opted for that choice.

Denton said that he was planning to fly home, and he would be back on Monday morning.

Johnnie said he really wanted to be there to greet the bus, but he had a date in Baltimore with Mary and planned to wine and dine her.

Alex pointed at the door and said that was the way out for everyone.

On the way back to the apartment, she asked Johnnie to give Mary her greetings and that she wanted to treat the two of them to a bottle of their favorite wine.

Johnnie joked back that it only cost him two dollars for a gallon of his favorite wine, but he would make sure the receipt would hit at least fifty dollars.

14 Bus Surprise

Zelda was as upset as when she had lived at home and was constantly remined by her mother that she was second best and that she should be more like her sister.

The last few weeks had not gone the way she wanted. Her frustration had grown as she listened to the meeting conversations that the RCMP Chief held with his counterparts.

She had listened to more talk about Fishing and Golfing than she could stand. They were two activities that were at the top of her list of boring sports.

She was almost as frustrated at her inability to improve her marksmanship with the 308.

Her range instructor had commented that many people got to stuck at a certain level. He suggested taking lessons from a woman who specialized in improving peoples posture or the way they held their weapons that often resulted in significant improvement.

She tried that but the woman's composure reminded her too much of Aada, so she dropped her.

She changed gun ranges in hopes that doing so might make a difference.

It did.

The range was newer and more automated, and it cost more.

Her performance did not change.

Her frustration rose higher.

There was no icing on her cake there was only a large soft pile of sloppy moose scat that smelled of failure.

She had lost a month on her trip along the border and that seemed to be the catalyst to get another look at the person who was the cause of the holdup.

She decided to take an impromptu weekend trip to Cincinnati. She rented a room on the Kentucky side that was close to the "Purple People Bridge." She decided that she would not rent a car but spend the weekend in downtown Cincinnati. She arrived early on Saturday and after checking in, she walked across the river on the purple bridge.

She first walked back to toward the ballpark to where she had stood and seen a bicyclist that she was convinced had been Alex Evercrest. She turned and walked toward the downtown. She made her way to the apartment building where Alex lived and sat at a metal bench a block away for a few minutes. She decided to have a sandwich for lunch. As she entered the park, she followed her ears to an area filled with people listening to an orchestra.

The sign identified the area as the Procter and Gamble Pavilion. She sat down at the top of the green area.

The grand piano and the music made Zelda think that the composer of the music was Chopin. Several violins were giving the piano a charming backing.

She looked across the crowd and wondered if Alex might be sitting within vision. She saw two women that fit the description and waited to see if she could get a better view when the concert broke up.

She wasn't sure what she would achieve by seeing her. She needed to eliminate her but at the moment she was unarmed and had no idea how she would eliminate her even if she met her face to face.

As she sat listening to the piano she realized that her fixation with Alex was because she had put her in the number one category.

She had also caused her a delay in going ever westward with her project.

That delay was causing her anguish.

She knew that Alex was coming to Canada to see the leader of the RCMP and was invited to go fishing. She needed to find out where the fishing outing was and see if it would give her the opportunity to kill her.

The concert ended and the crowd seemed to disperse in wave of people walking past her. She tried to relocate the two women that she had earlier considered Alex possibilities, but she could not find either of them.

She decided to walk up along the river. When she got to a round, restaurant that featured a river view she considered having an early dinner. She decided against it and walked back toward the area where the concert had been. She decided that she might take in the Aquarium on the Kentucky side and then call it a day. She was disappointed by the fact that she had not seen Alex.

She went up the steps to the walking bridge and stopped to look along the Serpentine Wall. She was just about to turn and head across the bridge when her eyes fell on a group of people standing midway at the top of the Serpentine Steps. There were four black people and one goateed white man, and a man and woman chatting and smiling.

The two black women looked very much like sisters, but she could tell that it was probably mother and daughter. Clearly the daughter was Alex. She was standing next to a young, tall handsome man that she was sure had been riding next to Alex the first time she had seen Alex ride past her the last time she was in Cincinnati.

She moved along on the bridge as the five people walked toward the bridge. She watched as they walked along the path in the direction from where she had just returned.

She decided to follow and observe. She was a bit jealous as she watched how Alex and her mother would walk holding hands, then periodically laugh and hug. The three men followed behind but they two seemed to be joyfully engaged. The other two were holding hands and were clearly a couple.

It seemed unfair that people could be so enriched and she on the other hand had not one person with whom she shared that kind of interaction.

The five of them turned and entered the restaurant.

Zelda decided that she would wait for a moment and then go in and have dinner. She entered and asked if there was room for one with a view of the river. The Hostess pointed to a seat at the corner of the bar and said that was the last seat available.

Zelda had been reading the name of the people and saw Alex's name and when she looked over to the seat at the end of the bar she realized that she would be shielded by two people but would have a direct view of where Alex was sitting. She was relieved to see that Alex would have her back to her.

She accepted the seating and when the Hostess asked her name she gave it as Z Smith.

Alex and Matt had spent a relaxed morning and had then gone to the concert in the park. The feeling of being watched started as she sat comfortably in her hooded sweatshirt leaning against Matt. When the concert ended they had walked to the very end where the walk met the ballpark. They had just turned to walk back when they got a call from Rupert that the bus was parked and that he and everyone with him would meet her at the top of the Serpentine Steps. Alex called ahead to the restaurant and updated her river view table reservation.

As they approached the Serpentine Steps, Alex gave Matt a hug and asked who he saw waiting with Rupert. Matt asked if she was talking about the three white people that he did not know or the two Black people that he did know.

Alex laughed and ran ahead and gave her mother and father hugs and the shook hands with Rebecca and Evan. She gave Rupert a hug and complemented him on how well he dressed.

Alex felt a shiver run through her. She felt like she was being watched but saw now one that was obviously doing so.

She called ahead and added two to her reservation and said they had about ten minutes to get to the other end of the River Front Walk.

She looked back several times but there were just too many people for her to spot the person who might be doing the watching.

She had been seated only a short time when the feeling of being watched returned. The restaurant was full of people enjoying their meals. She could not get the feeling to leave. She focused on her mother's story about deciding to ride the bus to Cincinnati with Rupert. She said that it was a very relaxing and enjoyable ride. She had rented a room for the night and was planning to fly out after lunch on Sunday.

Rupert said he was on the same flight back. He smiled that he had expensed the trip, and he was flying back first class on her bill.

Alex said that he was welcome but due to her mother's excellent contract the bill was going to the RMCP and the FBI.

Her mother laughed and said that she and her father were both riding back first class, but she had used the points that Alex had given her to upgrade her tickets.

Alex smiled and said she was happy to see the points go to such good use.

Zelda absorbed the good vibes coming from Alex's table. She realized she was witnessing a different view of life.

It was as if she were standing looking through a magic mirror and seeing a dream world. She did not ever remember ever having such a family experience. In fact, she could no longer remember what her father looked like.

When she saw the check being taken to Alex's table she paid her tab and left the restaurant.

On the way-out Alex stopped by the Hostess station and stood toward the back of the group as she engaged the Hostess closest to her. She was looking at the seating chart as she let the hostess know that she had really enjoyed the meal and that she should let the manager know that the service and the seating had been perfect.

She gave both hostesses five-dollar tips, she leaned in as she gave the other hostess a five and was able to pick up the name for a person sitting at the bar, Z Smith. She looked back at the seating and was sure that whomever Z was it was the person doing the watching.

She asked if the Hostess remember who Z Smith happened to be. The Hostess said that she had never seen the woman before.

Alex joined the rest of her group, and they got into two different cabs that would take them to the bus.

Matt asked what was up.

Alex said that she had felt watched again.

Matt asked if she had gotten what she needed from the hostesses.

Alex said that maybe but her magician was in Baltimore so she would wait until Monday to see if the person they were after had made a mistake.

Zelda was standing back in the trees on some steps that went down to the river walk when Alex came out and everyone got into two taxi's and left the lot.

She had seen Alex and satisfied that urge.

She realized that it did nothing to clarify where the investigation that Alex was leading was going but she now felt she knew more about the person who she might have to kill.

When they arrived at the bus, Matt let out a whistle as he walked down its side. He said it was plainly a beautiful bus.

Alex commented that it could not be both plain and beautiful.

Matt then said it was gorgeous.

Rupert was all smiles, he said they should all go in and celebrate the delivery and if they wanted they could all sleep in the bus and have breakfast in when they got up in the morning.

Matt was the last one in. When he stepped in he stopped and stared. He commented that he had never imagined that a bus could be so….he hesitated and said that he needed some better words than beautiful and gorgeous.

Alex smiled and said that perhaps, stunning, magnificent, wonderfully striking, dazzling, exquisite might all fit the bill.

Rupert said that it was one of his top creations. He pointed to the windows and said that he had added bullet proofing on the inside when Alex asked for bullet proofing on the sitting area up on the deck. He said he would demonstrate the decks use after breakfast in the morning.

Alex said that she was not prepared to spend the night but was looking forward to breakfast in the morning.

Rupert held up a bottle of wine and pointed out it was her favorite and thanks to her mother's guidance it was nonalcoholic.

Alex said she was ready for a glass. She took Matt's hand and guided him back for a tour of the bus.

Her mother joined them and said that she had prepared the back bedroom for use. She and a decorator friend had detailed it.

Alex declared that she liked the simple look and the excellent mix of light colors. She got onto the bed and commented that Rupert had changed the mattress.

Her mother said that the mattress was new but the same brand and firmness of the bed in her home bedroom.

She and Matt stayed a couple of hours before going back to the apartment.

Sunday turned into a flurry of activity. It was breakfast, then Rupert demonstrated how the observation deck operated. He highlighted the shielding that he had added and how comfortable the webbed seats with thick leather backrests were.

It turned out to be a great seat from which to watch the riding of the mini motorcycles.

Then they ate a quick lunch at a pizzeria that her mother wanted try. After lunch Rupert and her parents headed for the airport.

The arrival of the Chief, Mary-Anne, Bill, Travis and their wives and more mini motor bike riding took up the afternoon. Seeing the Chief, Matt, Bill, and Travis all riding at one time as she sat on the deck reminded Alex of the circus clowns coming into the big top and doing tricks on little motorcycles.

Alex and Matt returned to the apartment and enjoyed a quiet evening.

She was pleased with how Rebbeca, who wished to be called Beca, and Evan facilitated the whole day. Evan had pointed out the gas supply for the mini motorbikes and the maintenance tools that Rupert had added. He also mentioned the fact that Rupert had a satellite link, cable, and wireless internet connections so that the bus would always have internet available.

Matt had commented that Rupert had provided a bus that was externally beautiful, with an interior that was magnificent, and a deck that was amazing and safe.

He said he thought that the bus was worth every penny that the RMCP and the FBI were paying for it.

Alex replied that it was a deal that was a good one for everyone involved. She commented that she liked the fact that it was in time to be in use on the following weekend.

Zelda had returned to Toronto feeling somewhat relieved. She put Alex in the league of people that were happy and saw the world through the happy lens.

She figured that those people could never imagine someone who had set out to set a world record in killing men.

She herself had not started with such an idea but when she started inspecting the conditions of the border crossings as one of the key parts of her job things had just clicked.

She thought about herself as somewhat of a black widow. She always killed her victim after sex as they relaxed. It usually also happened after an evening of self-indulgence of some fashion. So, she figured her victims at least died happy.

All she knew was that it was time for another such evening.

15 Armed

Monday morning Alex was at Johnnie's for breakfast. She asked how his weekend had gone and learned that Mary had decided to move to Cincinnati and no she was not moving in with him.

She wanted her own place and if possible one that was not downtown. In fact, she wanted to live somewhere around the Kenwood shopping area. She had a cousin living there and figured she would like to reconnect.

Alex said that sounded great. Her favorite ice cream shop was there.

She shared that she thought that she might have a lead on who the person they were looking for might be. She needed him to see if he could locate a Z Smith.

Johnnie asked if she was trying to pull his leg. He was J Smith.

Alex shared how she had felt that someone was watching her and that the name she had obtained was Z Smith.

She figured it was a made-up name, but she wanted to get him to see if it showed up in any hotel or car rental. She suggested he should also to search the Canadian government records for the name.

Johnnie said he would get on it the first thing but there might be a delay since they had drone flying practice starting at nine.

Alex said that she understood the timing and that her request was secondary to the drone flying.

In the office as the team was drinking coffee and eating their rolls, she suggested that they make the trip to Montreal part of the first Family Weekend vacation. She said that she was thinking of having Nolan, Linda, and Laurie ride on the bus. She asked Bill and Trevor if it was Ok for them to fly up first class and meet the bus in Montreal.

Trevor put on a sad face and said that he would suffer the flight so she could enjoy playing with the kids on "her" bus.

Bill shook his head and said that it was preferable to being on the bus with excited kids and it fit what he and his wife had talked about. He liked the frosting to the cake being able to ride first class.

The Chief had walked out to their desks and had caught the gist of what was going on and took on a hurt look and said that he for once agreed with Trevor about missing the bus ride.

Trevor got a big smile and said, "see I told you all what a great guy the Chief really was."

The Chief shook his head and said that maybe he had made a mistake and should praise Bill for his adult approach since he and Rose-Anne had indeed talked about flying up and having dinner Friday night in Montreal.

Trey said he would let Lindsey know about the bus ride. He said he was sure the kids would be thrilled. He added that Lindsey would let Annie know.

They all went to their drone flying lesson where they were introduced to the actual camera drones they would be using.

Alex took her drone up and knew that she was flying a drone that seemed to handle more like she had thought it would. She took hers through several loops and dives and then landed it. She then flew the second drone that she had ordered. It was a drone that had a camera, but the main feature was that it was weaponized. It had a gun that looked like a barrel stuck in a square box. The box held six bullets in a magazine. Alex took it up, maneuvered it around the park, brought it down, and said she was going to the gun firing range and practice shooting with it so she could master hitting a moving target.

She left the park carrying her armed drone and walked back to the station and out to the firing range. She surprised the firing range master who asked if she was going to do it with a blind fold on.

She laughed at his joke and replied that she would try to keep the bullets from her drone going toward the target.

She learned that the drone fired a nine-millimeter bullet and had a fifteen-bullet magazine versus the six she had thought it had. She and Ted the range master verified that the standard nine mill bullets that the department used fit the gun on the drone.

He loaded the magazine and said that the drone was ready.

Alex launched the drone and flew it up to the target and back several times to get a hand of controlling it in the range. She then brought the drone to her end. She realized that the drone featured a laser light as the aiming aid. She put the laser on the center of the target and fired. The bullet hit the target where the laser had been pointing. She was surprised by how far back the drone had recoiled. She lined up the drone again but turned the laser off and fired at the target using the camera and her eyes. The first shot hit the target, but it hit toward the bottom. She continued practicing without the laser until her final three shots hit the bullseye.

Ted commented that she was always bringing him something new to think about. He had not considered armed drones as a weapon the department might want to consider but now that he thought about it, that capability would mean that an officer could be back in the safety of his car in a gun battle.

Alex agreed and said that the capability had just made it into her team, and she would have all of them in on the following day getting their first practice.

She walked to the pub where everyone had gathered for lunch and shared her experience with the rest of the team. She let them know that the gun on the drone used standard nine-millimeter rounds and Ted could show them how to load the gun.

She asked that they each schedule time at the range and go practice on using the drone. She had only ordered one of the drones.

Nabi said that it was a first for their drone distributorship, but her boss was interested in supplying more if Alex wanted.

Alex looked over at the chief and said that she was thinking of ordering one for each member of the team.

The Chief said that he was all for keeping the team in the lead. He said that he would want to practice using it so he could decide how to position it for the whole police organization. He said that it would be a great way to get his boss into the position to suggest it to the City Council.

Nabi asked whether she could try the drone out. Alex said that she would accompany her to the target range. She looked at Luca and Lucus and asked if they wanted a try. They both replied that it would be great if they could. Nabi asked if her boss might join them.

Alex said that they could have an hour of her time on the following day right after the drone practice in the park and before lunch. Then they would all go to lunch, and all the drones would be sent to be loaded in the bus.

She wanted the team to spend Thursday and Friday focused on digging into and sorting through all the information they had to deal with.

Bill said that he had called Ted and he and Trevor had a slot at the range that afternoon. Trey said that he had one the next morning. The Chief said that he would set something up when he got back to the office.

Johnnie looked at Alex and asked that she set up some time for him but when he got back to his desk he was on the hunt for Z Smith.

Alex suggested that he skip the Cincinnati search and focus on the organizations associated with supporting the Canadian border. She said that she thought that person would have some support role that allowed her natural and a somewhat low-profile access to the border stations. She was expecting the person to be doing some short of checking at the stations.

Johnnie agreed with trying the support organization and asked whether he should hack or ask for legal access.

Alex smiled and said that hacking was faster, but she would call Reg and get him to grant access and assign someone to be his RCMP internal partner.

They all walked back to the office. She suggested they split the work up and asked Bill and Trevor to review their plan and adjust the timing based on driving the bus to the first and second border crossings so they could get firsthand looks at the grave sites.

She asked Trey to organize the first weekend activities in Montreal.

She was going to call Reg and then work with Johnnie to see if they could track down the serial killer.

The Chief said he was going to his office to work through the politics of having to supported the buying of a bus that might only get used for one trip.

Alex reminded him that the bus would most likely be needed for the rest of the year or beyond looking for bodies that were not on the immediate Canadian border crossing properties. She said that he should put his feet up on his desk and enjoy his coffee and the fact that his excellent team was going to crack a case that neither the RCMP nor the FBI had even identified.

The Chief nodded and said that her suggestion was superior to the work he had been contemplating.

Alex looked over at Johnnie and suggested they go to a huddle room and work there.

She called Reg and asked him for permission to peruse the various data bases that his organization might have. She suggested that if that was possible that he then assign someone to work with Johnnie.

She told him they had glimmer of a lead that might help identify the person behind the hacking and the bodies at the border stations.

Reg said that his person would need to be the one going directly into the data bases, but she and Johnnie could direct this person on what to look for and where. He said that he would have the person call her shortly and they could then figure out how they would work the search.

After Alex got off the line, Johnnie let her know that the arrangement might slow down the search and he was willing to hack through any barriers.

Alex said that she knew he could do that, but she said that she preferred letting the RCMP step up. It would allow them to save face when they caught the person, and that person turned out to be a trusted government worker.

It would be a worker who had passed previous background checks. She would be considered a trusted individual and even a close check might not have uncovered he insane behavior. She had demonstrated an uncanny ability to find victims that did not cause a search for them to be done.

A call came in and a Lennard Wilkins introduced himself as a senior IT specialist for the RCMP and that they should call him Len. He had access to all the government data bases and had been asked to work with her and a Johnnie Smith.

Alex handed her phone to Johnnie and told him to set up whatever interface he had in mind with Len.

Johnnie chatted with Len.

Alex listened and realized that the two were speaking in computer-ease in English and she had no idea what they were saying. She realized that Johnnie had trained himself to be up at the top level of the professionals in the IT world. She would needed to share this with the Chief to see if Johnnie deserved a raise or redesignation to a higher level.

Johnnie turned on the big screen and lines of code appeared. He and Len kept a running dialogue going.

She could tell that the two of them were getting along well and seemed to be going from data base to data base more rapidly than she could grasp what they were doing.

She relaxed and watched as they jumped from data base to data base.

Johnnie commented that the data bases needed to be modernized and synchronized. Ted agreed and said they were in the process of doing so but the organizations that used the data bases needed to be synchronized before the data bases had a change of getting done.

Alex was doing a practice profile of an individual that would have the kind of personality that would lead her to commit so many killings.

She began by saying that her home life had caused her to feel unloved or somehow diminished. She thought that perhaps some sort of sibling struggle was involved.

She then focused on the fact that the male figure had somehow fractured her physique, and her mind had put them in the cross hairs of her desire to eliminate these valueless beings.

Alex thought that perhaps the woman used sex to lure the selected victim before killing them.

Alex was most interested in how the killer was able to repeatedly select the men who could disappear and not raise a red flag when they disappeared.

She figured that it might have to do with the work the man was in. She would have to see if learning who the men were, where they worked, and their personal life would give her some insight in her killers keen ability in identifying her victims.

She created a profile of the man that could be killed and not somehow draw the attention to his disappearance. Her profile described a man that had a temporary job or was in between jobs, no strong connections to family or friends, traveling, a loner, frequented bars and sat at the counter or in the corner when he was drinking.

She looked at the clock and realized that Johnnie had been working with Ted for almost three hours and the workday was over.

She interrupted the dialogue going on between Johnnie and Ted and suggested they find a break point and continue in the morning.

Ted thanked her for interrupting and that he had evening plans with the family. He suggested they begin at nine in the morning.

Johnnie said the timing was fine.

After they disconnected, she listened as Johnnie commented that the RCMP systems were worse than most systems he had encountered, and they were in ancient code.

Alex asked whether he had any dinner plans. She suggested a burger or a Ruben sandwich and named a shop that featured both that was only three blocks from their apartment building.

Johnnie replied that it sounded great. They could ride home, clean up and go to dinner. He asked if Matt was joining them.

Alex replied that Matt was doing some extra hours so he could have the weekend off.

Johnnie said that Mary was excited about the weekend in Montreal. He then said that Mary had told him to give Alex a hug.

Alex smiled and said that she was going to tell on him because he had not given her a hug since his return.

16 On the Way

The next morning Alex stayed with Johnnie until he connected with Len and the two started conversing in ITeze.

She excused herself and spent the time before drone training improving the profiles of the killer and victims.

She reviewed her earlier analysis and added that the killer was thought to be a good worker and excellent at her job. She needed little supervision and worked best when left alone. She was, however, not the best coach and most likely would remain at her current level.

Alex then put herself in the killers position and added that she did not make the salary that she deserved. She was frustrated because if she pressed for more pay, what she was doing might get too much scrutiny. This was causing her to accelerate he desire to kill the next man that she could find. Her killing frequency had increased.

That thought put finding out the dates of death as one of the critical items that she needed to get from the exhumed bodies.

She and the team went to the park and set up their drones for their final practice at nine. That Johnnie was missing was no surprise to Alex. She was sure he was surfing through data base after database and would find the person they were looking for.

Alex flew her drone and practiced using only coordinates. She learned that the response of the drone was a little slower than that of the training drones had been and spent her time getting the feel for the response times for various flight changes.

She realized that her practice was being watched not only by the trainers but by the other members of the team when Trevor asked if she had taken up drinking Kentucky Bourbon.

She let out a whoop and flew her drone about a foot off the ground and swept by everyone standing by the green and then pulled the drone up into the air in as steep a climb as it would take. She did a wiggle and then had it dive down toward her and gently land at her feet.

She smiled and told everyone when they could duplicate her flight they could sit on the deck of the bus. She declared that she had to go practice with her other drone and see if she could learn to shoot blind folded.

She put her drone in its carrier and headed toward the station. She smiled when she heard Trevor shout after her that he loved her too.

Trey caught up with her and said that he had been told he was qualified, but he said he would never be able to fly his drone with the skill she had just demonstrated. He added that he would practice missing trees and keeping his drone from crashing and that he was not going to try to best her.

Alex nodded and said that she loved flying the drones and it would most likely be a toy that she would enjoy flying on many weekends to come. She added that she thought she might get into using it to take unique nature pictures.

Trey said that he thought it would be a great activity to do with Nolan.

They both went to the shooting range and for the next hour they took turns using the armed drone. Alex had learned how to use it so that she could hit the target at the center without the laser.

Trey was almost as good but had a little more of a scatter. He and the drone did not have as tight of a synchronization bond as Alex had.

The range master commented that the two of them had put on an impressive show. He admitted to having used the drone to get a feel for it. He said that he was one step behind Trey. He added that he had gotten permission to order the same model drone and asked for the contact name and number.

Alex said that she would bring the person he needed to talk to back after lunch.

Alex had forgotten that it was the team's graduation lunch, and she had agreed to pay for the lunch, but Nora wanted to pick up desert and to hand out certificates to her team.

Alex realized that Johnnie had picked the restaurant where she had shot and the thug that was after him.

She went into the huddle room and interrupted the session he and Len had going and said that it was lunch time, and he was expected to attend. She, Trey, and Johnnie were the last to arrive. They were led to a separate room where everyone had already ordered their starters. The Chief pointed to the starters in front of the three empty seats and said that he had ordered for them.

Alex thanked him and asked how the rest of the training had gone.

Trevor replied that it had gone very well until they had each tried the Black Alex Radical Flight. He then said that in capital letters it was spelled BARF, and they had all tried BARFing but failed.

Bill commented that Trevor's jokes were really hitting the bottom.

Alex looked over to Nora and said that she might not need to buy desert or hand out completion diplomas.

Nora smiled and said that her trainers had told her that they had never worked with such a talented group. She looked at Johnnie and said that he owed her one more training session. He could arrange it whenever he had the time.

There had only been three mains to choose from: Salmon, T-bone, or Filet Mignon. Alex chose the Filet and said that if Trey and Johnnie each took an order of the other two mains they could all share some with each other.

When they returned to the office, the Chief commented that the lunch was a huge success, and he looked forward to the team using the new technology. He added that they needed to catch the serial killer. He asked Johnnie if he was getting any closer to finding her.

Johnnie said that by a process of elimination he and Len, the RCMP IT, were getting to the point they would either strike gold or start their search over.

Alex suggested that Z might have somehow removed her personnel records. They should check the payroll names versus personnel records.

Johnnie said that he would suggest that to Len. He added that they had both gone IT crazy versus user crazy.

Alex smiled and said that sometimes it was so easy to slide into the normal versus the practical. She shared the fact that when he got the name, no one that worked with that person they were looking for would believe that she could possibly be the person that had killed nearly a hundred men.

She reminded everyone to bring personal things that they needed to the bus in the morning. She said they should make sure they had the medicines they might need.

She said that she would ask Rebecca and Will to arrange for laundry service as they traveled. This would let them travel light. However, there was plenty of room in the luggage storage area so folks could bring their tuxedos if they wanted.

Trevor said that he could not put any of his expensive tuxedos in a suitcase and the closets on the bus were too small, so he was planning on only wearing his old blue jeans.

Alex replied that she had decided the same thing about all her evening dresses.

Bill commented that he was going to stop by the pharmacy and get a supply of depressants to put in Trevor's drinks.

Alex then reminded everyone to get their drones put in the bus before evening. She volunteered to take anyone's drone when she went out to the bus.

She shared that the bus would leave at six the following evening. There would be refreshments and light snacks and then they would all hit their racks and Will and Rebbeca would drive overnight and get them to Montreal for breakfast.

They all had hotel reservations for Saturday and Sunday. After that, the team would be sleeping on the bus.

Trevor took on a hurt look and said that only her favorites, Trey and Johnnie were going to enjoy the comfort of the bus ride, the really valuable members of the team had to ride out on the wing of some biplane to get there.

Bill said he was going to add sleeping pills to the items to pick up to put in Trevor's coffee.

Alex said that Bill should take it easy on his partner because after all riding in "First" class carried a class stigma that might be affecting him.

The Chief said that he had real work to do and went into his office.

Alex reminded everyone that the armed drone was at the firing range, and she would wait until the end of Friday before taking it to the bus.

Trevor commented that the armed drone was one weapon that he wanted to master. He said that the two major gun battles the team had gone through on two of their cases would have been significantly different had they been able to use armed drones. He planned to keep practicing until he could put every round into the center.

Alex said that she felt the same about the use of the armed drone. She suggested that once he got the hang of hitting the target with the drone holding a steady position and be able to fly it like it was a fighter plane and hit the target as the drone danced around the firing range she would make sure he got one of his own..

Trevor said he'd give it a try but first he had to develop consistency with a drone that hovered in one position.

Trey agreed and shared the fact that the range master had challenged Alex to do her blindfold trick with the drone.

Alex shook her head and suggested they all get to work. She went back to her profiling work and became sure that the person who had signed in for dinner two evenings before was indeed the person who she was looking for. She hoped that signing as Z Smith had been a mistake on her perps part.

She decided that if she only got one ride on the bus it would be a supreme victory, and she would happily buy the bus.

Zelda got an alarm from a monitor that she had set up. It was alarmed when someone was searching data bases using the letter Z or her name. She knew that whoever was searching was looking for the letter Z. She immediately hid her personnel records by changing the file name and erasing the letter Z from all the reports in the folder. But she knew that she was no longer safe. Someone was hunting her, and she intuitively knew that it was the person she had just spied on.

She figured the time to being identified was now a matter of days. She let her boss know that she was taking the afternoon off.

She had been looking at a used black pickup that had a camper top on the back and had a back passenger seat. It was in great shape and drove like a dream. It was ten years old and had a reasonable asking price. She asked about a discount and got a ten percent discount. She paid cash which made the lot owner smile. He told her in French that she had made his day.

She wanted to tell him she had made his day because he would probably keep the transaction off the books.

She simply replied, "'en prie," as he handed her the keys. She asked to pick up her paperwork at his lot and he agreed to get it sent back to him.

She went to her current rental and packed all her things. She had regularly moved so everything she possessed fit into three large trunks that were on wheels.

She put in a pole in the camper section and put all her hanging closes into the pickup and then moved all three trunks in. One of the things that had attracted her was that the camper portion had a fold down bed along one side and a set of shelves on the other side that had latched covers. She bought a foam mattress for the fold down and felt that she was set.

She then set up several new internet login accounts and looped the previous ones to randomly change their addresses. She hoped to wear out anyone trying to follow her internet journey and get them lost in the forest of accounts and never make it through.

She then connected back into the system at work. It was one of many backdoors that she had designed. This backdoor was the account of the RCMP's chief. She figured that someone might find out the fact that she had the ability to ease drop on his support, but they would miss the back door to the chief himself. She went from that location and searched around to see if she could learn anything.

She took another step and bugged every support secretary so that she could intercept messages sent to them.

This was a risk, but she needed immediate information about what Alex might be finding out.

She looked at the time and realized that she had reservations at her gun range. She figured it was time to retrieve her weapons. She now had the original 308 that she had started with, and she had added a top of the line 405 lever action, four shot, with a walnut stock and with a specialty scope mounted on it. It a had cost her a small fortune. It was the most expensive item that she had ever purchased. It had cost more than the pickup she had just purchased. It was known as a rifle a rhino hunter could rely on. She learned almost immediately that the 308 had a much lighter kick. Lucky for her she had a foam harness on her shoulder to take up some of the impact of the 405. Her first few shots had almost knocked her down. She loved the fact that when she hit the target, the entire solid red center part disappeared.

She used her range time to practice with both rifles and then checked them both out and let the range master know that she was going to use them in the next few weeks and would come back and let him know how hunting had been.

When she returned to her newly rented cottage she put her two rifles into the large containers in the back of the truck where she had left room to carry them.

She went online and went into the system at work and went to yet another account that she had set up that was her bosses support. It allowed her to spy directly on her boss. She found out that an inquiry about her had been made.

She had no idea how anyone could possibly have tracked her.

There were no names mentioned but the city of Cincinnati was in one sentence. She knew who was doing the searching. The message mentioned attending a face to face on Monday with the RCMP Chief to review the evidence being brought to him in person.

She knew that she had to get herself into position to take out the person she now knew was a superior hunter. She knew visitors were always asked to enter the front of the building where the Chief had his office. She knew exactly where she would be when Alex was climbing up the stairs to the front door.

She would kill her and then disappear to somewhere. She thought about where that somewhere should be. She knew Canada like the back of her hand, but she had never thought about where to hide. She thought about it and decided to stay in the woods along the St. Croix River. She knew that her truck parked in the woods would look like any hunter's rig and would not draw any attention.

That was as far as she got when the alarm she had set if someone found her files came through.

She could not believe what was happening. She was being exposed on all fronts. She kept mumbling, "how was it possible," She wanted to find out and kill whom ever had collapsed the good life that she had built. She kept thinking that she should have somehow killed this Alex in Cincinnati.

Alex had finished Friday feeling exhausted but feeling that she was making progress on the case. She had her things on the bus and she and Matt were discussing what games they would play with the kids until it was bedtime.

Alex suggested they let the kids have a quick mini motorcycle ride in the lot area, then load up and play the game of choice that might interest the three. Alex pointed out that all games would be online, and she had the controllers that let up to four people play at a time.

Trey arrived with everyone in his minivan, and everyone piled out.

Matt asked who wanted to try a mini motorcycle. He laughed when everyone, but Trey raise their hands. He and Will got five ready and gave everyone instructions on how to ride and how to control them.

Lindsey took the lead and Annie took the back. The five took three trips around the park.

Alex waved them in and said they should get all their things on board while the bikes got put away.

Then they would be on the way.

<u>17 Arrival</u>

Trey had done the research for the weekend and had decided that they would hit the top breakfast place in downtown Montreal and afterwards they would go to the campground where the bus could be parked. He had selected a campground to the southwest of the Montreal proper that featured fishing, paddle boarding, canoeing, hiking, and biking.

He had inquired whether mini motorcycles were allowed and had learned that there was a dirt trail that went out into the forest that could be ridden on as long as they were not too loud.

He had asked everyone what other activities they wanted to do.

He had a couple of requests for any historic sites that might be interesting.

The younger set was quick to say they were not interested in Museums.

After getting everyone's input he set up a tour on Sunday that ended at the La Ronde amusement park that featured Six Flags rides.

He said they would spend the afternoon and have lunch and an early dinner there. The group flying back to Cincinnati had to leave by five in the afternoon to catch their flights. He had arranged transportation that would pick them up at the entrance to the park and the bus would be there when they arrived so everyone could get their luggage put on the bus.

They arrived in Montreal and went to the hotel that was within walking distance from the campground. He had negotiated dinner in the hotel where everyone that had not ridden in on the bus was staying. They were to be met there by the group that had flown in and were in the hotel.

As they all gathered for dinner he decided it was the right time to share the weekend itinerary.

When he finished, Trevor said that Alex had given Trey the easy place to identify entertainment where everyone would have a good time, and he was relegate to the finding weekend entertainment in the wilderness.

Alex smiled and said that she had indeed done so because she knew that he was a superior planner and would surely be able to outdo Trey.

The next day, after breakfast while the bus drove to the campground, Trey highlighted all the sites that he could show on the screen.

The Chief commented that he had not realized he had a detective that he might lose to some tourist agency. He complemented him on selecting a great hotel. He would have to go back to the office and make sure that his compensation was appropriate to his demonstrated capability.

Alex looked over at Trevor and said that the two of them needed to sharpen their party planning skills so they too could see about raises.

Bill looked at Alex and told her to quit baiting his partner.

They were shown their camping spot that was surrounded by trees and was right on the shore.

Alex thought about fishing, then she thought about a bike ride, then she thought about a hike, then she saw a reclining lounge chair under the trees and decided that was where she was going to take a nap. Matt let her know that he was going out on the pier and try his hand at fishing.

Johnnie chose to sit on top of the bus with Mary who had joined them during breakfast. The two of them were laughing and joking and a little later they climbed down and went for a walk.

Trey and the kids were out on the dock fishing. Lesley, and Annie were out demonstrating their paddle boarding skills.

The Chief and Mary-Anne had gone for a walk.

Evan and Rebecca were in the bus sleeping.

Alex woke from her nap and went to see how the fishing was going.

She noted the time. She had to get ready to have dinner with Reginald and his wife, the Chief and Mary-Ann were also going as was the rest of the team. She had learned that Denton and his boss were also going to attend.

She was surprised at the attendance but thought it was a good way to make sure all the organizations were aligned.

Mary, Lesley, and Annie were staying with the kids. They had decided to take a couple of pizzas out of the freezer and had ordered some desert to be delivered. They hoped everyone would have as good of a time as they were planning to have.

Alex and Reg had decided to go to one of his favorite French Restaurants that was located in the downtown district.

She was in a simple black pants outfit that she hoped was dressy enough. Matt was stunning in his dark navy-blue suit. She was so used to seeing everyone in plain work clothes that it was strange to see everyone in suits. They arrived at the restaurant and were escorted into a private room where Reg and his wife were waiting. He had also invited, Lenard, the IT that was working with Johnnie.

They all sat down, and the waiter rattled off the selections that they could choose from. She, Matt, Trey, and Johnnie made their usual deal and they each chose one of the main dishes.

She thanked Reg for being so gracious as to set up the dinner. She said that she hoped that they could continue their great relationship and coordination.

She complemented Len and Johnnie in finding Z, the mysterious and soon to be the infamous serial killer that they would bring in.

Reg said that he did not want to discuss the case but just enjoy each other's company but on Monday he was going to really dig in and question who they were accusing.

Alex raised her glass and said, "to friends, to compatriots, to success and to Monday. Our border makes us good neighbors."

The conversation turned to what they were all doing. Trey had the spotlight as he described the concept that the team practiced of "Weekend Vacations" as a means of keeping work and family life in balance as the team tackled out of town engagements. He smiled and said that if they had to travel the Canadian-US border it would be one of the longest out of town engagements that the team had ever undertaken.

Reg said that he was impressed with that approach. He asked the Chief how he could afford such a team.

The Chief smiled and said that he had the best contract negotiator, Alex's mother, who had deftly put all the expenses in the contract that the RCMP and the FBI had cosigned. He chuckled and added that like Reg he did not want to talk business over dinner.

Reg nodded and asked what everyone thought of the food.

The Chief said that it was outstanding and that he was looking forward to the desert.

Reg asked if they wanted to see any of the Montreal night life.

Alex replied that she was planning to call it a day after dinner.

The Chief, the FBI director, Johnnie, and Lenard said they would like to see some of Montreal's night life.

Alex thought that would work well for all three organizations. She knew that Johnnie would work on Reg and get closer to Lenard. He would make Monday a verification day versus a contentious day.

As they were riding back to the bus. Matt asked what was on her mind. Alex commented that she suspected that her prey might have discovered that she was being hunted. She shared the fact that Z had made at least two visits to Cincinnati. She must have put out extra feelers linked to several support persons as she tried to find out what was going on internally. Alex said that she had been profiling Z and felt that if Z got desperate, she would strike out.

Alex was worried about where and when.

Trey was sitting in front. He turned and said that they would need to be extra cautious on Monday.

He added that he felt that Sunday would be a safe day because there was no way that Z would have any idea where they were. However, on Monday they would be going to meet with Reg and if Z knew, she might choose their arrival or departure to make a move.

He said if he were in her shoes he would be a sniper.

Alex said that she agreed with him, and they should keep the conversation they just had to themselves and come back to it when everyone had departed on Sunday afternoon.

Matt said that he would call his boss and delay his return.

Alex replied that he should do what he had originally planned. His presence would distract her. She said that she had a partner who had her back. He had saved her countless times, and she knew that he was fearless.

Matt gave her a kiss and said that she made sense.

When they arrived, Rebecca and Evan were relaxing in their lounge chairs outside and sipping on a beer. They greeted Alex, Matt and Trey and asked if they wanted a cold one.

Alex thanked them and said she was going in and see how things were going in the bus.

She went in and was surprised at how quiet it was. She looked at what movie they were watching and was surprised to see that Fiddler on the Roof was on.

She went to the back and got out of her dress clothes. She and Matt came back and took a seat at what she considered the kitchen table.

Trey came out in casual clothes and looked the way that Alex thought of him.

He asked if Matt wanted anything and said he was going to make some popcorn.

He had said it loudly and got the response he had expected.

He got up and put on a large stainless-steel pan that had a thick bottom and poured in enough oil to cover three test kernels of popcorn. He then let the oil heat until the three kernels popped. He pulled the pan to the side and covered the bottom with popcorn and put the pan back on the burner.

A few moments later the popping was persistent and then died down.

Trey pulled the pan off the burner and distributed the popcorn into four large bowls. He melted a bowl of butter and pour it liberally over the popcorn in the bowls, sprinkled some salt on the popcorn and then put a top on each bowl as he shook it.

He took two bowls and put it on the table in front of those watching the movie. He put one bowl on the Kitchen table and took one bowl out to Rebecca and Evan.

He took three tall glasses and filled them with ice and put them on the kitchen table with three bottles of sparkling water.

He sat down and said he thought it had been a great day, a great dinner and so far a great family weekend.

Alex agreed and said that she was looking forward to their tour on the following day.

Trey said that he had hired a local tour guide, and she would be at the hotel when they picked up the folks staying there.

Alex said that she thought the approach he had chosen of only visiting the Art museum and driving by the other sites was perfect. She hoped the tour guide was used to giving bus tours.

Trey said that the company where she worked usually did the tours in their buses, but Trey had insisted on using their bus. He had gotten a slight decrease in the tour fee but not as much as he had hoped. He had checked on the route and found out that there were no low over passes, and they would be able to sit on the bus roof during the drive through.

Alex suggested they check to see if the armor that she had ordered could be kept down otherwise the bus would be higher than most double deck busses.

Try said he had not thought about that critical detail and that perhaps they might need to use the tour bus after all.

Alex said they should worry about it in the morning and if necessary they could make the switch during breakfast.

Zelda had a rough day on Saturday. She had moved out of her cottage and had worked all day to set up several additional nefarious nodes in the web to trap and snag anyone trying to trace her. She figured she that her web would have any IT person on their knees or so confused that like a spider she would have them encased.

It was a gloriously clear day. The weather was cool, and it was what she considered perfect. She decided to go fishing so that she could contemplate what she had to do to get out of the mess she was finding herself in.

She knew she could not yet go back to work but had to first get rid of anyone that was trying to track her. She did not think they could link her to any of the bodies, but they could implicate her and ruin her career. She was going to take out anyone that she felt might cause that to happen.

Fishing was a huge success. She caught two large trout and figured she would enjoy them for dinner. On the way back from fishing, she stopped by a local convenience store and bought a six pack and some chips.

She decided on a show and picked one that over the years she had watched multiple time. Little did she know that she was watching the same show as the person that she wanted to eliminate, and that person was within walking distance.

Alex let out her breath as a cold shiver ran down her back.

Matt asked what was up.

Alex said that she felt the person that they were seeking was close by.

Matt asked how she could possibly know that.

Alex said she had no idea.

Trey asked if he should be worried.

Alex said that there was nothing to do but to enjoy some great popcorn and a sip of her sparkling ice water.

Matt asked Trey if Alex was always this way. Trey said that he counted on her premonitions because they had saved both of them countless times.

He reminded Matt of his own experience when he had first met Alex. It was her personal radar that had saved the two of them that day in Wiggins, Mississippi.

Matt thanked Trey for reminding him. He was just worried about the current situation. It was going to drive him nuts when he got back to Cincinnati.

Trey said that he could not keep him from worrying but Matt had to know that not only he would have her back but so would Bill and Trevor. They were both fearless and were both super protective of Alex. He added that Johnnie would also be doing the same.

Matt thanked him and said it helped to know that Alex had a fearless team.

Alex pointed to the kids. Two were already asleep and Lorie was flirting with sleep.

Trey picked Nolan up and took him to his bunk and put him in. Lindsey had made Nolan wear pajamas to watch the movie. She had also been in her pj's and had fallen asleep as well. Trey nudge her and she smiled and asked if it was bedtime. She said good night and took the bunk below Nolan's.

Trey brushed his teeth and changed into his sleeping clothes and climbed into the top bunk.

Annie said good night as she put Linda and Lauri in their bunks and climbed into the top one. She said that it had been a great day and thanked Alex.

Alex let Rebecca and Evan know that everyone inside was either in bed or going there.

They thanked her for letting them know and as soon as they finished watching the episode of one of their favorite shows they would come in and hit the sack as well.

Alex took Matt by the hand and said that it was time for them to enjoy the great bed that was in her room in the back. She said that they should really shower first before getting in the bed.

Matt said that would be better than the desert he had enjoyed at the restaurant.

18 Tour and the Park

The next morning when they woke up they were already at the hotel. Rebecca said that they had made a decision that it would be easier for the folks on the bus to take their time getting ready knowing that they only needed to walk from the bus to breakfast.

Alex complimented them on making a good decision. She had been planning to make coffee but chose instead to go in and get coffee and breakfast at the restaurant.

She and Matt got out and walked into the hotel.

She walked in and saw one other person in the breakfast area and approached her and asked if she by chance happened to be the tour guide.

The tour guide held up her tablet and said that she indeed was and introduced herself as Silvia Preston and said that she was waiting for a Trey McGregor.

Alex said that he would be coming in soon. She asked if she and Matt could sit with her.

Alex went and got two cups of coffee and returned to the table. She asked Silvia if breakfast was self-serve or did they need to order.

Silvia replied that she was not sure, but she had watched the serving area being set up and a waitress had asked if she was planning to order breakfast, so she figured it was a breakfast that you ordered but most of it was ready except for the eggs or maybe the waffles.

As if on que the waitress came over and asked what they wanted for breakfast. She asked for their room number.

Alex explained that this was the McGregor party and there would be more joining soon.

The waitress nodded and said that they had been notified about that arrangement and welcomed them to the hotel and to Canada. She took their order and said that she would be back shortly.

Alex asked Silvia if it was possible to use the tour companies touring bus. She said that the bus that was parked outside had a top deck, but the seats faced to one side. She figured the touring bus would have better seating.

Silvia said that would be no problem and asked whether they could ride the bus outside to where the tour bus was parked, and then change over to it. She said that she would put in a call to her driver who had dropped her off at the hotel.

She stopped and asked whether Alex could authorize the fifteen percent that would be added back on the tour contract.

Alex nodded and said that she would make sure that Trey would sign for the additional cost.

Silvia made the call and after letting her driver know that they would use the company bus and after a few "sure, that would be good and a yea me too," Silvia said that her driver was happy because he only got paid when he was driving, and he said he would drive back and pickup everyone at the hotel.

Alex thanked her and said that the change in arrangement would simplify the logistics. She asked if there was room on the bus for luggage and if by chance they delivered people to the airport.

Silvia said that they did provide that service but that would be an additional fee.

Alex asked her what the cost would be to take nine people to the airport. All of them would go there at one time.

Silvia replied that it they would need to take three taxis from the theme park to the airport. That would cost them sixty Canadian dollars per cab or one hundred and eighty Canadian dollars by cab. She could do that trip for one hundred and she would include dropping the rest of the people off at the hotel.

Silvia had just agreed to the arrangement when Trey walked in the door with Lindsey and Nolan and headed toward where Alex was sitting.

Alex stood up and introduced Trey, Lindsey, and Nolan.

She let Trey know that she had just convinced Silvia to handle all the logistics.

Trey replied that it was a great call

His entry seemed to be the trigger for everyone else to arrive for breakfast.

Silvia introduced herself and said that she would come around and get everyone's name and give them a name tag so she wouldn't lose anyone.

A few moments later, an older man walked over to Silvia. Silvia stood up and introduced Rene Gauthier, her French speaking bus driver. She smiled and added that he spoke fluid Canadian English and was the best driver in the company.

Rene said he was pleased to be driving, and he added that he had wiped down all the seats and the bus was ready. He said that seating was available both on the top open deck or inside. He added that the top deck was shielded from the wind by plexiglass shields that he had raised but he could lower them if they were in the way of taking photos. He smiled and said that the ride on top was fun and was like riding in a convertible.

Alex saw that breakfast seemed to be over, and she said they should all take a ten minute break and then assemble out by the bus. She said that those returning to Cincinnati should bring their luggage out to the tour van because it would take them to the airport from the amusement park.

Alex refreshed her coffee and put it into a paper cup. She asked Silvia if coffee was allowed on the bus.

Silvia said that it was and that the bus was stocked with soft drinks including coffee in a bottle.

Alex smiled and said that Trey had picked the right tour company.

Silvia nodded and said that she was right about the company, but she had to credit Trey with the selection of drinks and snacks. She said that there was a bowl of fruit inside and one on the top deck.

Alex put on her name tag and walked out to the bus.

Rene was standing by the open back doors of the van.

Alex engaged him in some small talk and found out that he had grown up in Trois-Rivières-Way a city that was half-way between Montreal and Québec City and that he had been married for twenty years and had one son at the University of Toronto and a daughter in her senior year in high school.

Trey came to the van carrying two medium sized suitcases and was followed by Nolan and Lindsey.

Alex asked Nolan if he was ready for the day. He nodded and said he was going to ride on top.

Silvia helped pin Nolan's name tag on and then showed him where the steps up were located.

Annie, Linda, and Lorie were next, and they all left their luggage, got their name tags, and climbed up to the top deck.

Matt brought out his things and asked if Alex was sitting on top.

She nodded and said she would be up as soon as everyone got on.

The Chief, Mary-Anne, Mary, Johnnie, her mother, and father all said they were riding inside.

Rebbeca and Evan came over and asked if they could join the tour. They said that hotel expected to have the bus parked there all day and they figured they might as well take in Montreal and enjoy the park.

Alex looked at Silvia and asked her to add them and make any adjustments necessary.

Alex climbed up the steps to the top deck.

Matt had the very first seat and had one next to him. She had an open area in front of her and a clear view out the side. He said that he was designating her the photographer for both of them.

Trey and Lindsey had the seats on the other side.

Alex looked back and saw that Nolan, Linda, and Lorie each had an individual seat. Annie was sitting at the center of the back bench seat and had her art supplies out.

Alex knew that Annie sketched and painted and only took photographs to capture the scene she was planning to paint.

Silvia began her tour as they left the hotel parking lot. She shared some of the history of the growth of Montreal and the significance of some of the small villages they passed.

French and English battles had raged along the St. Lawrence River and the early settlers, and fur trappers had all played a part.

Silvia let them know when they got to the art museum they would go up the elevator to the top where there was an Inuit art collection, they then would ride down the elevator and see one piece on each floor that followed a timeline approaching the present.

They would then go to Michal and Renata Hornstein Pavilion for Peace.

As they entered Montreal, Silvia explained that Montreal was similar to New York City because it too was located on an Island. Laval was the other less known city that was also on an Island, and they had just driven across it.

She then highlighted two parks that were near the city center making the comparison to New York even closer. She then pointed out that New York was ten times bigger and so was Central Park.

The bus then stopped in front of the Montreal Museum of Fine arts. Silvia said that this would be the only walk in part of the tour and the others would be videos shown on the bus and a drive by the exterior of the museum.

She highlighted the fact that in 1972 the museum experienced the largest art heist in Canada's history. It was given the moniker, "The Skylight Caper" because the thieves had entered through an under repair skylight.

The thieves left rapidly when the alarm went off and left the two most valuable paintings but got away with two hundred million dollars' worth of art that to date had never been recovered.

Silvia led the way, and they took an elevator up to the top level where Inuit art was feature. She led them through a brief walk and then took the elevator to the next level down and did the same. As she brought them down she commented that each level brought them one hundred years closer to the present. It was clear to Alex that Silvia was well versed on all the art they were walking by that she briefly explained.

They had gone one level into the basement and then climbed the stairs back to the first floor. Silvia said that either the Center needed to add a floor on top or dig deeper because they had a great deal of art stored away.

She said that the bus was waiting at the base of the steps, and the rest of the tour would be on the bus.

The bus left the Museum, and a short time later entered Dorchester Square and circled it once as Silvia pointed to a variety of Statues. They then circled the Mary, Queen of the World Cathedral and then were heading back when suddenly Alex felt a shiver when they stopped at the light.

She looked down and saw a single helmeted, cyclist it a dark green riding outfit, wearing dark riding glasses waiting for the light to turn green. She felt certain she was looking at Z. She was getting ready to run down when Z looked up and immediately sprinted across the intersection and turned down the next alley.

Zelda had ridden the bus into the city and brought her bike. She had decided to spend the day enjoying doing some shopping, riding her bike, and walking through Dorchester Square and visiting the Mary, Queen of the World Cathedral where she often had gone to enjoy the interior.

She planned to treat herself to an exclusive lunch at either the most expensive sea food restaurant or to a just as expensive steak restaurant for an early lunch. She decided on steak and when she entered she found out she was the first and so far the only customer. She was relieved because she had left her bike out at the entrance and had dawned a wrap to act as a skirt and wasn't sure she would be adequately dressed.

The steak was superb, and the customers were just starting to arrive as she took her bike to the elevator and went down to street level. She rode up to the light that turned red as she was approaching.

She was suddenly in a shadow as a bus stopped next to her. She looked up and almost fell off her bike when she saw the person she was thinking of killing looking down at her and snapping a picture. She launched her bike across the intersection and turned immediately down the next alley.

She was peddling as if the devil was after her. She kept looking into her helmet mirror to see if anyone was following. She went through several more turns and alleys until she was sure she was not being followed.

She decided that her trip downtown was over, and she was going to head back to her cottage and sharpen her plan to get rid of Alex. At the next bus stop she got off and then figured out the right busses to get her home.

As the rider began her sprint, Alex had a clear view of Z sprinting her bike across the intersection and almost being hit by a car entering the intersection. When she saw the bike turn into the alley, she knew that she would not be able to catch Z.

She sat down and let out her breath.

Matt asked her what had just happened.

Alex said that she had looked down at a cyclist that was stopped next to the bus. She said that the cyclist looked up and then she sprinted across the intersection and disappeared down the first alley way. She said that she thought she had just looked down at Z.

She said that she was going to let Johnnie know.

Johnnie said that he had not noticed but he said that it was good to know she was in Montreal since it would help to narrow where to find the end of the string of internet nodes.

Alex returned to her seat and slowly sipped the cold coffee. It was hard to concentrate on the remaining part of the bus tour.

She came back to the tour when they arrived at the amusement park.

She got off and asked Silvia about where to eat.

Silvia said that all the places were fast food. And that she felt that the grill at the far end of the park offered the most complete meal, and that they also had table seating.

Silvia escorted them in gave the tickets for everyone to the attended at the entrance.

Alex let everyone know where she was going for lunch and began the walk across the park. She walked by various rides and said that she was staying off most of them. She commented that some of them frightened her more than being in a gun fight.

She looked back and saw Trey and his gaggle break off and go to a hotdog looking stand. The rest were walking behind.

There was about three hours of play time and then it would be time to get to the airport.

She let Matt know she was not in the mood for any of the parks rides. She suggested he go find where Trey was and join him and play with Nolan and the girls.

Matt knew the situation and he knew Alex's disposition. He said he was going to go play and left the restaurant.

Her mother came over and ask what was up. When Alex said, "nothing" Rose-Anne knew that "something big" was up.

She invited Alex to go with her to a Pizzeria that was supposed to serve the best pizza in Montreal, and she was going there to see if she could get them to give her the rights to feature it at Rose-Annc's Pizzeria.

Alex said that seemed like a good idea. She thought it was a good idea to get out of the boisterous theme park. She walked with her mother to the front of the park and after getting their hands stamped so they could re-enter they caught a cab and went to the pizzeria.

Rose-Anne led the way into the shop and asked for the owner. The owner came out and asked how he could be of help. The two sat at one of the tables and chatted for a short time. They stood up and shook hands and Rose-Anne waved to Alex to follow her.

Alex had been sitting and playing out various possible attack scenarios that she might face. The quiet had helped her relax.

She got up and walked out with her mother. As they waited for the taxi to come to pick them up she learned that her mother had made a deal that she would share her best pizza recipe and the owner she had been talking to would share his secret recipe. They would each share the proceeds of their sales with each other. The owner Rodolfo Roberto would come to her shop and teach her chef how to make his pizza, and he would verify that the pizzas were to his standards.

Rose-Anne said that they would get back to the theme park just in time to catch the bus to the airport.

Alex looked at the time and said that indeed it was that time.

19 The Beginning

The fifteen-minute trip to the airport gave everyone a chance to say goodbye. Everyone agreed that it had been a whirl wind weekend, but it had been fun. They all said they were looking forward to their first-class flights and the meal that came along with it. Except for the three kids no one had eaten dinner.

As she watched everyone pull their suitcases and head for the counters, Alex felt a weight getting off her shoulder.

Spotting Z from the tour bus had raised her level of concern. She felt better with everyone leaving and getting away from her.

She knew that she was a target if Z had figured out that she was a suspect. She was raising her assessment of Z's capabilities. She was a cyclist, and her sprint had demonstrated that she was also in good physical shape. She had also kept two very IT capable guys at bay for several days. She had quietly lured and killed close to one hundred men.

Alex put Z into the most dangerous type of adversary category.

She raised Z's to one where she was going to work with Trey on how they should improve their approach to working in the field.

She at first thought about moving the bus to another location but then changed her mind. The bus had been in the hotel parking lot, and the tour bus would be returning to wherever it was kept.

When they got to the hotel parking lot, Alex paid for all the adjustments she had made to the tour contract and also paid for the waiting time and then she added a twenty percent tip.

Both Silvia and Rene thanked her for her generous tip and said that they had a good time as well.

They all rode the bus back and when it was parked, Alex asked if anyone had eaten dinner.

Trey said that none of the folks with him except the kids had. He learned that the flight would serve a meal in first class, so he had played until it was time to get on the bus.

Johnnie said that he and Mary had decided against another meal in the park. Mary said she had an energy bar and would get something when she got to the airport if she was hungry.

Bill said that he and Trevor had done pretty much what everyone else had done and both of their wives had decided that the food in first class would be better than the fast food in the park.

Rebecca said that she and Evan had talked about cooking something when they got back.

Alex asked if they were up for some Thai food, if so she would get some delivered and they could all eat on the bus. It they wanted to; they could go and eat at the restaurant.

Trey said that he preferred to eat on the bus.

Trevor and Bill seconded that idea.

Everyone agreed that they were ready to take it easy.

Alex called up the menu and they selected several starters, an order of Thai beef, two orders of Thai Shrimp, two orders of Thai Scallops, Thai fish, and an order of frog legs.

Alex said that it would come with rice.

Trevor asked if he could add noodles.

Alex let Rebecca and Evan know that the meal would fall into the category of family style because they would all share a little of everything.

Trevor commented that whoever ate frog legs must really be hungry, but his joke was ignored.

Rebecca said that family style would be just fine.

Alex said that she wanted to set the stage for their morning meeting with the leadership of the RCMP. Reg had let her know that the regional leaders from each of the provinces where a body had been found would be in attendance. He was not sure about the other leaders, and they might show up just so they would not be left out of the loop. All but the Quebec leader would attend virtually.

She shared the fact that she was upping the threat she thought that Z represented and shared why she was doing so.

Everyone on the team agreed with her.

She said she wanted to arrive a few minutes early. She said the bus was to park in front of the building and that the deck get raised as a precaution to Z being in position to shoot. She asked Trey where he would locate if he were setting up to shoot someone.

Trey said that he would go to the top of a building that had a clear view of the entrance to the RCMP headquarters. He would take a building that was far enough away so he could make his escape after taking his shots.

He added that putting up the deck shield was a waste of time. The shooter would have an angle that would put the shot well above the deck shields.

Alex said that she agreed and said they would leave the deck alone. She asked if Trey had a suggestion on how they should enter the building.

Trey said that she should go out ahead of him.

He would have his weapon at the ready and walk sidewards looking one way. He wanted Trevor to do the same but to walk sidewards looking the other way. The two of them would be shoulder to shoulder. Bill would have his gun drawn but would face backward and walk backwards toward the building.

He suggested that all of them should have their Kevlar body suits on.

He added that if he detected the possibility of a shot being taken he would shout, "incoming." And everyone should take cover.

He then asked Johnnie whether he had earned his certificates for flying the drones.

Johnnie said that he had qualified on both the larger search drone and had also qualified on the weaponized drone.

Trey said that before any of them got off the bus, he wanted Johnnie to launch the weaponized drone and fly it to the build they selected as the most likely to be the one to be where Z would locate. His job was to fly the drone up and see if it was possible to get a shot at Z.

Johnnie smiled and said he liked the weaponized drone and was naming it Gunjfor. He explained that the weapon was magical like the spear of Odin, he had given the name to the drone for two reasons the name "Gunjfor." It had a gun, but he felt the drone had a little magic as well.

Alex laughed and said that she would be happy with the drone just getting to the target and taking a shot.

She looked at Rebecca and Evan and asked them whether they were prepared to continue driving the bus based on what they were learning.

Evan said that the bullet proof glass had increased their level of concern. The discussion they were hearing raised that a little higher.

Rebecca asked if by chance she and Evan could get a set of Kevlar suits.

Alex asked if anyone had any extra sets because hers would be too small.

Both Trevor and Bill said that they had an extra set that might fit the two. They would bring them out so they could be tried on. They were in the luggage carrier so after dinner they would get them out.

Johnnie said that it would be a good time to bring out Gunjfor as well.

Alex asked that when they arrived at the RCMP building Rebecca and Evan to sit on the bus stairs after they turned off the bus engine. This would put them in the safest spot.

Alex asked Trey to be in charge of their engagement plan and take them all through it once more before dinner was delivered. Then they would focus on eating. After dinner she suggested doing their first walk through outside before it got dark.

She said that in the morning at seven she wanted to do another walk through before they left the park.

She looked at her phone and said that it was time to set the table because the order was at the door.

Trevor stood in the doorway and handed in the bags of food. He gave a generous tip and closed the door.

Alex thanked him for handling the delivery.

The dinner was great. She enjoyed the mix of food. She especially liked the breaded shrimp, the scallops, and the frog legs. She skipped the rice and ate a few bites of all the other items.

The practice went well, and Trey asked them to repeat it.

She had no trouble falling asleep, but she missed not having Matt next to her.

The next morning, she was up early. She made coffee, toast and sat down at the table where she buttered her toast and spread jelly on the two pieces she planned to eat.

Trey and Johnnie were the next two and they both said they were going to emulate her breakfast. They both said they were surprised at how well they slept after eating the mix of food at such a late dinner.

Trevor was next and he said that he really enjoyed all the food and was surprised that he really liked frog legs.

He took out a small frying pan threw in a half a cup of brown rice and the scrambled in two eggs for his breakfast.

Bill came in and fried two eggs and heated up some of the stir-fried beef left over from the night before.

Alex said that they needed to be at practice in five minutes.

Both Rebecca and Evan announced that they were up but had stayed out of the way so that they all could get their breakfast.

Alex looked at Trey and said, "let's do it."

Trey stood up and said, "the bus just arrived at the RCMP building. He was looked out the bus window, pointed, and said that one."

Johnnie was standing beside him, and he turned, took the drone out to the back wheel of the bus, and turned on his drone.

He gave Alex a thumbs up.

Alex stepped down the steps and stepped out so that Trey could take his position. When Johnnie gave his thumbs up, Alex began a steady walked away from the bus.

Trey waited until Alex was about ten feet away then began his side stepping. He was pleased with how close Trevor was and he looked back and saw that Bill was exactly where he wanted him.

He saw that Johnnie was flying his drone a few feet above the water out over the lake.

He shouted, "incoming."

Alex did not wait for Trey to finish his word but immediately jumped behind a tree.

Trey turned and moved back to the bus and went around the back and ran away from the bus. Trevor and Bill were right behind him.

Johnnie had shot the drone straight up into the air and, said, bang, bang. He then landed the drone at his feet and folded it. He took it in and put a new charged battery in and put the battery that he had used into the charger.

Alex thanked everyone and said that it was time to get underway.

Evan was driving and chatting with Rebecca. They were wearing their Kevlar out fits on the outside of their clothes.

Alex asked Trey how he rated their exercises.

Trey said that everyone had demonstrated doing exactly what they needed to do. He suggested that Alex climb the stairs up the right side and get up the first couple of stairs rapidly so she would be up by the column which would provide a place to take cover.

Alex said she would, but she hoped nothing would happen.

Evan said that they were arriving. He slowed down and brought the bus to the front of the building, turned off the engine and a he and Rebecca got into the stairwell.

Trey pointed to the building he would select if he were the sniper. Johnnie said he had it and stepped out of the bus and into position. A moment later he gave his thumbs up signal

Alex started her walk, took a quick glance back and saw Trey, Trevor and Bill doing their walk.

She followed Trey's advice and was just taking the third step when she heard the "I" in incoming and jumped behind the pillar.

She watched a huge chunk of the step that was at the height where she was standing, blown away. She realized that had she been any slower the shot would have hit about waist high and torn her in half.

The next shot took a huge chunk of the pillar at about her waist level. She felt some of the small shards hit her. She turned to reduce her profile. The next two shots hit the pillar in front.

She waited a moment and figured the shooter was done or was making her escape and she raced to the side of the bus.

She heard Johnnie curse.

Johnnie said that when he cleared the roof a gust of wind had hit Gunjfor. He had shot seven rounds as Z made for the stairwell door. He was sure that he had scored at least one hit, but she was still on her feet.

Alex could hear the sirens as several police cars came rushing toward the bus.

She told Johnnie to put Gungnir away and store it out of sight. She asked Rebecca and Evan to stand away from the bus and raise their hands.

She put her weapon six feet in front of her and raised her hands. She had her badge in her left hand.

The front door of the building seemed to burst open and at least a dozen RCMP came out with their guns drawn and aimed at them and the bus.

Alex called out her name and said they were friendly. She then added please be advised that three of my team has entered the building at the end of the street in pursuit of the sniper.

Reg came out and told everyone to stand down. He asked the sergeant that was in charge to take a contingent and see how they could assist Alex's team that had gone into the building and to send a contingent to surround the building.

He walked over to where the chunk of the step was laying. He commented that the sniper had to be using a very powerful weapon to have blown off that large of a piece from the granite step. He put his hand where the pillar was missing another large chunk and then looked at the two hits at the front of the pillar.

He commented that Alex had been very lucky.

Alex held out the right side of her jacket that had a series of holes in it and said that luck was only a small part of the outcome. She and the team had practiced for the encounter, and it had worked out exactly as they had practiced. The only remaining piece was what the rest of her team would find in the building.

Zelda had taken her position early in the morning. She was experiencing some gusts of wind, but she was looking down at the trees and they were not experiencing anything.

She felt confident that she would get some good shots. She turned on the laser on her scope and zeroed in on the RCMP headquarter steps.

She felt confident she would hit her target.

Her heart skipped a beat when a black bus stopped in front of the building. It was beautiful. There seemed to be a moments delay and then she saw Alex.

She decided to use her laser to make sure she would get the shot she wanted. She slowly raise her barrel and was just squeezing the trigger when Alex leaped behind the Pillar that was one step up from her. The trigger had already been pulled and a second later she saw a huge chunk of the step being blown away.

She saw a flap of what she took to be Alex's jacket and took the next shot in hopes of having the shrapnel from the side of the pillar take Alex out. The next two shots were shots of frustration.

She was getting ready to pick up the bullet casings when suddenly a drone with a gun rose over the edge of the roof. She made a mad dash for the door. The wind gust saved her, but she got hit in the thigh and she thought one might have gone through her arm.

The leg wound was bleeding, but the bullet had not hit any arteries. She ignored the pain in her leg and ran down the stairs and got to her bike. She threw her rifle into its holder and rode away as fast as she could.

She had to stop to take care of the bleeding from her leg. She realized that the other bullet had hit the fleshy part of her arm, and the bullet had gone through and had adhered to her windbreaker. She rode several more blocks and then caught a bus and headed back to where she had parked the pickup. She was going to leave Montreal.

She wondered how Alex could possibly have known that she was going to be on the roof. She also wondered about the armed drone.

She decided that she needed some intel and would need to stay in Montreal for a few days. She could stay in her pickup and do the gathering of intel. She would use public Wi-Fi but would do it from a different location each time.

Once she found out what the next steps that Alex was taking she would position herself and take the shot that would eliminate her deadly opponent.

Then she would melt away and disappear.

<u>20 The Middle</u>

A taxi was let through the barrier that was across the road and Denton and his FBI boss got out and walked up towards them.

Reg suggested that they have the meeting that they had planned. He was now anxious to understand the situation and see how his folks could help, apprehend the sniper and most likely the killer of many, many people.

After introductions and a quick update of the shooting that had just occurred. He introduce Denton and his boss as the FBI partners who had worked with them for close to a year.

He then introduced Alex as the huntress that seemed to have flushed out a very dangerous person.

She stood and said that she was hunting a person they had designated as Z because they believed that person either had a first or last name beginning with the letter Z. She shared the belief that Z had great hacking skills and was able to intercept the e-mail of some of the RCMP leadership or their supports.

She introduced Johnnie and she pointed to Lennard his RCMP counterpart and said that the two must be getting very close to finding Z because she figured they had been the catalysts for the attack out in front of the building.

She introduced Trey as her partner who had organized how she and the team would arrive at the headquarters and survive a sniper attack. She pointed at Bill and Trevor and said they were the other two defenders who had rushed the building where the sniper had been located.

She said that the team had come prepared for a potential attack but neither she nor the rest of the team had expected to face the fire power that had been used.

She took off her jacket and held it up so the light would shine thorough the holes. She said that it had cost her a jacket to attend the meeting, but her team had saved her life. She sat down and took a sip from the glass of water.

She then stated how she understood the case and how she was slowly unraveling it and determining the timeline of all the killings. She said that she expected the forensics to confirm a theory that Johnnie had postulate that the killings started three of four years ago. That a body had been found at the first crossing at St Stephen, New Brunswick. She was waiting to find out the time when that killing had occurred.

She and the team were going there to get a feel for the situation and then they were going to go from crossing to crossing to the crossing where a body had not been found.

They anticipated another attack at that crossing. They would find that body and if necessary find other bodies as they worked on closing the case. Once they captured Z her team would leave the prosecution to the RCMP and the FBI to handle. She and her team would continue to support the closure of the case, but they would return to Cincinnati and await assignment to their next case.

The question about the body count surfaced and it was obvious that doubt remained about the number.

Reg spoke up and said that as far as he was concerned the model of one body per crossing was confirmed since sixty bodies had so far been located and the missing ones seemed to be at crossings where the crossing service area had little or no space. These were crossings that would take additional time to find the bodies that he was convinced would be found.

He asked how Alex planned to identify the western most body.

Alex shared that she planned to jump over the next border crossing just west of where the current western most body had been found. She would do this until no body was found and then work back until she located the western most. She added that she hoped they had already found the western most. She added that she hoped that her team had interrupted Z enough to have prevented her from killing the next person.

She said that she did not have much else to share and asked if the rest of the team hand anything to share.

Trey said that he had followed a trail of blood spots for about two blocks where it had stopped. He said that Z had most likely stopped long enough to stop the bleeding.

Bill pulled an evidence bag out that had five very large cartridge casings in it. He smiled and said that Johnnie's drone attack must have rushed Z because she had left the casings and her fingerprints behind.

Trevor added that Johnnie must have hit her more than once because there was blood on the floor and blood on the doorknobs of the doors that Z opened on her way out.

Reg signaled one of the men standing by the door and asked them to take the evidence to the lab for inspection.

He asked Alex about the weaponized drone.

Alex nodded and said that she would have Johnnie take the drone to the lab, but she wanted it to be examined and then returned immediately before she left Montreal. It was a key part of the offense she needed in case Z tried to kill her again.

She asked Johnnie to get the drone to the lab.

Johnnie stood and walked out of the meeting.

Reg asked if there was anything else that should be shared.

The participants in the meeting were all quiet.

He then declared the meeting over and the video was cut.

He asked if anyone wanted to accompany him to the lab and smiled when everyone in the room said yes. He said that they could all go but when they got to the small lab only he and Alex would go to the evidence table where he was sure the evidence would be located, and the rest would need to stand by the entrance.

He led the way.

Alex was surprised at how small the lab was and asked where the bodies were processed.

Reg said that they were in a different room that was about twice the size of the room they were in.

Alex took in the chunk of step and the chunk of the column and the pile of chips by each of those objects.

The four casings Bill had turned over were each in a holder and the fingerprints were clearly visible.

There were several Petri dishes that had blood samples in them.

The armed drone was sitting on top of white paper, and the gun had been taken apart and a technician was taking swab samples.

The Principal Investigator began his explanation by pointing at the granite chunk of the step and the white marble. He commented that had either bullet hit a person, that person would not have survived.

He said that he had never analyzed a situation where such fire power had been used. He pointed at the casings and said that he had a partial of an index finger and an almost a full print of a thumb of someone's right hand.

He pointed at the two Petri dishes and confirmed that the blood was from two different parts of the body based on the location where the blood samples had been taken. He said that he expected to get the fingerprint information very shortly and if those prints were in any RCMP personnel records they would have a name. The blood sample was an A negative that was fairly rare so it and the fingerprints would pinpoint the person.

It would be very good evidence.

He added that the drone was a new one on him, but the caliber was a common one used by many police departments. He said that he had been asked to process it quickly and return it.

Alex confirmed that the drone had most likely saved her, and she needed it in her possession.

She held up her coat and showed the investigator the holes in her jacket.

He asked if she was handing it over as evidence.

Alex nodded and said that her outfit had died in her place out on the steps.

The investigator asked if she had been hit at all.

Alex showed him her right side lifted her blouse to expose her Kevlar pullover and said that she thought only her coat had been hit.

The investigator asked if she were willing to give him the whole outfit. After the case was over he would return her clothes. He said he had a very fashionable paper coverall she could wear until she could change into another outfit.

Alex laughed and said that she should have kept her dead jacket out of his hands and asked where she could get into his fashionable coveralls.

She took the bag containing the coverall and stepped into the rest room and changed out of her outfit.

She returned and joked with Reg that coming to his meeting so far was the highlight of her current trip and she appreciated his generous gift of a new fashion look.

They were all getting ready to leave when the investigator shouted out that they had a name. The shooter was a Zelda Mulhaney.

Reg said that he wanted to reward everyone and take them out for lunch.

Alex said that sounded good to her. She asked if she could invite the drivers of her bus as well.

Trey complimented her for her new outfit as they walked out to the bus. He said that he was feeling the after effects of having gone through the mornings action.

Alex said that they would all most likely have some of those after effects and would need to sit down during their evening drive and talk about it. She said that she was still riding high on her adrenaline, but she would most likely be down by evening.

She went in and changed and as she was rubbing her hands on her side, she felt something and with her fingernail she picked out a tiny piece of granite. She wondered how it had made it all the way through to her body.

She looked in the mirror and smiled.

She figured that a powerful hand had shielded her.

She placed the tiny piece of marble on a piece of paper towel and then wrapped it in plastic wrap.

When she got out off the bus she handed the plastic wrap to one of the RCMP officers standing outside of the bus and asked him to deliver it to the lab and let the case investigator know that the sliver was embedded in her side just above her left waistline.

She walked over to where Reg and Trey were standing. She noted that the two were almost the same height.

Reg suggested they ride down in several of his cars and leave her bus in front of the station.

Alex agreed and they all rode to a top end restaurant that had a superb menu. The lunch was a great way to slowly come down from the mornings action. She asked Reg what he thought about her teams impact on the case so far.

Reg smiled and shook his head. He said that he had had spent the weekend thinking that it was on the wrong track but the action this morning verified Alex's theory that the serial killer was a part of the RCMP network.

He hoped that Zelda was not directly in his organization but none the less she had infiltrated it and was a danger to the whole organization.

He looked over to where Johnnie and Len were sitting and complemented them for shaking the hornets' nest and getting one of the hornets to react.

He added that now it was only a matter of time before they had Zelda.

Alex nodded and added that she hoped that she was keeping her so off balance that she had no time to find and kill her next victim.

Zelda had made it off the roof and had ridden her bike away before the police had arrived.

She was in the back of her pickup patching herself together and was in a state of shock.

She now knew that her preparation to leave Montreal had been the right step.

Once she was done she went online to see if she could determine if she was being hunted or if she could find out where Alex would be next.

She was more determined than ever to kill the bitch.

She got angrier every time she thought about the fact that her life as she knew it was over. She was now going to be a fugitive.

She had bank accounts in multiple banks and needed to get the money out so she could disappear.

She had enough cash that she would be able to have a good comfortable life.

She would begin by taking the money she had in three different banks in Montreal.

Alex looked over to where Johnnie and Len were working on Johnnie's computer. She asked what Johnnie was up to.

Johnnie smiled and said that he had followed the advice that she had given him on one of their cases, to follow the money. He looked over at Reg and said that he and Len were hacking into a Zelda Mulhaney's bank accounts and sending the money they found there to an account that Len had set up at the RCMP.

They were leaving a hundred dollars behind so that they would not be needing to close the accounts.

He added that they would do the next two accounts that he had found and the RCMP account would have three million dollars in it.

He was expanding his search of additional bank accounts for Zelda Mulhaney across all the banks in Canada.

He smiled and said that Zelda would soon be destitute and living under a bridge if he could arrange it.

Reg said that he was hard of hearing and asked Alex if she had understood what Johnnie had just said.

Alex smiled and said that Johnnie and Len were just sharing how they were doing at a new game they were playing.

Zelda parked her pickup and walked into the bank. She said that she would like to withdraw her money and would like to close her bank account.

The teller asked for her account number and two identifications with her picture on them.

The teller asked in what denominations she wanted the money.

Zelda replied that hundreds made the most sense. She had carried in a large square brief case in which she figured the money would fit.

She watched as the teller opened her cash drawer and took out a hundred-dollar bill, pushed to her, and put the id cards on top of it and asked if she could help her with anything else.

Zelda stood for a moment in a state of shock. She then asked the bank clerk to give her a printout of her bank statement for the last month.

She looked at it and stepped away from the counter and went and sat down in one of the chairs in the lobby. The three quarters of a million dollars she had in the bank had been transferred out no more than an hour before.

She rushed to the second bank, and then the third and each time found the same thing. She knew that the banks had been hacked, and her money move out of her hands.

She now knew that whomever the person was that worked for Alex was a very talented hacker and she knew that she had to get to her other bank accounts where she had her money, or she would be penniless.

She had twenty thousand dollars in the pickup and that was it. She had another three million in the remaining accounts, but she had to get to them before those accounts were discovered and emptied.

She got on the phone, called those banks, opened new accounts, and transferred the money to them. She left twenty thousand in each of her old accounts to see if she could keep the hacker from looking beyond that account.

She also needed to get to the banks and get the cash in her hands.

Alex asked Johnnie how his ribs tasted.

Johnnie smiled and said that they were delicious, and the cash sauce made it taste even better. He said he had set up a routine that was checking the banks in Eastern Canada for Zelda.

Reg looked at her and said that he hoped that Johnnie would not infect Len with the hacking disease.

Len smiled and said that he had no clue what Johnnie had just done and probably would never have that level of skill.

Alex nodded and said that he was her magician who was responsible for having given her the secret sauce to solve every case that she had been on.

Johnnie smiled and shook his head and said that he had only followed her suggestions at every turn and following the money had been her guidance.

This time he had just been slow at it and had kept his head in the IT world and had missed the money world.

He commented that if he and Len were successful they would have Zelda living under the bridge by the evening.

He added that based on the money she had she was frugal person, but she had kept the money in savings and checking accounts and had not invested it or she might have had twice the money she currently had in the bank.

He put up his hand and said he had a hit and would get back in a moment.

He said he did want desert.

Alex looked at Reg and said that Johnnie was relentless when he pursued someone on the internet. She commented that the term under the bridge was a term that the two of them used often because Johnnie had done so for many years.

Len said he was not sure how legal what was happening was, but he would figure out how to handle it later. He said that he was all for confiscating all her wealth in the short term. He would make sure to get an account set up that would keep things straight.

Johnnie said that he had just moved three million more into the RCMP-Zelda account and so far there were no other hits.

He added that he thought Zelda was onto the fact that her bank accounts were being emptied because she had just moved her money trying to hide it. He smiled and said that she might be a prolific killer, but she was neither a good hack nor a person who knew how to hide her money.

He said that she was down to the six hundred he had left in the banks and whatever cash she had on her at the start of the day.

Len shook his head and said that he wanted to have whatever Johnnie ordered for desert. He hoped it would help him get just a little better at his IT role.

Alex said that Johnnie's talents had been developed in the Cincinnati Library where he went every morning and freeloaded of the free sweet rolls and coffee that different groups gave out as part of their presentations.

She added that he had also used the library as the background to convince her to hire him and find him a place to live.

Johnnie chuckled and said that was exactly how he remembered it.

21 Destitute and Desperate

Zelda sat in the back of her pickup in a stunned stupor. Her bank accounts had been drained and the banks insisted that she had made the transfers that had been executed. She asked for and got the routing number to the account where the money was located. When she tried to hack in she got a winking smiley face back in code ;) and with the phrase, "its warmer under the bridge," which threw her for a loop. She had no idea what that meant.

She was going to try again when her computer blinked and went out. Then a message in large white lettering scrolled slowly across the screen telling her if she turned herself in her computer would be turned back on.

She wanted to scream but she was parked in a quiet neighborhood and did not want someone calling the police.

Johnnie started laughing and everyone looked over at him.

He shook his head and said that he wanted the sweetest desert possible with a side of vanilla ice cream with honey on top of it.

Alex asked what he had done to deserve such a treat. He said that he had drained all the money from Zelda's accounts, and he had infected her computer with a trojan horse that disabled it. She was locked out until she could get another computer and get it online and connected to the points she had set up.

He said that if she was good at hacking she might be able to get back online in about two days.

Reg said that he was impressed, and he authorized two servings of desert for him. He then asked if all her entry and hacking connections could be removed.

Johnnie said that they could, but it would be hard to find them. It would be better for Len to reinstall all the systems and at the same time load in the new features of the system that would make future hacking more challenging. He added that the mafia and the drug cartels had better software protection than the RCMP.

Reg said that he would welcome Johnnie's input in getting a stronger system put in place.

Johnnie said that Len had the system improvements ready to go but it had been stalled because someone in finance said the cost was significant and she was not sure they needed the upgrade at this time.

Reg shook his head and said he would take care of that when he got back to his office.

He then asked what Zelda might do next.

Alex replied that she thought that she would go into hiding in a territory that was known to her and where she would not be noticed. She would want a place where there were few people but it should be close enough so she could get online. She would be reaching back into the RCMP system trying to get information. She suggested holding off in removing the places that allowed her access. They should put in the information that the team decided would draw her to them.

Reg said that sounded dangerous.

Alex agreed but she said that Canada was a huge country where a person who wanted could stay hidden, even when they had little money, if they could live off the land. She reminded him that parking in front of the RCMP building had been dangerous.

Reg agreed and asked what the RCMP could do to help.

Alex suggested that he contact the personnel at each of the border crossings that she planned to visit and make sure they knew of her arrival and that she was authorized to do surveillance in their area.

Trey suggested that a RCMP officer got added to the team so that Denton had someone to play cards with.

Denton laughed and said that he had been told that getting qualified on the drone gave him a seat on top of the bus not under it. He figured his new skill would allow Trey to sit in the sun and get a tan.

Reg looked at Alex and asked whether the request for a representative was a serious one.

Alex smiled and said that it was, but the representative would return with the same infection that had already taken over the FBI rep that had joined the team.

Reg said that he figured it was worth the risk. He asked whether his rep could be taught to fly a drone.

Alex assured him that she would gladly put drone flight training on the teams schedule, and she would sit in the sun with Trey to work on her tan while the RCMP officer flew her drone searching for a grave.

Reg said that maybe he would volunteer so he could get out of his stuffy office for a few weeks. He commented that Alex and her team had only just arrived and were only a little over a month into the case and had flushed and almost captured a serial killer that had not been on the radar screen before then. He asked whether she would take on the case of the missing women after she had captured Zelda.

Alex said that she had a soft spot for the plight of women who were in trouble and that too many cases of missing women went unsolved. She shared that she had set up a foundation to help women that needed her help, and she had a retreat and an education program she funded. However, she did not think of his missing women's listing as a single case but perhaps dozens. She would take a closer look but said she was making no commitments.

Reg said that sounded fair he looked over to his FBI counter part and asked what he thought.

Denton's boss said that he now agreed with Alex. He would give her all the information his department had but he had gone back through the missing cases reports for the women and when he took another look in the light of the connections Alex had made, they did not seem to be the work of one person.

Alex was sipping on her tea watching Johnnie enjoy his ice cream.

He had just made a huge breakthrough.

She was trying to figure out how to reward him for his latest huge contribution.

Trey was watching her and said that he agreed with her.

She looked at him and said that she hadn't uttered a word.

Trey said that she didn't need to. She was thinking of how to reward Johnnie. Trey said that the ice cream and their gratitude was the only thing Johnnie needed.

Johnnie looked up, smiled, and said that he agreed with everything Trey had just said but he had left off that his great drone shooting ability needed to be on the list.

Alex asked if the RCMP representative could meet them at the Four Corners New Brunswick border crossing, in the next couple of days. She wanted to leave and head there after lunch.

Reg said that he would have him there when she got there as long as her bus kept to the legal speed limit. He said he knew she moved fast but wanted to make sure he did not get a report of a speeding black bus.

Alex looked at Rebecca and Evan and asked if they ever went faster than the speed limit.

They smiled and said they were always five of ten kilometers per hour slower than the speed limit. Rebecca smiled and added that she also had some great land in Florida that she was trying to sell to some willing Canadian.

Reg shook his head and said that every person on her team had been infected and now he was sure he would get his RCMP representative back in the same condition.

Alex smiled and said that was the price he had to pay for having signed the contract for her teams services.

Reg nodded and said that the contract was getting clearer and clearer every day.

Alex stood up and thanked Reg for a great lunch. She said she was ready for a nap and hoped that her bus drivers were ready for the road. As soon as she said it she knew that she indeed was going to take a nap when she got back to the bus. The after effects of the morning were starting to set in.

It was as short ride to the bus. Denton went to the car that he had arrived in with his boss and took out his suitcase and gave it to Evan and said that he had his small carry on which had all he needed in the bus. He followed Trevor, Bill, Trey, and Johnnie into the bus.

Alex thanked Reg and Denton's boss for their support and said that she intended to close the case by capturing and turning Zelda over to them.

She figured she would capture her on the Canadian side so the RCMP was the organization that should be getting their lawyers ready to prosecute.

She pointed out that they should make sure that Zelda paid for her own lawyers and used her confiscated money to do so. She added that the trial judge should be informed of the situation and be asked not to grant parole or to allow a lawyer to be assigned gratis to the case. She said she was not vindictive, but she felt that Zelda did not warrant any state aid.

She said that she would deliver Zelda, but Reg had to make sure the Canadian government delivered the maximum penalty allowed under the law. She wanted to make sure that her attack that had just occurred was one of the charges against Zelda but only after she got charged for every person she had killed.

Reg said he understood, and he would work with the prosecutor to make sure that Zelda would remain in prison for the rest of her life.

Once on the bus, Alex asked Rebecca and Evan to drive to the Four Corners Border crossing. She smiled and said that the speed limit would be fine.

She then said that she wanted to quickly hear from everyone and get their take on how they might set themselves up to capture Zelda.

Trey said that the first two places, the 774 and the Calais, crossings had found bodies, and they were currently waiting for the forensics reports from those finds. He said they should be prepared but he did not expect Zelda to strike them there. He suggested that the third crossing at Saint Croix had also found a body and it was the next report they were waiting for.

The fourth crossing was US 95 and Canada 95 where a body had been found. The fifth crossing was Boundary line Road and 190 where they were still looking for a body. This might be a point where Zelda might attack but getting away would be a challenge. He felt it would depend on her desire to get even versus her desire to escape and where she was hiding.

Both Travis and Bill said they deferred to Tray's analysis.

Johnnie said that he thought he could make Zelda as mad as a hornet by screwing with her new computer.

Alex suggested that he do that but to keep her computer online so she could find the information they wanted to feed her.

She thanked them for the input and said that she was going to freshen up and then go to sleep until she felt like getting up.

She said good night to Rebecca and Evan and asked if they needed anything. They said that they would have the bus at the first crossing in the morning. They might make a stop for gas but that would be the only reason to stop.

Alex went to the room in back, took a shower and got into bed. She called Matt and was surprised to get through. He normally blocked incoming calls when he was at work.

He asked how everything was going and if anything, exciting had happened during the early part of the day. Alex said that getting shot at and surviving had been the only thing of any significance and that she had met with the RCMP and FBI leadership afterwards and she now had organizations that believed the teams theory.

She shared that Johnnie had worked his magic and had found out that Z was Zelda Mulhaney. Zelda was now wounded and was down to whatever money she might have in her possession because Johnnie had hacked into her bank accounts and moved close to eight million dollars to an RCMP account.

She said that she had called to say goodnight because she was on the bus, and they were on the way to the first border crossing and then they would work their way along the border until they reached the first crossing that had yet to find a body. She added that if there was any action it would most likely happen then.

She added that Trey had been the one that had set up the approach that saved her life.

Zelda had tried to kill her by taking a position on the top of a building and shooting a very high-powered rifle that had blown huge pieces of the granite steps and the marble column off.

She shared the fact that Johnnie had used the armed drone and had hit Zelda at least two times as she tried to escape from the building roof. She had gotten away, but she was now financially down on her luck.

Matt laughed and complimented her on having such a nice calm morning. He said that he wished he could be with her but knew that he would only be a distraction.

Alex sighed and said that he was a distraction that she wished was on the bus with her but that it was time to give her love, and she was going to get some sleep.

22 Crossings One, Two, Three, Four

Lubec, Maine was where the first US-Canada border crossing was located. It was roughly eight hours from Montreal and the best route was through Maine. Alex slept all the way and only came awake when the bus stopped and was maneuvering and getting set up.

She freshened up and came out.

Everyone was gathered in the front and relaxing. They asked whether she was going to be able to go to sleep again.

They pointed to the final setting of the sun that they could see from the front bus windows. The sky had a clear red rising on the far horizon, and the grey of the evening could be seen slowly making its way towards them. The ripples in the water seemed to be flipping between black and red as the evening breeze swept in towards them.

Alex asked if anyone was hungry and if they should order some carryout.

Trevor replied that there seemed to be only one restaurant that had a substantial dinner menu and if they each ordered a different item they would hit all but one menu item.

Bill said he was for Trevor ordering one of everything including the extra. He said the mix would let them all have something they liked. He suggested they order two pitchers of tea and a two six packs of beer.

Trevor did not hesitate and called in the order. The person at the other end said that the order would be ready in about thirty minutes, and they needed to pick it up at that time because the restaurant was closing.

Alex was just going to suggest they get a couple of their mini motorcycles out when her phone vibrated on the table. She picked it up and after a moment, she said that yes, she had something that he could do before joining the team. She smiled and gave the name of the restaurant where he could pick up an order for a Travis. She let Jay know that the order had been paid and a tip had already been added. She said she was looking forward to him joining the team. She let him know the RV camp they were in. She smiled when he said that he knew the bus because he had stood guard on it while it was parked in front of the RCMP station and there was only one RV park in Lubec.

Alex let the rest of the team know that their RCMP team member was joining them. He would bring their food order out.

Johnnie said that he must have flown down to have arrived so soon. He said that there must be a small airstrip on the Canadian side.

Alex nodded and said that Jay had arrived several hours ago and had been sitting with his American border crossing friends at the American facility.

She said she was taking a walk around the bus and get a quick glimpse of the surroundings before sitting down to dinner. She asked if someone knew where they were parked.

Johnnie answered that she was looking out over a bay named after their boss.

Trevor laughed and said they had driven all this way, to park on the shores of Johnson Bay.

A black Ford sedan with special plates pulled up.

Alex watched as the two persons in front got out of the car and put on their green hats with the dark brown leather bands They both had on green jackets with shoulder insignia and a badge attached on the corner of the left pocket flap. Both were armed and had their guns in holsters that were on their right hips positioned to the back. They both wore black shoes or boots that had been spit polished or were coated to look that way.

Alex smiled as the person in back got out. He slowly put on his tan hat with its darker brown band. She noted that his hat had four indents that made it four dented with a peak at its center.

His red jacket with its high neck collar, black trim in front were highlighted out at each side by black shoulder patches. The gold buttons on the front of the red coat and a wide brown belt with holstered weapon was the look that the RCMP were famous for. His black trousers and glimmering brown boots finished the portrait. His appearance was a contrast to the more typical border guard look displayed by the other two with which she was more familiar.

He came forward and introduced himself as Sergeant Jay Bird of the RCMP, Ontario Unit.

Alex shook his hand and welcomed him.

He in turn introduced his two, "American friends" who had driven him out and who wanted to meet her and her team."

Alex welcomed them and invited them to stay for a while if they could.

The driver thanked her but said they had left their partner alone at the crossing, but they had listened to Jay for several hours recount the gun battle in Montreal and the fact that she and her team were responsible for having found the bodies of the men killed and buried on the Canadian side of the border. They both saluted and thanked the team. They turned to Jay and said they would bring his two trunks to the bus, and he had a ton of food to get out of the back seat.

Evan asked where Jay wanted the trunks.

Jay said that he needed to get some things from the black trunk, but the aluminum case held the weapons he had brought out at Alex's request. He said the enveloped taped to the front held all the paperwork that would be needed when they crossed back into Canada. He said the weapons could legally be used in the US by Alex's team. He was not authorized to do so until he was back in Canada. He handed Alex a plastic card that looked like a credit card and said it certified that guns were legal.

Rebecca had been carrying the food into the bus and said that she would get it ready for the team.

Alex waved as the two US border patrol backed out and drove away.

She took Jay in and showed him around the interior and the bunk he would be using. She said he should make himself comfortable and when ready he was welcome to join them as they ate a late dinner.

She went to the front and put a variety of food on a large paper plate that by the time she sat down had a little of everything on it. She found the noodles and clams to be her favorite and when she looked, she realized it had been everyone's favorite as well because it was all gone.

Jay came out in a casual pair of blue jeans and a grey V necked pull over.

Alex asked if hc wanted something to eat or drink.

Jay said that he had eaten in Montreal, but he would go for a beer.

Alex asked him to share a little of his background with the team and then she would ask everyone to share a little about theirs.

Jay began by saying that he felt like he had won the lottery. He said he had been surprised to be called into the Commissioner's office and to be asked if he were willing to be temporarily assigned to be a team member with the Cincinnati detective unit. He said that I was the only single person that was immediately available. I was thrilled and said that I was pleased to be selected. He told me to get my things and go to the airport to a specific hangar.

When he got there, the gun case was already on the plane, and the pilot put his bag next to it. He said that two hours after her bus left Montreal he was in the air.

Alex thanked him for coming. She then briefly introduced everyone.

Trevor smiled and asked Jay for his last name.

It was clear to Alex where he was going. She stopped Trevor and said that he should enjoy a sip of his beer or take a bite of his pie.

Jay smiled and said that he had heard jokes about his name all his life. He gave out the series of chirps and said that it was the Canadian Jay bird's "Whisper song." He then made as series of snapping sounds and said that it was the sound a Jay bird made when chasing away an intruder or in his case a rude person.

Trevor smiled and said that he would fit right in with the team.

Alex then spent a few moments explaining to Jay that the team was visiting each of the early sites to get an in the field feel for the situation.

She was going to plant perennial flowers at each grave site as they went along the border crossings. They were doing this while they waited for the lab results on the bodies that had recently been dug up at the crossings.

She and the team believed that these were the first bodies and that the ones found out to the west were among the last. The lab results would give them the timeline of the serial killings. The timing would help in identifying who the victims were.

She said that they were also trying to lure out the person who had tried to kill her in Montreal and who was the serial killer.

She asked him if he was qualified on the weapons he had brought with him.

Jay said that he was certified and practiced with them often.

She asked how often he had used the weapons in the field.

He admitted that he did not hunt and had only used the weapons at the firing range.

Eager, well trained, top of his class but green went through Alex's mind.

She figured he would go back to his team field tested, and more mature.

She then called out the order and timing of their stops at each crossing point. She started at seven thirty at the Lubeck Crossing, then at nine at Calais, eleven thirty at Saint Croix where they would have Pizza or steak from their freezer. She wanted to go to two more crossings in the afternoon.

She asked Bill and Travis to check out the restaurants in Woodstock and suggest a place for dinner.

She asked Rebbeca to find a place to Park either in the Woodstock area or some place on the way to the 110 highway crossing.

She said that at the crossing she had just named, they were not expecting to do anything but plant the perennials at the grave sites. However, Trey had said that the following day both Highway 110 and the Highway 190 crossings seemed to be the ones that he would select to attack them if he were in the vicinity and knew that Alex was coming to look for the yet undiscovered bodies at these locations. He said that after looking at the surrounding territory he would be on the 190 crossing, but they should treat both of them equally.

Alex then asked Trey how he would prepare for an attack.

He suggested the Johnnie once again fly the armed drone. At each location he should set up his drone on the far end of their seating row and have the drone out in front of him on the deck. He would send his drone high and out to where the shooter was located.

Bill and Trevor would come in from the sides ready to crash their drones into the shooter if they had the chance.

Alex would sit at her position and launch her drone.

He suggested that Jay lay prone on the deck ready to take a shot at any person shooting at them.

He said that the only worry he had was whether the plexiglass shield was strong enough.

He would be making his attack on the ground.

Jay asked if the team had made this detailed preparation for the attack in Montreal.

Alex said that they had, and they had practiced it multiple times before they had driven to the front of the station. Since he had reminded her she was changing their schedule in the morning and first thing in the morning they would practice what Trey had just described.

Jay started to apologize but Bill put up his hand and said, thank you for reminding us. We value our practices because we have learned that in every case it has saved our butts.

He added that they also wore full Kevlar outfits that so far had not been mentioned but he was planning to wear his.

Jay nodded and then added that he did not have a Kevlar outfit.

Trey said he had one that would most likely fit him. He thanked Bill for bringing that up. It was second nature to him to put it on when he was thinking about a gun fight.

He smiled and said that the gunfight at the gun club that had left him looking like a dark purple prune where the Kevlar body suit had saved all their lives was a lesson imprinted forever in his mind.

Trevor nodded and added that he too was a convert and gave daily thanks to the god Kevlar.

Jay started to ask if there was such a god and then laughed and said that he would have to get use to the banter the team seemed to constantly engage in.

Rebecca said they had contacted a hotel in Woodstock that held conventions and had been glad to rent them a place to park their bus where convention buses parked. It had full facilities. The charge was three hundred dollars per night.

Alex told her to book it.

Trevor said he had a restaurant and in the morning he would see if they took reservations. He would make reservations for seven.

Alex looked at the clock and thanked everyone for staying engaged until ten-thirty in the evening and they should consider getting a good night's sleep. She pulled out a big trash bag and began throwing in paper plates and used plastic ware and empty paper cups.

Everyone joined in and soon the bus was back to its pristine clean state.

Rebecca said she would do a little more cleaning before she went to sleep. She asked what she should either order in for breakfast or get ready.

Alex said that coffee and toast, butter and jam was all she was planning to have for breakfast. That seemed to be the general consensus. Bill added he might fry up an egg and bacon, but he would decide in the morning.

Alex walked back to her room and then stood under the hot shower and let her neck muscles soak in the heat.

She called Matt and asked how his day had been. He laughed and said it was still going because his team was involved in a multicar accident that had occurred on Seventy at the little Miami bridge and it was still getting resolved.

Alex listened to Matt and asked if he would get time to sleep.

Matt replied that his boss had already let the team know that they had the next day off.

He asked what her team would be doing the next day. He commented he felt better about the fact that she did not expect any action the next day.

Alex replied that the day after might be a confrontation day, but they had already made an action plan that would be practiced several times in the morning.

She said goodnight sind that she would be dreaming of him.

Talking to Matt had been the remedy that she had needed for the tension that was the result of the previous day's action in Montreal.

She was going to make sure everyone had processed that action and that no one was having any recurrence of the PTSD symptoms they and all experienced after the two cases where they all had survived massive gun battles and fights with machete swinging druggies.

She was feeling a little guilty about stressing her team when suddenly she realized that she had fallen asleep and that it was five in the morning. She laughed and said she wondered what she had thought about while she was awake and what she had dreamt.

She stayed in bed and thought through what Trey had laid out as the teams battle plan.

She valued his keen battle skills. He was the person who had been the main hero in each of the gun battles the team had face. She had never seen a person purposely walk fearlessly towards a shooter. She remember the FBI agent who had a picture of Trey's weapon that had an AR 15 bullet lodged in its barrel. She had a picture on her desk of him standing in the tattered police issued armor and the Kevlar vest under it embed with flattened bullets. In the picture he was smiling and pointing to his chest.

She had also noted that Trevor no longer teased Trey. He had recognized Trey as a true hero as well.

She and Trevor continued the banter with her because they both knew that it did not affect them in the same way that it affected Trey.

She and Trey also participated in AA meetings which brought them very close together. It helped her that Lindsey had let her know that it had made a huge difference at home. There were no longer hidden bottles of alcohol anywhere in the house. She said that the old Trey from their school days was back, and he was a great dad.

Alex got up and got ready for the new day.

<u>*23 Crossings Five, Six, Seven*</u>

*A*lex got a cup of coffee and went out into the grey of the early morning dawn.

She could see the thin contrast line of the sun as it moved to make its way into the sky.

She looked up at the white moon that seemed to be receding and fading. She sat down on the old weather-beaten bench and cupped her mug in her hands. She had brought her favorite cup, with the picture that had Trey, Lesley, Nolan, She and Matt on one side and a picture of her standing with Annie, Linda, and Laurie on the other. It was a cup that reminded her each morning how lucky she was.

When she climbed into the bus, she was greeted by everyone enjoying their breakfast. She took note that Bill had decided to have his normal fried eggs and bacon. She sat down and buttered a piece of toast and put a spoon of blueberry jam on it. After refilling her coffee, she asked how everyone had slept.

Travis said, "like a baby." And everyone but Jay agreed.

He said that he had a dream where his firearm was misfiring but would not fire when he pulled the trigger.

Trey smiled and said that such a dream was common when new soldiers went into combat.

Alex asked Trey to lead the team through three practices while they were in the campground and then repeat it once at each border crossing station.

Their three practices went smoothly and quickly. Jay decided to make a tie down area on the top deck where he secured his 308 so that he did not need to carry it up the steps on the side of the bus.

Trey complimented him on figuring out how to be more effective. He then suggested that Jay not wear his red jacket.

He then reminded everyone that their Kevlar jacket would probably not protect them from the 405 that Zelda was using.

They drove to the crossing and crossed back into Canada, planted the flowers at the grave of the victim buried there, and said a prayer.

Alex had Jay explain to the guards what they were going to do and then they practiced for an attack.

Throughout the day they repeated the routine.

They arrived at the Highway 95 crossing in the late afternoon and followed the same routine.

They decided to do dinner in the restaurant but first went to the convention hotel where they would keep the bus. After their arrival and getting situated, Alex suggested taking taxi's to the restaurant.

Once they were seated and looked at the menu, Trevor suggested that everyone order the meal they wanted but there could be no duplicate orders. When the waitress figured out what they would be doing, she volunteered to keep the meats separate and would serve the mashed potatoes, noodles, and sweet potatoes on separate plates. She said then it would be more like family style.

Trevor agreed and thanked her.

Alex asked if there were any improvements in the exercise they were doing.

Bill spoke up and said that they should get into position before they got on border crossing property. They did not have a grave to put flowers on and when they drove onto the station property they would be ready to start their search.

Trey said that he thought it was a good idea. He said that he was not going to be at his seat but would be on the ground.

Johnnie asked whether he should stay on the ground as well.

Trey shook his head and said that Johnnie should stay on the platform. He said that flying the armed drone from the bus platform put him in an elevated position that might be advantageous. He added that Rebecca and Evan needed to keep the bus running and ready to move.

He would jump back on the bus if they were going to pursue Zelda, so the door needed to be kept open.

Jay commented that Trey reminded him of his drill instructor at the academy. That instructor had been in Iraq with a Canadian unit.

Trevor smiled and commented that old war veterans all sounded much the same.

Bill shook his head and commented that once again his partner was taking a cheap shot.

Trevor smiled and replied that he had to work with what he was given, and Jay had been put off limits and he could not duplicated the song of a Jay.

The meal arrived and they all dug in.

The evening on the bus was rather quiet but enjoyable.

Alex suggested they get to sleep early and be ready for the next day. She reminded them that it would be the first time that the search drones would be in full use looking for a grave site.

She was rinsing and putting away her cup when Johnnie said that the reports for the first three bodies were in. They had the time of death for each, and they had been able to identify the first body. He was Dillon Olinger who had been reported missing six years ago in Conception Bay South on Newfoundland.

Alex asked if that was close to where Zelda had grown up.

A few moments later, Johnnie said that Zelda had grown up in a small town called Paradise that was near St. John's where she had attended University.

He commented that her name came up with the mysterious disappearance of her sister, Aada.

Then a few years later her mother had moved out of the area and had left no forwarding address.

Zelda had graduated and taken a Job with the agency where she was still employed.

Alex said that Dillon might have a story to tell them and asked Johnnie to dig into his past. She suggested doing some more digging about Aada as well. She said that he still had armed drone duty but while he was waiting to fly it he could keep busy getting information about the three people in Zelda's background.

She asked about the times of death of the other two bodies.

Johnnie looked and said there seemed to be six months between each of the three bodies. The first body was three months after Zelda was hired and then six months between the next two.

Alex nodded and commented that the frequency of the killings had increased. She then asked to verify the start date of the serial killings. She added the date did not change the number of bodies, but it might tell them about where she had been at the time and where the people she killed would be reported missing.

She thanked Johnnie for the extra information about where Zelda had gone to school. She wondered if any of the professors at the University had any recollection about Zelda or if the school had anything on record.

She looked at Johnnie and said that she was now hunting for any information that would help a prosecutor put her away for life.

She then said good night and walked back to her bedroom. She took a shower and then called Matt to let him know that it had been a full but quiet day.

The next morning, she was drinking coffee, eating her toast, and getting caught up on the news scene.

Johnnie came in and said that he had found out that Zelda's sister had disappeared in a mysterious fashion and that the local police had suspected Zelda but had never been able to get anything to make an arrest.

The mother had disappeared a year later, but no one ever filed a complaint or a missing person's request.

He said that the missing person's report for Dillon came in three months later but a connection to Zelda was never made.

Johnnie smiled and said that in the University Junior yearbook he discovered that Dillon and Aada had a photo that had them sitting together in the soccer stands. In digging into Dillon, he discovered that he was a womanizer that had pictures with many of the good looking students. There was one with he and Zelda as well.

Alex shook her head and said that it sounded like Dillon had created a situation that put the two sisters at each other. She wondered if Aada had been killed by Zelda or what had happened to her.

She then asked Johnnie to see if there was anything in the network that Zelda's mother or Aada might have posted to friends or acquaintances.

Then said that it was time to get underway to border crossing number five.

They got to 110 and stopped a mile from the border. They were in the process of getting into place when Jay pointed to a point ahead of them where an Albino deer was standing and observing them. He said that the deer conveyed the message that the power of nature was not easily subdued. He added that it was also thought to be a symbol of good luck and that those seeing it should reflect on their spirituality.

Alex thanked Jay for sharing the story of the white deer and they were going see if it brought the team good luck.

They all got into position except for Jay who would let the rangers at the station know of their arrival, their search for the grave site and the potential for a confrontation.

They drove into the station area and Jay interacted with the border guards. He returned and said they been expecting them, and the bus should take any position that they wished to.

Johnnie said that they had passed a dirt road leading to the Big Presque Isle Stream about two football fields back along 110. They should set up there and search along the creek near where the dirt road hit the stream. Evan drove the bus there and backed up into a side area that let the team face the stream.

Everyone launched their search drones and began to look for a spot that might be a grave.

Alex felt a little strange to have an empty seat next to hers where Trey normally sat. She concentrated on flying her search drone. She and Bill has split Trey's search area.

Bill quietly said that he thought he might have something and took his drone down to near ground level.

Alex brought hers down from a different angle and she agreed that he may have found it.

She asked everyone to bring their drones in and take a break. She asked Jay to call the border crossing and ask them to bring out the ground radar unit that they had at the crossing point. She had wanted to have one with her but had been reassured there would be one at every station that had yet to find the body at their crossing.

She climbed down and asked Trey if they should walk to the site where the body might be located.

He smiled and asked if he was being asked or told.

Alex said that she would hold up until the body radar detection unit was brought down.

A pickup with the Canadian leaf pained on its side stopped and asked if they wanted a ride down.

Alex replied that they would walk down.

Travis and Bill led the way down and she and Trey followed.

Bill indicated the area were the radar should be used.

A few minutes later they had pictures of bones and then they got one of the skull. Bill had found the grave, in Trey's area some forty five minutes after the start of the search.

The two Canadian border guards said that the area that they had chosen to search in was outside of the area that had been previously searched. He said that it had probably been buried in this location because of the dirt road that came down from 110 to the creek.

Alex asked that the area get taped off. That a report get send in and that exhumation and analysis be scheduled.

She looked at Jay and said that perhaps the white deer had brought them good luck and that the team should pack up and go to the next border crossing.

They all got back on the bus and continued to the next border crossing.

Trey said that he had missed this crossing in his previous assessment. He said that he did not expect it to be a place where they would be attacked. The body had been found and was in for analysis. The getaway would be too difficult, and they would be there only long enough to plant flowers.

They agreed to an early lunch at a restaurant near the St. John's River about a half hour at the border and then a drive to the border that was the most likely to be the place that Zelda would attempt anything.

Johnnie said that he had been posting taunts and insults that should have Zelda fuming. He had also "leaked" location and timing information as if it was coming from a disgruntled RCMP person in the know. He figured she would be at the next crossing.

Alex asked why this crossing had not found a body.

Trevor looked at the layout of the facility and suggested that it was too neat and perhaps too well lit, had lots of cameras that had discouraged Zelda. He pointed to the area north of the border crossing and said on a dark night he would be able to drive along the border until he was in the trees.

She then asked Trey where they should park the bus. He pointed to the area that Trevor had suggested and said to park the bus at a forty-five to the border, looking north.

They exited the restaurant and got set up to go to the border.

It was a ten-minute ride out. Trey guided Rebecca as she parked the bus where he wanted. He took his position at the front corner of the bus. He thought he could feel her presence, but he knew that was the feeling he had before every fire fight. He took a couple deep breaths to settle himself down. He did not want to trigger one of his PTSD episodes.

Alex launched her drone and was approaching the woods when suddenly she heard the metal in front, between her legs clink and then the metal shield behind her legs clinked. The plexiglass in front of her blossomed into a glistening white flower and an object fell on her computer keyboard.

The sound of gunfire seemed to be out of synch with the blossom and came afterwards.

She moved immediately to Trey's seat so she could land her camera drone. Almost immediately the plexiglass shield in front of her seat shattered, her computer lid was slammed down, and a hole appeared in the cushion of her chair.

That was three incoming that had successfully done its job. She heard Johnnie say he had her in his sights and was firing his drone.

Zelda was furious at whoever the hacker that was taunting her. She recognized that he was significantly better than she, but she was getting the intel she needed in spite of him. Her network of backdoors to the support personnel had surfaced one disgruntled employee that had fed her the agenda and timing for the border visits that the black bus would be making. She had carefully checked out the crossing at the Route 190 crossing. She found one house that seemed to be closed for the coming season and decided to take a chance and park her truck in the shed near the house. There was electricity and she could connect with the internet. She figured she could just sit and wait. She decided that she should also have a hiding spot that she could move to after she killed Alex.

She would slowly depart along Oldline Rd and then cross the river on highway 10 and go out to some place in the woods where she would park for a few days.

She was all set. She walked the edge of the woods near the crossing point and decided that a low limb of a large old oak provided a perfect spot to rest the 457. She had come to love the weapon and hate its weight. She had doubled the thickness of the kick pad but every time she pulled the trigger she had to force her body back into position.

When she saw the bus pulling into position she knew she had picked her spot well. She saw Alex seated at the very end spot.

She drew a bead on her head and when she fired she realized almost immediately that she had not allowed for the drop. She adjusted and fired a second then a third shot in rapid order.

Suddenly the limb she was using seemed to explode and a piece hit her in the face and knocked her protective glasses off. She turned and began running through the woods. She knew instinctively that she was being chased and suddenly she felt the sting on her neck. She did not slow down but ran into the shed, jumped in her pickup, and drove it out of the shed. She had not opened the doors and when she looked in her rear-view mirror she noted that only the edge of the door remained. The wound on her neck was bleeding but it was not too bad. She realized that she must also have been hit on her buttock because it seemed she could feel a bullet.

She was wondering if she had killed Alex. The shield had been shattered but she had not seen Alex.

She looked to see if there was any one following and was relieved to see that no one was following. After she got across the St John's she felt like she had gotten away. She proceeded slowly down the gravel road that led back into the forest. She pulled in and drove slowly into the woods so that the truck would not be seen from the air. She got out and went to the back and climbed in so she could bandage her wounds.

She was hurt but mentally feeling good. She was sure her third shot had kill Alex.

<u>*24 Capture*</u>

*T*rey shouted for everyone to get ready to move and told them to get their drones in. He got in and told Rebecca to head down the 309 as fast as she could.

Alex hollered down that all drones were on the deck and folded. She got out and brought hers inside the sitting area. She watched as the rest of team did the same. She saw that Jay had secured his weapon and was lying on his side with his back to the wind. The team had not practiced this part of the dance.

Tray put his head up through the roof window and said that once they crossed the St John's river they should all look for some small road into the forest. Then they would stop and search to see if they could spot the pickup.

Johnnie shouted out that he had hit her twice but had no clue where. He had been aiming at her back but flying, shooting, and recovering from having shot was very challenging.

Bill was the one that called out a road to the right and Rebecca got the bus to slow down enough to be able to make the turn in. Trey asked her to pull over almost immediately.

He got everyone out by the side and said that they needed to fly their drones high and see if they could find the pickup. He said he was sure it would be under some trees, but it might still be visible. He wanted to find her keep her from using the four-fifty-seven.

Trevor was the one who spotted the pickup, about three football fields back in the woods. He gave his coordinates and Johnnie said he had the truck.

Trey led the team toward the pickup.

Johnnie said he had eyes on the back and the cab.

When they were about twenty feet from the truck, Alex called out, "Zelda Mulhaney, this is the police, you are under arrest. Come out with your hands in the air."

The back of the camper burst open, and Zelda jumped out with the 457 and began to raise it.

Johnnie shot her through the arm, but Zelda kept raising the weapon.

Alex shot her in the leg and Zelda dropped to her knees but seemed determined to raise her weapon.

Alex then shot her in the wrist and the 457 fell to the ground and Trey, Bill and Trevor rushed in and pushed her the rest of the way to the ground.

Alex asked Jay to have the RCMP, or the regional police come for Zelda, and he should request an EMT as well.

She went and sat on an old log, placed a call to Reg, and let him know they had captured Zelda, and he needed to get his judge and prosecutor ready.

She added that Zelda would need some medical treatment for gunshot wounds and a possible broken wrist. She added that Zelda was already complaining about cruel and harsh treatment.

Reg said that he could not believe the pace she had set.

Alex said that her next actions would be out west to find the west most body and then she was going to visit Zelda's hometown to see if she could find out any useful information.

Reg asked if she would be passing through Montreal.

Alex said that she was so she could drop Jay Bird off then then proceed out to the west.

Her next call was to Matt to let him know they had caught Zelda. She could hear the approaching sirens and said she would fill him in later.

Trey had called to the bus and had a towel brought down and placed their weapons on it. The 457 was laying were it had fallen. Bill and Travis had moved Zelda and leaned her against a tree.

Zelda looked at Alex and called her a black witch surrounded by her ignorant minions. She was going to sue them all for what they had done to her.

Alex chose to ignore her. She asked Johnnie where they should eat dinner.

Suddenly they were surrounded by a host of policemen and women.

She told Jay that it was now his show to conduct. She and the team stood back and watched as the EMT team loaded Zelda into the emergency vehicle. She heard Zelda screaming that she was going to get even with the black bitch.

Alex smiled as she thought that she preferred black witch.

She asked Jay to make sure the team weapons, including his, would be sent to the lab in Montreal. She wanted to get them back before heading west.

She watched as Jay took control of the interface with the local police, and he stood by as the person who was in charge of the scene talked to Reg.

It was clear to her that Jay was now going to be listened to.

The leader came over and introduced himself as Les and said she must be a very good friend of the RCMP Chief because he told me to do whatever you asked.

Alex shook her head, pointed to Jay, and said he was in charge of the scene, and she trusted him to do a fine job.

She thanked Les for taking control and said that after Zelda, the person that had been apprehended, was treated she should immediately be sent to Montreal. She said that Zelda was very personable but should be restrained so she could not escape.

Les pointed at the 457 and asked if she had done much damage with that size of a cannon.

Alex said that his team needed to get pictures of the bus and that there was a crime scene at the Border Crossing as well. She said that he would see firsthand what a four-fifty-seven could do at about one hundred fifty meters.

Les nodded and asked if Sergeant Jay knew all of what she had just shared.

Alex smiled and said yes but this was his first time handling a crime scene and she said she would appreciate Les giving him some slack and some coaching.

Les smiled and said he would do so. He asked if the team had any plans for dinner because it would take a couple of hours to work the three crime scenes: the pickup, the bus, and the site back by the crossing. He said if they were in a celebratory mood they could still catch happy hour at a place on the board walk and then perhaps enjoy snacks and eat off a great dinner menu.

He could have them dropped off there and they could relax while his men worked the sites.

Alex looked around to see how the team felt about the idea.

Johnnie spoke up and said it beat standing in the woods with hands in his pockets or slapping at the biting flies.

Alex checked with Rebecca and Evan who both said they would stay with the bus and as soon as it was released they would come to wherever the team ended up. They could then decide whether to drive on Montreal or stay overnight. They would take turns napping while they waited for the police to process the scene up on the deck.

They said they had looked at where Alex had been sitting said she should go out and buy all the lotto tickets she could.

Alex climbed up on the deck and stood in front of her seat. She took note of the bullet hole in the metal plating below the table. She peered into the hole and could see the bullet flattened against the back steel plate. She looked at the back of her computer lid and saw the grove put there by the third bullet that had shattered the glass and was now embedded in the seat cushion at about her heart level.

She would always think of it as the heart shot that had missed. She remember that the first bullet that had made it through the plexiglass had fallen on the computer keyboard She gave credit to Zelda for having become proficient with her 457. She had just come back down when the field analysis crew arrived to process the scene.

She got into the front seat of the police car and said she was ready for the bar. Trey said he was too and were the two of them going off the bandwagon.

Alex looked over her shoulder and said no but she was going to have the blackest tea that she could order.

They made happy hour. Johnnie, Denton, Bill, and Trevor ordered their drinks. Alex ordered the one nonalcoholic wine on the menu and shared the bottle with Trey.

She asked them how it felt to capture the person who had killed so many people.

Bill commented that they had accomplished it faster than he had anticipated, and it seemed that instead of following any of their original plans they had stepped from one change to another and had somehow come out the other end of the tunnel as winners.

Johnnie chuckled and asked how that was any different than most of their cases.

Trevor took the bait and commented that their leader was just a poor planner that had to be rescued by the rest of her team.

Trey smiled and added that she was the one that had done the shooting that had kept Zelda from being able to fire the cannon she was using, and he didn't care about her planning skills he cared about her aim.

Denton said he was ready to resign from the FBI if he could become a team member.

They all laughed, and Trevor smiled and made a toast to their sharp shooting leader.

They were just getting ready to order desert when she got a text from Rebecca who said that they had been cleared to leave the crime scene and asked where they were.

Alex let her know and invited the two of them to join them. Rebecca said that would be great. She said that there would be three of them because Jay was coming with them.

When Jay walked in in his red RCMP suit the restaurant went silent. He waved and said he was here to celebrate, and everyone should relax. He sat down and said that sometimes he felt like he was under the microscope.

He looked at the desert menu and said he would go for warm apple pie and a scoop of vanilla, and he would have a glass of whatever Alex was drinking.

Rebbeca let them know that they were staying in a Castle parking lot for the evening. They would maintenance the bus in the morning and then head for Montreal. She figured they would get to Montreal by three in the afternoon.

Alex asked Jay to call his big boss in the morning and give him an update on the capture and let him know when they were arriving.

Alex said she was thinking of taking one of the detours that Bill had mentioned she wanted to back track and go to St. John's where Zelda had grown up and see what they could learn of her early years. That might provide the reason for her career as a serial killer.

She suggested they take a two-prong approach. Johnnie and Jay would work with the western border crossings and see if they could find the bodies. She and the rest of the team would see about getting a series of interviews with people that knew the victim, Zelda, her sister, and mother.

She said that the trip would take two days of solid travel and would take them back to their first grave site.

They would most likely spend a few days in St. John's and then make the reverse trip.

Jay asked if they could have the bus go to Montreal after they dropped they were dropped off at Bathurst and they could fly to St. Johns and when they finished they could fly to Montreal. He said that would shorten their travel and still accomplish what Alex wanted to do.

Alex looked around at the team and asked what they thought of that idea.

Trevor said that it sounded better than a twenty seven hour bus ride.

Alex asked Jay to set up the flight and suggested if there was a first or business class he should book it.

She called Reg and let him know of the change in plans and explained her desire to do some investigation into Zelda's early years.

She asked Johnnie to begin researching Zelda's high school and college time periods.

She asked Bill and Trevor to list the people they should interview and see if Johnnie could identify specific individuals and get phone numbers.

She said she and Denton would see about the hotel and transportation when they got to St. John's.

They all boarded the bus and worked on their part of the trip to St. John's. The different parts came together, and they all felt they were ready by the time that Alex was ready to get some sleep.

The next morning, they took their short flight. They discovered that they had the choice of one car and one van that had a bench seat in back and a very large carrying area. They figured the van was useful to carry their two drones and all their luggage.

Alex said that she, Jay, and Johnnie were going to the police headquarters and let them know about the visit and their goals.

She let Jay know that she was using him to get close to the local police. He should use his connection to Reg to open the door and gain access to all the pertinent files. She said it would be great to work with someone in the local police department who had been involved in Aada' and her mother's disappearances.

Jay smiled and asked if he was the cases poster boy.

Alex shook her head and asked how he felt of his participation so far on the team.

He replied that he felt great about it and said he was just kidding about being a poster boy. He said that every step of the way he felt listened to, trusted, and put in charge, like being the person that worked the scene where they had captured Zelda. He added that it was a first for him and it felt great.

Alex replied that she and the team were impressed with his capability and if he had not measured up he would be back in Montreal. She added that he needed to be the authority in the coming meeting. She and the team were the Americans aiding the RCMP.

Johnnie smiled and said that he was as handsome as Jay was and had never gotten that kind of a compliment.

Alex smiled and said that he had too many sins that he needed to rectify before she could even think about such a compliment.

She then said that she wanted him to make friends with the appropriate computer person and gain access to the police data bases and any databases they had access to.

Johnny nodded and said that he would do so.

They arrived at the station, parked, and walked in.

Jay took the lead and very quickly they were sitting in the office of the local Chief of Police. Jay had a letter of introduction that his boss had given him and shared it with the Chief of Police.

He then introduced Alex and Johnnie as a part of team of eight that had come to St. John's to check into the past of Zelda Mulhaney.

He gave a brief background on the fact that she was in custody of the RCMP and accused of murder. He and the support team were investigating her past and were aware of the fact that her sister, Aada, and her mother were both missing.

The Chief read the letter and handed it back to Jay. He said they should call him Jasen. He had attended a leadership meeting where Chief Huntington was the featured speaker.

He then said that he had been one of the two persons that had looked into the mysterious disappearance of Aada. He said that he was not aware of the missing mother, and he did not think any missing persons request had ever been turned in.

He then added that that they thought that one of two people may have murdered Aada. Her sister or the young man that had most recently dated her.

The young man had a solid alibi, and the main suspect was Zelda. She had a very weak alibi but without a body the case went cold.

As far as he knew they were the first to be looking into that situation since the file on that situation had been closed.

He said that he would link Johnnie to their IT support who was an external contractor cleared to access all the police data bases. He speculated that this IT person most likely handled all the secure data bases in St. John's. He added that she was extremely talented and hoped that Johnnie could keep up with her.

He said if they gave him a moment he would see if he could connect her.

He introduced Monica Alister and put her on speaker. He then explained why he was calling. Monica suggested they meet over lunch and then they would see how she could help.

After that call he made a call out to his support and asked her to send Peter in.

Alex took Peter to be about Johnnie's age.

When the Chief explained the situation, Peter said that was a case where he felt certain that Zelda had disposed of her sister in some fashion. He had heard rumors about her mother but there had not been a police involvement in that situation.

He said that after all this time, he doubted that any new information would surface.

Alex nodded and agreed but she would appreciate talking to him and getting his help in seeing if they could come up with something that might be pertinent to the case of Zelda facing multiple murder charges.

Peter said that he hoped that she would get nailed because he was ninety-five percent sure she had killed her sister.

He suggested he get out the records, organize them, and see if there was anything entered in the computer files. He added that the department was in the process of digitizing all their records and he was not as good with the computer access to files, but he could point them out.

Alex said that Johnnie was her IT magician and would be the one that went after the information in the computer files.

They walked out to the parking lot and got into the car. She called Trey to see what the rest of the team had come up with.

She found out that Trey had gone to both the high school and to the university and had gotten them to loan him the year books that included Zelda and Aada.

He added that they had wanted to keep his police badge and credit card number to loan him the books.

He had left them with his credit card information to get the year books.

He, Denton, Bill, and Travis were going through the year books to see if they could find who they might want to talk to. He added that they had the names of the teachers, principals, school counselors and even a couple of janitors that had made the year books. He added that he was returning the university year books because he had been told that they were now all online and had gotten the website where they could be found.

He added that they had a list of six friends of Aada, but it seemed that Zelda was the ugly duckling that had no friends. He gave the names of the six and said that after lunch he and the rest of the team would spend their time calling.

Alex shook her head as she said they were meeting at lunch with Monica, one of the persons on his list. She was now in business as an IT specialist.

Trey said, "Wow" it was a small world.

Alex replied that they were in a small town, and it did not surprise her so much. She added that her first job was as a deputy in a small town. Everybody knew everybody and many of the people were related to each other.

Alex let Trey know the restaurant where they were eating and said she would see him there.

She looked at the time and asked if Jay was up to driving by Zelda's neighborhood, her high school, and the University.

Then they could go to the restaurant.

<u>*25 Memories and Reality*</u>

Zelda's child home was in a neat, well kept, lower middle-class neighborhood. It had flower beds around the houses and around the front light posts. Alex took it as a place where kids would play safely in the street, and everyone got along. She asked Johnnie to get the house numbers around Zelda's old home and see who was still in their homes since Zelda's time. They should be added to the interview list.

They were going past the high school when Johnnie said that lunch was going to be even more interesting than he thought and said that the house on the same street as Zelda's was where Monica lived. She had taken over the ownership of the home just a year ago from her parents. He did not know the circumstances of that transfer, but they were going to be able to find out at lunch.

Alex said that she was glad that she had invited Monica to lunch.

The Memorial University of Newfoundland was well laid out and was a very functional and business-oriented campus. It was not scenic and did not seem to be oriented to exterior student activity. Alex would have loved to see the interior of the facilities to see if they were tuned to the students.

They drove through and then headed to the restaurant that was apply named St. John's Fish Place. As they walked in Alex stopped to read a handwritten menu. The waitress asked if she had a reservation. She said that the reservation was most likely under the name of Travis. The waitress looked and said that yes she was part of a party of ten that they had just set the tables for. Alex followed the waitress to her table knowing that she was going to order Mussels, the Surf and Turf Skewer, her normal iced tea and then she would find out about desert.

A few moments later, Trey walked in with the rest of the team, and they were shown to the table.

They were all looking at the menu when Monica walked in and was brought to the table. Monica briefly introduced herself and asked if she were at the right table.

Alex said that she was, and she introduced Johnnie as the IT person in their midst. She then introduced everyone around the table. She suggested that Monica order lunch and then they were interested in not only getting her support but in interviewing her because she was a person of interest to them.

Monica smiled and said that she found them not only an overwhelming group but one with an introduction that had her worried about what made her a person of interest.

The two waitresses returned to take the orders. Alex put in her order first and the two waitresses worked in opposite directions around the table. She noted that one waitress was much faster than the other and got twice as many of the orders.

Alex took a sip of her tea and addressed Monica. She let her know that they were working on a case where Zelda Mulhaney was being charged with murder.

Monica blurted out and asked if they had found Aada.

Alex shook her head and asked if she knew a Dillon Olinger.

Monica stopped and said that yes, she had dated him but dropped him because he was after any girl that would go to bed with him. She gave a small laugh and said that at that time she had no interest, now she wondered where all the available men were hiding.

Alex let her know that Dillon was one of several killings that Zelda was being charged with.

Monica shook her head and blurted out, "You must be kidding."

Alex let her know that her team had come to St. John's to find out more about Zelda's missing sister, Aada, and her missing mother.

Monica said that she would give them all the help she could. She said she was convinced that Zelda had killed her sister.

Alex nodded and said that they were going to be looking for Aada's body, but they currently had no idea of where to start and perhaps Monica could be of help.

Alex said that Bill and Trevor would be the two that would interview her and see what she could remember about both Aada and Zelda. She was more interested where the two sisters would most often go, such as a beach or a hiking trail, or a place to go fishing.

Monica said that was easy and she had told this to the police. Neither of them liked to fish or to go hiking but they liked to go to Middle Cove Beach. She added that Aada always seemed to be defensive of Zelda except for the time she had caught Dillon and Zelda kissing. She had confided to her that she was going to disown her sister for stealing her boyfriend. Monica said that this was the first time she had put everything together. She said that it was probably during that confrontation that Zelda had killed her.

Alex asked where Aada would have confronted Zelda.

Monica said she did not know where, but she thought she knew when. It would have been on a Thursday. Normally on Friday night several of the group they partied with, which included Aada, would have a beer at the student union and then decide what they were doing for the rest of Friday night. A couple of the girls often had their dates with them mend for several of the get togethers Aada had Dillon with her.

That night neither of them were present. She saw Dillon on campus afterwards for a while, but she never saw Aada again.

Alex said that she wanted to have Johnnie work with her to dig into both police data bases and the data bases for the high school and university.

Alex added that she was also interested to talk to any neighbors that had lived in the neighborhood and get their memories about the Mulhaney family. She then asked about the fact that Monica had recently assumed the ownership of the home she had grown up in.

Monica said she was impressed with how quickly Alex's team was gathering information. She said that she had worked for her Father who owned Nagle Information Services. When she received her Engineering Degree he had made her a partner. She had expanded the business by getting contracts with the police, the high school, and the university. Her parents were now called Canadian Snowbirds and had relocated just south of Tampa, Florida. A year or so ago she had changed the title to the house to her name so she could keep the taxes straight.

She added that she was beginning to think that Alex and her team were going to do what others had not been able to do back when things happened. She volunteered to contact all of the people she knew that knew Aada and Zelda and get them to step forward with what they remembered.

Alex said that would be a big help and she asked that she first review the list that Bill and Trevor had made. The two of them were planning to contact the people on the list starting sometime after lunch.

Monica said that if the two didn't mind she would like to join them for the interviews. She added that she wanted whatever happened years ago to come to light. She felt this was the first time she had some hope of finding out what had happened to her friend.

She knew she was dead, but her death had never been solved.

Bill said she was welcome to join.

Trevor added that she could probably help them a lot.

Lunch came to an end, and they split into two groups, Alex, Trey, Denton, and Jay returned to the hotel and picked up the two drones.

They then drove up to Middle Cove Beach and took the drones down to the beach. Alex noted that a fight on the beach could easily turn deadly if the two sisters used the stones that were elongated and about the size of a medium sized apple. She commented they all looked like hand axes.

She asked Denton and Jay to walk to the right along the beach and check it out for places where a body might be hidden.

She and Trey would walk to the left to do the same. Then they would return and launch the two drones and check the area from the air.

They walked along the beach and Alex pointed out that there was a good covering of pine and broad leaf trees and there were crevasses that came down from the higher ground. She walked along until the beach seemed to have been blocked by an almost vertical stone and earth wall.

She turned and walked briskly back to the beach where they had left the drones in front of a thick flat granite seat with an inscription on a brass plaque asking that the sea bring back the sailors with large catches of fish.

She watched as Denton set up the small drone. Its weapon had been part of the crime scene evidence that had been sent back to Montreal. She commented that Gunjfor might be hard to fly and suggested putting a beach stone where the pistol normally was located. She told Denton if he had any problems then bring Gunjfor in.

She got her drone ready and checked to see that it had a good interface to the computer. She launched and took a spin around where they were sitting and then sent it up and went along the ridge to the left. She was several tree heights up and was getting a good view of all the crevasses. Most had a few boulders that had fallen in, but otherwise they were clean. She spotted one that had quite a bit of stone caved in from the sides. She asked Trey what he saw and took another flight across the area. He said that he thought she had found the crevasse where Aada's body would be found.

Alex said that it seemed too easy.

Denton said that the stone idea had given Gunjfor enough ballast that he had been able to fly along the hill to the right. He and Jay had agreed that there was nothing of interest on their side.

She had both Jay and Denton look at the crevasses on her computer. They agreed with Trey.

They asked if they should go up and start digging.

Alex shook her head and said they should all drive back to the police station. They would show Chief Mosucter the footage and ask him to get a crew to come to the beach and remove the stones from the crevasse.

She wanted to let them make the discovery and then file the charges against Zelda. She and the team would be mentioned in the charge, but they would not be directly making the accusation. She said she was trying hard to keep the across border issues to a minimum.

Chief Mosucter and his friend Peter who had worked the case viewed the video that Alex shared and asked what had made her go to the beach to conduct a search.

Alex explained that the conversation with Monica was the reason. Monica had shared that it was the favorite place for Aada and Zelda.

He said he would get a crew out to the site that day to mark it off as a crime scene and assess what they would need to clear the trench. He looked at Peter and asked if he would go out with the digging crew and be in charge of the marking off the scene.

Peter said that he was pleased to do so but he said he had his doubts that Alex could come in and in a day solve a crime that had eluded the department for months before it was declared a cold case.

Alex said that she agreed with him, but things often got lost in the heat of the moment. Additionally, she was able to use technology that was new to her that allowed her to see things from perspective that had not been available when he was doing the investigation.

She pointed out that the bodies found out west along the border had been thought to be female but a second analysis by a different team determined they were both male.

Peter's eyes opened a little wider and he asked if there were more bodies.

Alex said there were many more and she wanted the person who was responsible to spend the rest of her life in prison and if she could arranged it, she would be put in a cell where she would never see the sun or sky again.

Peter said he would see to it that the stone was removed all the way to the bottom of the crevasse.

Alex thanked him and said she would be out when he got to the body. She was going to spend the morning following or doing interviews of anyone who was willing to discuss the Mulhaney family.

Chief Mosucter commented that it was a small community, and she might be talking to quite a few people reluctant to talk to an outsider.

Alex nodded and said that she was going to concentrate on talking to the college professors and other school personnel. She wanted to do a detailed profile of Aada and her mother.

She had done a preliminary one on Zelda that had led to her arrest. She said that she did not expect to find either of the two alive but wanted to provide the prosecution with the information and the profile that could be presented to the jury.

The Chief said that he would be following the case as close as he could. He would see if he could arrange to have an in-court camera feed so his department could sit in on the trial.

Alex left the station and drove to the hotel. She found Trevor, Bill, Johnnie, and Monica working away.

Johnnie and Monica were engaged and talking in IT-ese.

She asked Bill how they were doing. He said that they had almost a full day of interviews set up for the following day. They would need to have the team all join in so they could talk to that many folks. He commented that it seemed that every call they made they connected with a person who wanted to tell their story.

The professors and teachers were the only ones that had time constraints, but they had all provided at least thirty minutes based on their teaching or lecture schedule.

Alex said she was interested in talking to the professors and college personnel.

Trevor shook his head and said that once again she was taking the cream and leaving skimmed milk for the rest of the team to make butter with.

Alex said that it was not his fault that with his level of education he would struggle to talk to the well-educated professors. She added that she would make an exception and let him talk to the soccer coach.

Bill spoke up and said the problem was that Trevor didn't know anything about soccer.

Monica looked up and said that the team interaction reminded her of the chatter between her and her father.

She said she missed it.

Alex said that for the team it was about maintaining their sanity as they traveled among the so many bad people.

Monica said that for her it had been a way for her and her dad to enjoy each other.

Alex said that that was true for the team as well.

Alex had put five professors on her interview list for the following day. She asked Monica to give her a one liner for each professor.

Alex looked at the list and asked why one professor had, "Knows the most about the two Mulhaney.

Monica replied that Professor Benedetti had caught Aada writing an essay for Zelda and had failed them both. He had then let them write three essays each about integrity, honesty, and truthfulness. The highest grade that he had given them was a C.

She said that up to that point, Aada's grade point average had been close to being the highest in her class, but that grade wiped out any hope of her finishing anywhere near number one.

She said that Zelda had brazenly told the professor that she didn't care what he gave her. She was furious to find out later that he downgraded her to a D, and he had raised Aada's to a B. That later made Zelda have to take an extra semester to get her degree.

Alex called that professor and set up a ten o-clock meeting the next morning. She was not sure she would do all five interviews. It would depend on how quickly the clearance of the crevasse out at Middle Cove Beach would happen.

The next day, Professor Benedetti asked why Alex was asking him about the two sisters that he considered were polar opposites. Alex explained that Zelda was under arrest and being held by the RCMP on the charge of murder.

The Professor said that it did not surprise him. Zelda had privately threatened to kill him for having given her a D. He had been personally frightened and had stayed at a friend's house for more than a month. A few weeks later the police asked him if he knew where Aada could be. He moved to a new home but left his old address on all his paperwork until Zelda graduated and left.

He said that he hoped that she would not get out of jail because he regarded her as dangerous person.

Alex was just finishing the interview when a call came in to let her know a body had been discovered. She thanked the professor and said that she might soon know were Aada had ended up. She would let him know.

She also said that she was sure that Zelda would never see the outside of a maximum-security prison.

Professor Benedetti said that even after all these years knowing that would allow him to sleep better at night and feel safer going out in public.

Alex said that she agreed with him. She added that she had never met a person that she considered as evil. She considered Zelda to be rather intelligent but sly, deceptive, distrusting and a person who sought to be a person of status. She lacked empathy and viewed others as objects that were there to serve her needs.

<u>26 Buried Alive</u>

The call that came in was from Peter Nagle who was out at the site supervising the digging. He said that he had stopped the digging until the coroner, the Chief and she came out to the site. He said he was having pictures taken but the digging would need to be done by hand until they removed the skeleton that they had found. He said he would wait for them to come out before saying anything else.

Alex let Trey, Jay and Denton know that they were going to the Middle Cove Beach where the digging had stopped because of a find.

Alex asked Trey to call Bill to let him know that a body had been found and they should proceed to the beach.

The drive out seemed to take twice as long as the previous trip. She got there just as the Chief was getting out of his car with a person that he introduced as Coroner Adams.

Peter was waiting in the parking lot and said that the find had shocked everyone, and he had declared a break until Dr. Adams arrived and decided how to proceed.

Alex asked for them to wait a moment until the rest of the team got there.

When the team arrived, she was not surprised to see Monica get out of the car.

She asked the Chief if he was clearing her to be at the crime scene.

He said that it was appropriate since she had been the one to steer the search to the beach.

They all followed Peter up the hill and over to the crevasse.

As she peered down the slope into the ravine, Alex understood why Peter had called a halt to the digging. The skeleton of the person in the ravine was holding her hand above her head as if to shield the light from her eyes but Alex knew that what she had been trying to shield herself from was the massive slab of stone that Peter explained had been lifted out from the ravine. The skeleton was still standing because the soil had filled in around her. He flesh was gone and the soil must have slowly replaced it. The dress straps were over the exposed collar bones.

Dr. Adams shook his head and said that he would do most of the digging to get the skeleton out, but he was going to need help in getting the soil out from around the body. He said that he might be able to dig down and get whoever this person was out before it got dark but he asked that flood lights get put in place so he could eliminate any shadows the late afternoon might create.

He added that it was going to be tedious but at least it would not be so odorous that it would be nauseating. He added that what was nauseating was that he was sure the body they were looking at had been alive when the boulder had fallen across and over her.

The Chief looked at Alex and said he wished she had shown up a few years earlier.

Peter said that he had doubted that anything was going to be found but now he was wondering if there would be a second body in this same ravine.

Alex replied that she had not been sure before this discovery, but she was betting that Peter had discovered Zelda's mother, and Aada would be at the bottom of the ravine.

Monica said that Aada's mother had many dresses of the same style with straps over the shoulder and were square in front and back. She added that Aada never wore a dress if possible.

Peter nodded and said that he was going home. He said he was giving his wife a huge hug and he would see if he could get the courage to continue the digging in the morning. He was going to let the Dr. Adams extract the skeleton. He would be back in the morning and work with the crew to clear the ravine.

Alex sat down on the ground and watched Dr. Adams carefully brush the dirt into a bucket. He was working with a small whisk broom, a small garden shovel and a five-gallon bucket.

Peter had asked two workers to stay and assist him.

Trey was sitting next to her and commented that this was going to give him nightmares.

Alex said that she agreed with him, and she wanted the entire team to take some time to talk through what they were witnessing.

She said that the gun battles that the team had experienced were preferrable to witnessing a scene out of a horror movie where she was sure that the person in the ravine had been buried alive.

She quietly added, "buried alive by her own daughter." She added that it was a wonder that Zelda was still sane enough to be coherent.

Johnnie sat down on the other side of Alex and said that he didn't think he needed to do much more digging through records on the internet.

He added that the bodies would seal the case and whether Zelda spent the rest of her life in prison for killing her sister and mother or for some of the other bodies, he was sure now that she would indeed never see the outside of a prison.

He wondered how long she would last before she did go insane.

Trevor was sitting just to Trey's left side and commented that it was going to take him a while to get out of the bucket of despair before he would be in a joking mood again.

Alex said that they should cancel all the interviews the following day. They would return to the site when the crew was close to clearing the ravine. Then they would wrap things up and head home.

She looked at Jay and asked him to update his boss and get orders sent to Dr. Adams to do an initial analysis but then send the bodies to Montreal for more detailed analysis.

She said she would follow up with Jen, after the second body was found.

She added that the bus was going to be left in his boss's possession and she and her team were flying back to Cincinnati and would wait to be called to participate in the various phases of bringing Zelda to trial.

She was leaving the search for all additional bodies to the RCMP. There would be bodies all the way to out to where the first two had been found and then there might be some beyond.

She would share the technique she and the team had decided to use in an attempt to get ahead of Zelda but that plan no longer had any meaning. They had stopped her and now it was the RCMP's duty to find any additional bodies that she might have buried. Zelda might even be convinced to tell them where all the bodies were located so her body count could go up.

Bill said he was going to drive back to town and have a beer and then figure out what to have for dinner.

Alex said it was time for all of them to go. She wanted to have something sweet with ice cream.

Chief Mosucter said he was leaving as well. He was going to leave two units to secure the site and would periodically check in on Dr. Adams' progress. He said that he was sure that clearing the ravine would be accomplished the next day. He would ask Peter to call all of them when he was almost done.

Alex invited him to join the team for dinner.

The Chief declined and said he was going home. His daughter was coming over with her two and he was going to sit on the floor and enjoy them for the evening.

Alex smiled and said that maybe she needed to go with him and get some hugs.

He nodded and said that was what he was looking forward to. The two were his light.

Alex asked Trey to drive in so she could make a couple of quick calls.

She wanted her Chief to know about the find and she wanted to let Matt know that she was planning to close the case and return home. She wanted the two of them to spend at least the weekend at her parent's home.

She realized that the case had surfaced her desire to take a drink.

She asked if Trey was ready to go to their AA class. He looked over at her and said he had the same desire to drink a bottle of whisky that she was probably having and yes he was ready to attend a class.

He added that they should both drink hot black tea, eat chocolate ice cream, and have a big piece of carrot cake for dinner.

Alex nodded but said that she wanted Strawberry Ice Cream with her carrot cake.

Johnnie spoke up and said that he was going to join them at their next AA session, and he wanted to have a team session with their phycologist to discuss this case.

Alex asked him to set that up the appointment with the phycologist and she would get him a seat at the AA session.

At the restaurant, Trevor was the one that set the mood. He said he wanted them to remember going to dinner with the young woman who was the person that was supposed to be buried as the bottom tip of the heart made from the graves of eleven other young women were buried.

It was where they had faced a group armed with AR-15's that almost took Trey down, but he was a wild man and mowed them down.

It was the moment in time where Alex could truly complain about a pain in the butt and not be talking about him.

They had walked out of that battle because they were a team. He said that as a team they were going to overcome the macabre series of murders and the sinister and morbid act of a daughter burying her mother alive.

This time it was not bodily bruises that they as a team had experienced. Their bruises were mental shocks that were as deadly as the bullets that they had survived. This time their bruises were not visible, but they were just as painful as the ones they had experienced before and as a team they would bounce back as they had done before.

Alex smiled and looked at Bill and asked what he had allowed Trevor to drink all morning.

Bill said that he had purchased a bottle of smart pills and had been spiking Trevor's drinks with them.

Alex smiled and said she needed some of those pills and would gladly pay for them tomorrow if he gave her a couple today.

The waitress came to the table to get the order and Trevor said that he had it for the group. He went down the main course menu, one at a time until he had ordered the number of meals that matched the number of people at their table.

The waitress asked who got which meal.

Trevor said that the meals should be placed in the center, and each person would need a separate plate.

The waitress said she got it and that she would put all the like items on separate plates. That would make it easier to share.

She said that there were several great deserts and that she could put one of each on a platter and they could all share that as well.

She asked about drinks, and everyone agreed that black iced tea would be their drink for dinner.

The next day Alex decided that the team should relax until the second body was found. She suggested that they cancel all of the interviews and focus on writing the report for the case. She said that she was going to see if the Chief would like to go fishing out on the Lake and if, so she was going to set up a fishing outing. She said that they all needed to spend a few days doing nothing but enjoying the rising of the sun, some great meals and then the setting of the sun.

Trevor smiled and said that he would be glad to take a few more pills and do the analysis of the benefit of such an outing and convince the Chief it would increase the teams productivity.

It was just after two in the afternoon when Peter called.

Alex got the team together and let them know that the last large slab was going to be lifted from the ravine.

They arrived at the same time as the Chief. This time Monica stepped out of his car and greeted all of them before they all followed Peter to the ravine.

The work crew was sitting in the shade of one of the trees. One of them asked if there would be a body under the slab.

Alex replied that she was fairly certain that there would be a body.

Monica walked over to the person who had asked and quietly told him that Aada had been play mates with both of them.

She agreed with Alex.

She said maybe he should let someone else handle the crane to lift the slab from the ravine.

He shook his head, and wiped the tears form his eyes and said that he would operate the crane.

It was just that he hoped that she was not like her mother but had been dead when dumped into the ravine.

Alex said she thought that it was most likely that Aada had already been dead before she was dumped into the ravine.

Peter quietly said that it was time to get it over with.

The crew got into position. They had attached three ropes to the long slab so they could keep it from swinging as it was lifted and moved to a position at the lower end of the ravine. Once they got the slab down.

The crane operator went to the edge and let out a curse. He said that they were going to have to go down in the ravine and remove the loose stone.

Dr. Rogers said that he wanted to take it slowly. He would go down and put the stones in a bucket and they could set up a bucket rotation and get the stones removed. He said that exposing the bones slowly would help him determine how Aada had been killed.

The crane operator looked over to his three crew members and said he was going to sit on the crane and watch while they helped the doctor.

Alex asked Bill and Trevor to interview the crane operator and capture his recollection of both the Mulhaney sisters.

Alex sat down on the ground and counted buckets of rock and watched the pile grow next to the boulder. She wondered how long it took Zelda to get that much rock knocked loose and how she had managed to get the slap to break loose and fall on top of it all.

Dr. Adams called up that he had uncovered what was the side of a skull and that now the stone removal was into the sensitive phase. He was taking a picture each time he took out another bucket full of stone of the skeleton.

Monica asked if there were any cloth remnants.

The doctor replied that he might find remnants in the soil below the body but there were none that he could see.

Alex said that she and the team were going back to the hotel. She would wait for his initial analysis before taking the team home.

The Chief asked how she wanted to handle the press.

She pointed to Jay and said that it was up to the RCMP and the local Chief of Police to determine how to cover the news. She suggested that a simple announcement about a break in a cold case and that the suspect was in the custody of the RCMP. She and her team were happy to remain invisible.

Jay said that his boss had given him the responsibility to handle the news and that he should keep it low key.

As they walked back to the parking lot. Alex noted the conversation going on between Jay and Monica.

She knew the scene and was pleased that Jay would remain in St. Johns for a few weeks to wrap things up. She figured that during that time the two of them would figure out if they were meant for each other.

She called her Chief and let him know that the case was closed and that she was inviting the team to go fishing on Lake Michigan.

She laughed when he asked if there were any mad men out to get her or would this fishing trip only feature fish fighting to get off of hooks.

She then called Matt to let him know that she was coming home on the following day.

After that she called her parents and asked if they would host a fishing trip for the entire Cincinnati detective team.

Her mother brought tears to her eyes when she said, "what are parents for."

Indeed, she thought as she wiped the tears away.

The End

26 Buried Alive

Preview of: Body Parts

1 Business Success

Reston stood in front of the almost live sized human poster of a man with his hands out to its sides. He was surrounded by similar posters of both genders. He was learning the details of the new human body parts business he had been instructed to establish by his bosses in Italy. The poster graphics were detailed and captioned for both the exterior and internal body parts. He felt like a medical student. He was not going to do any memorization, but he knew he would be referring to the posters as the body parts orders came in.

He was use to trafficking in a wide variety of drugs and had never imagined that he would be getting into the business of trafficking in human body parts.

The posters had what each body part was worth. The arrow pointing to the skin indicated that it was worth thirty thousand dollars. The scalp was worth one thousand dollars.

He walked around the room, and it became clear that one body was worth more than a half a million dollars if all the parts could be sold.

He wondered about the people that were willing to pay for the body parts. He knew that he would be making more than the half a million per body. The black market would be many times more.

He had been informed that the legitimate body parts market was a billion-dollar industry. He figured that the black market would be worth to one hundred times more if properly managed

Adding the body parts business to the distribution of drugs had been a path that Reston had not envisioned getting into. He was surprised to find that the company had selected Cincinnati to be the central point of both production, acquisition, and distribution. Many of the body parts were stolen from various legal body parts distributors. The rest would be collected from the appropriate local people.

The posters covered eyes, liver, heart, pancreas, stomach, a large and small intestines, penises, the list went on to cover almost every organ in the body.

He had spent a great deal of time in setting up his own body part production operation. He knew that many of the bodies that he would be asked for would need to be harvested from individuals that he would need to identify that had the right match to some person willing to put up the money to obtain the body part they needed. He knew that speed and maintaining a supply of the most desired parts would be important.

He had spent a fair amount of time designing the layout of his parts production, inventory holding room, and distribution supply chain.

His "factory" was located in a warehouse that had all the legal licensing and had passed the required warehouse inspections so that he had a five-year window before the next inspection. He of course had set it up as a regular warehouse and later added the special features that turned it into a human parts production center.

The interior construction had been done by a special group out of the New York area that were all partners of the mafia. They had come in and used the drawings he and a new York architect had made. The work was quickly done in a quiet low-key way.

His few permanent employees were trusted mafia members who had been recruited, trained, and then sent to him.

Recruiting the right person to do the dissecting of the bodies was not as difficult as he had expected. He had forged papers that he presented to the surgeon that he recruited. This surgeon had been on a list of a dozen potentials that had been identified from their participation in a conference on human body parts. The surgeon was a resident at one of the local hospitals and deep in debt.

He activated his various connections in all the major cities along the East Coast and soon he had a list asking for almost every human body part.

The body parts business was significantly more lucrative than the drug business and distribution was relatively easy since the drug business had an established distribution network.

He kept an eye on the books and soon realized that the money being taken in warranted an expansion.

He was always short of some organ or another. He looked at the back orders and knew that he would need to enlist another surgeon to harvest more parts.

He would also need to be more aggressive in getting the right "donors' on the dissection table.

He had his acquisition leader get more referring doctors enlisted. He was ready to throw the net more broadly so that he could fulfill the surging parts requests.

He spent many an hour watching the harvesting process through an observation window. He had designed a business office that had a window that allowed him to see the dissection table.

He also participated in the inventory inspections of the parts stored in the cold room. Many of the body parts could be held for days and still be used by someone needing it and willing to pay to get around the various waiting lists that prevented them from getting the parts legally.

Those parts that aged beyond their viable period were processed and disposed of in a furnace that operated only at night.

He was making a small fortune running the business.

His surgeon was making one as well.

Reston had set up an offshore account for this surgeon but kept himself on record as a co-account owner. This ensured that the doctor could be kept in check if the working relationship went south. He also tracked much of the doctor's personal life and contacts. He did not want the good doctor to stray from the agreement that had him spending about two hours a day harvesting body parts.

He was currently watching one of the harvesting sessions being performed on specifically ordered body. The good doctor had already removed the eyes. This was an organ that was always in demand somewhere in the country. He was currently carefully sawing the rib cage open so that the heart, liver, and other organs could be carefully removed.

A series of containers were ready to receive each of the organs as they were removed. The process was handled very efficiently, and a body could be harvested in the allotted two hours unless some unique part had been requested.

He always stopped watching when it came time to skin the remains and harvest the skin tissue, the scalp, and any miscellaneous organ. It was the only time he got grossed out.

The young man that was on the table had been identified, tracked, and then brought to the warehouse and kept in a cell. He had been killed just prior to the harvesting session. This was one step that the doctor did know about.

He wondered if the good doctor recognized how fresh most of the bodies he dissected happened to be.

A few weeks later Reston received word that a second surgeon had been recruited. He informed the good doctor that he would be training the second surgeon on the harvesting procedures.

That was when he first got the word that the good doctor wanted to quit. Reston reminded the good doctor that he had made a small fortune, and that quitting was not an option.

The good doctor made the mistake of arguing with the position he was taking and threatened to expose the operation if necessary.

Reston knew immediately that he needed to take drastic and dramatic action to put the doctor back into his place.

Reston had his bodyguard do a little checking and learned that the good doctor had entered into a relationship with a surgical nurse at the hospital where he practiced. He figured that the relationship between the good doctor and the nurse was the reason for the good doctors change of heart. He came to an immediate solution.

The fact that the good doctor had more than ten million in the offshore account was probably an additional incentive to quit.

The nurse was very attractive. Reston obtained records and made note of the key DNA, blood type and other key attributes.

He waited until the right parts request came in. He was going to snuff out the superior attitude of the good doctor. He was going to emotionally destroy him.

A few weeks later after a couple more discussions about the desire to quit, Reston took the action he knew would totally change the good doctors attitude and ensure he had control of the situation.

He had the nurse, who the good doctor was having an affair with, snatched, and brought to the warehouse.

He waited until the good doctor was ready for the next body and walked in and handed him the extensive list of parts to be harvested. The list had every organ, a knee joint, an entire right leg, eyes, and the breast nipples on it.

He wanted to be in the room when the good doctor realized who his next harvest victim happened to be.

He stepped to the far end of the room with a direct view of the operating table. He had Dennis his bodyguard standing next to him in case he needed protection.

Sara was scared as she sat in the cage and watched the two men who had snatched her from the parking lot the day before as she got ready to go home. They had not replied to any of her questions or explained why they had snatched her.

Zack and Brent had exchanged a few quiet comments about their next victim. They agreed she was too pretty to be processed but they had their orders.

Zack got the call to prepare her for the next harvest. He opened the door to the cage and let her know that she could leave the cage.

As she stepped out of the cage, Brent hit her with the knuckles of his thumb on her two temples. She went out like a light when the switch was flipped.

They lifted her and put her face down on the processing table. Brent then slit each of her arteries in her neck. He then focused on undressing her as her blood pumped out and ran down into the collection bag. The blood would be filtered and sold to a blood bank.

He admired her beautiful body and was sorry that she had been selected but that was the bosses decision not his.

When the call came to wheel the body into the harvesting room they opened the door and pushed the table in.

James asked why Reston was in the room instead of behind the observation window. He was surprised to hear that Reston say that he had a surprise for him.

James watched as the table with the harvest body was pushed into the room and put next to the dissection table. He walked over to help in rolling the body over onto the table.

There was something familiar about the body, but he could not quite place the feeling.

As the body was turned over, his brain exploded, his life was shattered. It was Sara, the woman that he had fallen in love with.

He heard Reston call out, "surprise" as he picked up his scalpel.

He took the only action that flashed into his mind.

<u>2 The Nurse</u>

The large panoramic screen in the living room zoomed out to the mountains, then slowly panned along the river and finally on the campsite where her father was putting up the large tent that they had all shared. Her mother had just transferred all her family videos to the cloud and wanted to view a few. The family had traveled extensively around the country and had camped in many of the national or state parks. The clip that was on the screen had been taken in a campground near the Tetons. She remembered the cold stream water where she swam briefly in a clear pool where she could see the fish swimming below her. She also remembered catching some of those fish and watching her father clean and fry them over the open campfire. At that time, she was probably fourteen. It had been one of many bright memories of growing up.

The other memory of that trip was the drive through Yellow Stone, seeing the buffalo and Old Faithful. She was sure her mother would have extensive footage of that drive as well.

She took a sip of her wine and had to admit that she had grown up in a loving family as a spoiled young girl.

Her early school years were a blur, and she had little recall about specific events.

She considered her high school years to be rather busy and exciting. She had been on the school paper, a cheer leader, and was a lettered field hockey player. Her senior year was especially fun because of all the parties she had attended. The only thing that she regretted about that time was that she had not been very serious about what she was going to do after high school.

As graduation loomed, she decided to go into nursing and was admitted to the University of Cincinnati. That made her parents happy because she would stay near home. She was excited because she felt that she had found her way into a field that felt right for her. She realized that she enjoyed helping people and thought that nursing would satisfy her desires. Her mother had suggested becoming a doctor, but Sara knew she did not have the desire nor the grade point average that would get her accepted in most US schools.

She graduated and was pleased when she was hired by the UC hospital as a practicing nurse. She was first assigned to be a floor nurse. She worked hard and received excellent feedback on her performance.

A year later she applied for and got a position as a surgical assistant. This assignment at first was a little overwhelming and watching surgery took getting used to. She at first had a quesy stomach but slowly got over it.

Then she had assisted Dr. Westin during one of his surgeries. He was fast, accurate, and seemed to have a good sense of humor.

He seemed to like her and requested her by name for several subsequent surgeries.

Their relationship seemed to take a natural turn toward intimacy.

Sara had dated James for more than a year when he asked if she would go on a vacation trip with him. She had accepted and he had asked her to pick the vacation trip that she wanted to go on. She had thought about going to Yellowstone but was not sure that camping out would be that romantic. She decided that an Alaskan cruise sponsored by one of the famous magazines on one of the smaller ships would be just the thing.

They had a main deck cabin that had an outside view. The cruise departed Seattle and for fourteen days they spent their time together. They dined each evening with a number of the guests. Sara noted that there were thirty couples on the cruise and another handful of single people for about sixty people in total. The small number of people was what had attracted her to this particular cruise.

She knew that it was rather expensive, but James had let her know that the cost was no issue.

They had enjoyed hiking, biking, kayaking at various moments, and strolling through Petersburg and learning about its fishing industry. She had followed in her mother's footsteps and used her phone to capture most of what she saw. She of course took many selfies that she sent to her parents.

The tour ended in Sitka Alaska where they caught a flight back to Cincinnati.

Sara felt that it had turned out to be fourteen of the best days of her life.

On the way back to Cincinnati, James suggested that she move in with him. She accepted on the condition that they each had their own bedroom.

He had accepted and said that he currently rented a three-bedroom apartment a few blocks from the University hospital.

They agreed that she would move in as soon as her own apartment contract ended in two months.

Her mother asked her to come to dinner and share the highlights of the vacation. Sara knew that what her mother wanted was the inside scoop on the romance.

She was eager to share that news, but she also had a great video of the highlights of the vacation that she had purchased as part of the tour. It was professionally done, and she knew her mother and dad would love it.

Sara floated along in sort of a haze as she waited for her lease to end. She went to James apartment and was amazed at how spacious and comfortable it felt. She was ready to make the move.

After work, she was walking out to her car when suddenly she was grabbed and felt a cloth going over her mouth and nose. She identified the smell of chloroform before she passed out.

When she came to she was lying in a barred cell. She sat up and tried to get her bearings. She realized that she had been kidnapped and wondered what was happening. She spent the night awake and scared.

Then the next day a person that she did not know approached the cell and told her she was going to be just fine if she did as she was told.

She asked what was going on.

The reply that everything was going to be alright did not satisfy her.

Alright meant to not have been kidnapped.

A short time later, the first person returned with a second one. He said it was time for a surprise and opened the cell door and told her to come out.

She was warry but figured that getting out of the cell was better than resisting and staying in the cell. As she stepped beyond the door, suddenly she was hit on her two temples, and everything went dark.

Zack picked up the young woman and put her on the dissection transport table. They had been instructed to undress her, bleed her, and then turn her face down before pushing the gurney into the dissection room.

He nodded when Brent commented that it was pity to have to kill such a beautiful young woman. The two of them knew better than to question the bosses direction and they did as they were told.

A few moments later they had everything ready.

Thank for reading this far.

Go to the web site to purchase the book

<https://Remwriter95.net/>

About the Author

Ronald E. Mueller
remwriter95@gmail.com

Ron grew up in what is now Flint River State Park in Southeast Iowa. The 170-year-old house Ron lived in is built into a hillside. It faces a 125-foot-high cliff towering over the little Flint River. The house and the land talked to him about; the passing of time, the struggle to conquer the land, the struggles people faced and the wonder of nature.

He climbed the cliffs, crawled into the caves, dove from the swimming rock, collected clams from the bottom of the pond, gigged and skinned frogs for their legs. He trapped muskrats for fur, hunted raccoon in the dead of night, and with only a stick hunted rabbits in the dead of winter.

His young life was outdoors, and nature tested him.

He walked to a one room stone schoolhouse uphill both ways. A stern but warm-hearted teacher, Mrs. Henry was instrumental in shaping his character as she shepherded him from the fourth to the eighth grade.

It was a great way to grow up.

Ron graduated from Burlington, High School, went to Vietnam in the Navy. He graduated from The University of South Florida with a master's degree in engineering, worked for thirty eight years for Procter and Gamble, traveled around the world thirty times.

He has remained happily married for more than fifty years. His daughter and his two sons are all successful and his three grandchildren have all graduated.

His wife has humored and supported him as he became a full time professional story teller.

His experiences inter-twined with snippets of fantasy lend themselves to the adventures he leads the reader through.

Books by then Author

<u>**The Taelo Series**</u>
Taelo: The Early Years
Taelo: The Golden Feather
Taelo: Journey of Discovery
Taelo: Dangerous Passage
Taelo: Condor Clan Slingers
Taelo: Circumvention
Taelo: The Journey of Sages
Taelo: Collection
Taelo: Future Leaders Journey

<u>**A Taelo Story:**</u>
White Swan and Quiet Pheasant
The Child's Name
Floating Cloud
Quiet Rabbit
Busy Bee
Little Otter & Talking Wren
Broken Spear
Burley Bear & Meadow Flower
Taelo Story Collection

<u>**Science Fiction**</u>

The Savitar Series:
Journey's End
Savitar
Confluence
Savitar Series Collection

Bram Nielson Series
The Fold
The Message
Fold Wormhole
Negative Fold
Ripples in Time
Bram Nielson Collection

<u>**Single Science Fiction Books:**</u>
Current Past and Future
The Event
The Door
Viajante 7

Published by: Around the World Publishing LLC.

https://www.Remwriter95.net/